"[A] gorgeous novel. *The Places We Say Goodbye* is an outstanding story and comes highly recommended to you." ~ The Novel Approach

"A very emotional read... The book, which was well-written and interesting, kept me riveted from start to finish." ~ Bayou Book Junkie

"*The Places We Say Goodbye* is a wondrous story of love from so many different angles. I loved the journey." ~ Christina's Bookshelf

THE PLACES WE SAY GOODBYE

JORDAN TAYLOR

Published by
NineStar Press
PO Box 91792
Albuquerque, New Mexico, 87199
www.ninestarpress.com

Warning: This book contains moments of graphic gore, war-related violence, and a gun-assisted suicide of an incidental character.

Print ISBN #978-1-945952-03-6
Cover by Natasha Snow
Edited by Sasha Vorun

Dedication

For Libby Kresky. Thanks for the memories.

STAGE ONE

Sunday, June 19

Shouting voices mixed with chaotic noise, resonating in blackness. An explosion launched me sideways. I felt the rush of heat, heard the blast that obliterated screams. It left my ears ringing and my heart racing, yet I saw nothing.

My throat constricted with panic as I fought to call for someone. Someone I had to find.

Then I woke up.

Wednesday, June 22

Cold tonight. What else? Remembering is like writing a message in sand already covered by the tide.

There were two men beside me, all of us watching for something. What did we see? Darkness?

Odors remain. Cold and fear remain. A reek of death. So afraid. Then the explosion. Or was that from last night? All nights?

Thank you, Amélie, for the advice of starting this dream record. I need it since details fade as soon as I wake.

Find a pattern. All different. Yet all the same. For months now.

Torin asleep beside me. I type on the screen of my tablet, the bedroom darkened by blackout blinds.

More of the dreams. Cold that stung my eyes, freezing their moisture. It burned my lungs, made my throat ache and my hands and feet numb. Acrid, smoky odors mixed with something dead. Like the smell when I was ten and my mom poisoned rats in the basement of the rental dump we lived in. They died in the air ducts. The first time heat came on, blowing nauseatingly into our faces, she said she'd leave the rats alive next time. Same smell in the dream. But worse. So sickening that it nearly blotted out smoke and cold.

I smell it now, longing to get up and shower it off.

Why are my feet frozen? The bed feels warm, almost hot with Torin against me. For once, I did not wake him by thrashing or yelling in my sleep. He must be nearly as sick of this as I am.

Tingling needles of cold in my toes and fingers. Like being out in the City too long in winter. Walking through snow in Central Park. Waiting in line for a show in January.

I can't climb from bed now that I managed not to wake him all night. Or did I wake him and not know it?

I hate these dreams messing with us.

Safe bet that Torin would mention it if I kept him up though. A chronic extrovert, he is accustomed to bringing his suffering to the attention of those around him. And finding something to debate in the matter. I mean that in a good way—if you ever read this, Torin.

Thursday, June 23

Running. Dozens of others ran with me. I was shouting...something.

Crashing, grinding death sounds. The din of a thousand men screaming, a world self-destructing.

Sound stays with me this morning more than anything. My ears feel as if they are bleeding. I cannot hear the City outside, or white noise inside. I hear only carnage.

Sunday, June 26

I keep thinking of accidents. Natural disasters, derailing trains, even plane crashes. Sometimes there's fire. It could be a gas explosion. A car wreck. Every night, even if only a fragment—some odor or sound, one bit or another—it's the same.

Not an accident. I know what it is. I know what I have faced in darkness—what has trashed my sleep, invading my life, my relationships, my work—for the past four months. Yet, I do not understand.

How can it be possible that, night after night, I dream of war?

CHAPTER ONE

Torin grabs the thermal travel mug from the coffeemaker with his left hand, typing on his phone with his right.

"Time to go," he says, still looking at the screen

"You're not ready," Bell calls back from the living room. She stretches in front of the TV, watching a *Good Eats* rerun with her six-year-old sister.

"I am ready." Torin has to glance at his mug to find the lid. He touches "Send" without rereading what he typed and snaps the lid closed.

"Are not," his daughter again corrects him, her back to the kitchen. "You're getting coffee."

"Coffee's done. Shoes." Pushing his phone into his pocket, holding the mug, Torin opens the refrigerator with his elbow. "Ree, did you get enough to eat?"

Ree does not answer. Then, "Daddy, did you know you need one-eighth teaspoon of cream of tartar for each egg white?"

"Let's go." Torin finds the paper bag lunch for Bell and a bottle of water. She will not carry a lunchbox anymore since, apparently, lunchboxes are for babies.

He makes his way to the door with his hands full and adds the lunch sack and bottle to Isabelle's dance studio backpack—also babyish. She wants a messenger bag.

The TV remains on, Bell and Ree still in place before it.

Torin's phone chirps. He attempts to read while tying his shoes and looking for the door key. There's an answer from Flep that reads, *NP*.

Torin taps "Reply," the smartphone balanced on his knee. He sends a *Thx!*, finishes with his shoelaces, and grabs his keys.

"Isabelle! Carine!"

The TV goes silent. Light feet race around the couch toward the entry.

"Dad, can we have white asparagus?" Bell asks as she glides up to him on her toes. The world's most graceful eleven-year-old. Do all fathers think that? Too bad for the rest of them that they're wrong.

"Depends what's at the market," Torin says. "White doesn't have the same nutritional value as the green stuff."

And the white ones look like little penises—particularly the last batch they had from the Union Square Greenmarket. Torin wishes he had a dollar for every time he controlled impulsive speech since having children.

Ree, frowning, yanks at her hairband, which her older sister must have just fixed.

"Stop it, Ree." Bell tugs her hand away.

"Sesame chili salmon with white asparagus and basmati rice for dinner," Ree says. Like so many of her requests, she makes it sound like an order. Last week it had been jasmine rice.

Torin stands to snatch his wallet off the shelf just to the side of the front door.

"Get Flep to take you to the market this evening before they close," he says.

If Flep can stay awake. He has been so messed up lately. Torin meant to talk to him about his nightmares and insomnia this morning.

Flep only moved in with them this past March. He assured Torin all these sleep problems are new. Are they because of the move? This place? Torin cannot leave this apartment. The location is vital to his work.

"Flep can't cook!" Ree howls as she grabs her father's arm.

"He can shop—"

"No, he can't!"

Torin pushes open the door. "Do you have everything, Bell?"

"My bag stays packed, Dad," she answers. "As long as my lunch is in there, I have everything."

"*Daddy*—"

"I don't know what to tell you, Ree." Torin waves them out. "You can't go shopping and fix dinner on your own. You're not supposed to handle chilies or knives unsupervised. Work out a compromise."

He only just shuts the door, standing with both girls in the building's hallway, when he pushes it open to grab sunglasses. Bell swings her dance bag. Ree tugs her hairband off. Torin makes sure the door is locked after shoving the glasses on his head.

"Flep won't be able to make the sauce." Ree stretches her hairband as far as it will go, clutching it with little hands.

"Don't do that, Ree." Bell tries to snatch it, but her sister darts backward.

Torin hurries down the hall with Bell beside him and Ree trailing.

He wouldn't mind a little more sleep himself. He assumed he would miss some with Flep moving in. Part of the point, as they're still in the honeymoon phase—not that they're married. But the nature of this sleep deprivation makes all the difference.

Torin blinks as he jabs the elevator button. No, this has been more akin to bringing home a newborn than post-wedding nights.

Wasn't he supposed to say something else to Ree? The girls are still bickering behind him about hairbands.

"You can make sauce," Torin says, glancing at the clock on his phone. "And put on the rice, but let Flep do the rest. Just give him instructions."

"Broccoli and carrots if we don't get asparagus," Bell says to Ree.

"I want snow peas."

"Snow peas and carrots then. You've got your hair all messed up."

"*You* messed it up." Ree sticks out her lower lip. "It's too tight. You can have it." She shoves the hairband at her sister.

"No."

Ree scowls at this lack of gratitude.

"If it's too tight, you need a new one, Ree." Torin pushes the elevator button again. "Stretching the one you have is not the answer."

She glares at the pink band dangling sadly in her fingers. "I don't want it."

"Sweetheart, what's wrong?" Torin kneels, phone and wallet pocketed, and rests his hands on her small shoulders.

His daughter only looks at the hairband, then the floor.

"You don't have to wear it across your head. Want your hair back in a ponytail?"

The elevator door opens. They have it to themselves as they descend thirty floors to the lobby.

Torin asks again about pulling her hair back, to which Ree nods. Her silence is a bad sign. Eldest sister Isabelle is the one who takes after her mother. If that woman had a superpower, it would be death by silent gaze. But Carine is her father's daughter.

No time for it now. If she will not talk, he won't try to make her. He knows the hairband upset is only a manifestation. He doesn't blame her. He understands those feelings—upside down family feelings—but he can only do so much for his daughters in the next sixty seconds. Especially with brain fog from three hours of sleep last night.

He picks Ree up as they step off the elevator, swinging her through the air.

"You are such a gorgeous girl." He kisses her cheek. "You could shave your head and dye your eyebrows green and you'd still be perfect, Ree. I'll get you softer hairbands, but try not to worry about it in the meantime."

She goes limp for the ride. "Yellow. Yellow and blue."

Torin catches the eye of the doorman, Martin, and nods as they approach. Martin nods back and steps out to the street.

"Yellow and blue it is. Want one that says, 'I heart lobster'?"

He pushes open the first lobby door with his arm as Martin rushes back to help with the second. The cab already waits at the curb.

"More like, 'I heart TV,'" Bell says as she walks ahead of them.

"Good morning, Miss Isabelle," Martin says, lifting his hat to her.

"Lobster, lobster, lobster," Ree chants, her face lighting up.

"Morning, Martin." Torin lowers sunglasses over his eyes. "Efficient as always."

The rush and buzz, the smell and searing morning brightness of 2nd Avenue hits them as they cross the sidewalk to a yellow cab.

"Lobster, lobster!" Ree raises her voice above traffic and pedestrians talking around them.

Martin opens the cab door. Bell thanks him while Torin settles Ree into the seat.

All inside, Torin stems the lobster flow with a lifted finger and says, "Carnegie Hill. Madison. Nordisk Dance Studio."

The driver nods, pulling into traffic.

Bell frowns out the window. "Can't we all go to the market? You're not supposed to be at the restaurant on Mondays."

"I told you about this on Friday, Bell," Torin says. "Brent is out of town. It's just for this week."

"You're not even picking us up?" Ree asks on his other side.

Why did she have to say it like that? *We know you won't be here for dinner, won't be here in the evening. But* not even *picking us up?*

Torin tries to smile. "Flep will pick you up. I texted him."

"Flep is also working." Bell still does not look at him. "I'm done at two and Ree's kindergarten only lasts a few hours."

"More than that. He'll finish the day from home. You can shop on your way home at Whole Foods or the Greenmarket. And leave him in peace while he's working." Suppressing a yawn, Torin looks again at Ree.

"I want lobster," she says.

"Make the Thai salmon you wanted. Flep can't be responsible for lobster."

"Or a grilled cheese," Bell mutters. "Or boiling water."

Torin pretends not to hear. "I'll fix us lobster on Friday. The 4th of July is next Monday. We'll do something fun for that. Want to plan the party food?"

Ree nods, though doesn't meet his eyes. Menu planning is one of her greatest pleasures. Being asked by her chef father to plan one is even better.

"Can you bring home croquembouche tonight?" Bell asks, still looking outside.

"Croquembouche!" Ree bounces beside him. "Croquembouche!"

"That's not..."

Bell glances at him, then away. "It's okay. I know you don't always have them."

"No," Torin says quickly. "You should come down for late dessert tonight. Eat them fresh. I'll tell Flep you can stay up." Torin mentally winces. Stupid thing to say. Flep is probably hoping to be in bed by 9:00 p.m. himself.

Ree bounces more, smiling. "Croquembouche and lobster!"

"Are you even having them tonight?" Bell looks at Torin again.

"We are. And I'll make sure there are leftovers." Why is he saying this? Just tell them no. At least don't overpromise on behalf of others.

Bell smiles, though the gesture is fleeting.

"Sorry I won't be back to pick you up," Torin says.

She shrugs. "Sorry Mom has to stay at the office."

"Will you help in the kitchen? I don't want accidents with Flep and Ree working together."

"Like her bursting into tears, or him rubbing his eyes after he handled those serranos, or setting off the smoke alarm, or—?"

"Anything. Any mishaps. Keep an eye on things for me."

She nods, watching for the dance studio to come into view. "I can't make any promises."

"Do your best." Torin forces back another yawn.

Better send a text to Flep to say that he, Flep, will be up late. And one to Dominique at the restaurant warning her that they are making croquembouche today.

Torin blinks against the morning sun through the window and his glasses, head aching, eyes feeling cottony. He should have brewed extra coffee.

Monday, June 27

A dirt road stretched away, straight and flat, as far as I could see. I stood, then walked. Maybe I was walking all along, but didn't feel like I had moved.

A dozen horses lay along the road. Fat, white maggots emerged from their nostrils and eye sockets, wriggling over dark fur. Abdomens bulged, grossly distended below summer sun.

A man stepped up to me. Rows of men behind. Packs on their backs and rifles in their hands. Sunlight flashing off steel helmets. This man had a mustache and never glanced at the animals along the road.

"There's a farm ahead, sir. I'll have the lads check for a pump."

Then, in a gloomy building at night. Dust thick on the floor. Men talked around me. I was apart, away from them, beside only one other.

My companion tried to tell me something important. Like with the water pump man, I could not listen. He read from a notebook in his hand.

How could he ask my opinion on poetry? While maggots flopped and convulsed down sunken faces—so crowded, they forced each other out? While the young man in the corner scratched his own head until his fingers were bloody? While another sang about ghost horses as he smoked one cigarette after the next, lighting one with the butt of the last?

Still reading to me, insistent. He jabbed his finger at a page.

I wanted to shoot him. I scrambled to my feet. I said I had to write a postcard.

Then I stood in a river of mud, legs braced, shouting, "Get out of there, Attwater!"

I couldn't see him, couldn't feel him, and couldn't get away myself. Scorching metal flew past my face.

"Attwater!" Panic and mud sucked me back into that dark river.

I woke with a jolt, shivering and disoriented.

11

The TV plays a cooking competition show. Both girls riveted.

10:00 p.m. and I sit at the kitchen table, laptop open—working. Asleep sitting up. Fresh anxiety that the girls are not in bed. Then remember: Torin asked me to bring them to the restaurant tonight.

I open my mouth to tell Isabelle and Carine they can get ready to go. Parting my lips, I see flopping maggots—bloated like slugs—almost tasting them. I must shut both mouth and eyes for several minutes.

Hands shake on my keyboard. Still nauseated when I inform them we can go.

Only a dream. Only a dream. I wonder if I am trying to reassure— or trying to convince myself.

CHAPTER TWO

"Ready! Set!"

Flep watches in alarm as Carine dashes between tables like a hummingbird.

"Go," Isabelle finishes under her breath. She flops into the chair opposite Flep and takes a bite of a cream puff.

Her little sister is almost to the restaurant's front door before she looks around.

"You cheated!" Carine shrieks.

"Did not. Anyway, you skipped the count." Isabelle licks lemon cream from the center of a puff. "You won, so how could I have cheated?"

"You didn't even run!" Carine races back toward them.

Isabelle shrugs and pops the rest of the pastry into her mouth.

They sit toward the back of the dining room at Torin's restaurant, Chaleur. Renard, the host, just left—though noise from behind reminds them that there is still cleanup underway.

Flep finds the gloom depressing. His pulse quickens as half-formed images of dark nights in the cold fill his mind, listening as men die around him.

Chaleur is French fusion—regionally influenced, organic, and the topic of dozens of local and national write-ups, glowing reviews, and devoted fans. The place is such a success, Torin plans to open a second location soon.

If only it felt more inviting. Black and white, nothing generous with its presence. Torin is no designer, unless working on the canvas of a plate.

Flep notices Carine glance at him as she returns to their table and the leftover croquembouche.

She looks away. She will not ask him to race. Carine won't ask him to do anything with her. She will *allow* him to read to her or draw with her or attempt to help in the kitchen—as she did tonight for dinner, though her big sister mostly cooked their salmon and vegetables. Neither girl will ask.

Still too new to them, Flep knows. They can warm up to him at their own pace. Or...not. It has crossed his mind, though he keeps the worry at bay.

Watching Carine stalk to the table to grab a tiny pastry, Flep wonders if the girls' mother, Amélie, has any idea they are being allowed up so late. To eat dessert.

He would never have brought them to the restaurant after hours on his own. They are six and eleven. They shouldn't be up until midnight on a Monday—or any other night. Not his kids. Not his decision.

As much as for them, Flep wishes he were also not down here on Lexington Avenue while the chefs close and clean. He is the one falling asleep.

"Don't you want any?" Isabelle glances at Flep, pushing the plate toward him.

He smells sugar and lemon. It makes him feel sick.

Why did she have to offer? This is something he does not want to ignore, an invitation to a shared experience that he needs from them— longs for.

Flep opens his mouth, starting to shake his head. Carine looks up from where she leans on the table, standing between them to eat a lemony puff.

Why not offer IRS paperwork? Or the flu?

Could he hide it? Drop it? He has no coat pocket on this June night, still in black jeans and a light teal button-down from work.

Torin knows Flep can't do lemon in sweet things. Lemon on fish or salad dressing—okay. Not lemon pastry.

Torin, clad in black slacks and white chef's coat, had whisked the plate out to them fifteen minutes earlier, praising his daughters for recommending the dessert.

"A hit. You two are geniuses." He had rested the pastry tower before the girls, telling Flep he would be right back, and they could go home together. "They were so popular we only have this one lemon stack left," he added, giving Flep a wry smile.

Now, the sisters have not invited Flep into their games around lonely tables, yet Isabelle noticed him not eating and wishes to share.

Both girls watch him, one pair of blue eyes and one of brown boring into him.

He was scarcely older than Carine when his mother had brought home two bags of groceries that Flep never forgot. Usually, it was a loaf of bread, peanut butter, and dry beans in bulk. A treat meant cheddar cheese or an apple. On that autumn day, after picking Flep up from first grade, she opened the back of the old station wagon to reveal overflowing bags.

Flep had wondered if she got a bonus from the department store where she worked, or had there been a huge sale on groceries? But he didn't ask.

Arms around a sack, he clambered up two flights of stairs to their apartment. He unpacked on the card table they used for a kitchen table. So much that he left the half-gallon of milk and celery in a chair. Canned soups, canned tomatoes, canned green beans, an orange, potatoes, bread, cereal, eggs, even frozen chicken drumsticks.

"Let's have a feast." His mother put the chicken in a baking dish and washed potatoes at the sink, assuring Flep they would have real mashed potatoes with milk. "This will take a while. How about dessert first?"

From the bottom of a bag, she produced a miniature lemon pound cake, golden and wrapped in cellophane. Flep was again in awe.

They sat together at the table, a glass and plate before each. The milk was room temperature from being out in the bag. The cake tasted dry, not quite stale. It filled his mouth with a burst of lemon flavor, its sugar glaze like candy. With his tongue coated in sweet lemon, Flep talked about the watercolor he did in school while his mother asked questions and the radio played pop music.

With chicken in the oven and potatoes simmering, she left to rest before dinner.

Flep remained at the table with his medieval knights coloring book, looking up soon after to make note of the chicken timer. His mother had forgotten to set it.

He hurried to ease open her bedroom door. Words stuck in his throat as he glanced inside to drawn blinds and bars of gray light. She sat on her bed, hunched forward, face covered by tissue, shoulders shaking.

Flep had pulled the door back and fled to the table. He sat underneath—as he did when there was a thunderstorm, or his mother was upset about bills, or his school lunch was stolen and he couldn't tell her.

The taste of lemon cake still in his mouth, he did not know why she sobbed that afternoon while dinner cooked. He did not know until weeks later that the bags came from the local food bank. He did not know until many years later that it had been the first time in her life she experienced charity as a recipient rather than a donor.

Flep has never, in three decades, eaten another lemon pastry.

Still, Isabelle offers. Carine also watches with interest.

"Thanks, Bell." Flep smiles and reaches to take the smallest cream puff he can see, though all are beautifully uniform.

Crisp crust, smooth middle. He holds his breath, swallowing cream without chewing. Tart lemon spills into his mouth like toothpaste. Flep almost gags.

Carine has already moved on, trying to get her sister to play the animal guessing game she had learned in kindergarten today. Isabelle swings her feet and looks around to the kitchen for her father's return.

Flep swallows once more—not choking, not gagging. Only a cream puff. A glass of water would be nice. Or Irish coffee.

What will he do if she offers again?

At last, Torin sweeps back to their table, all smiles. He lifts Carine to spin her around, asking what she thought of her treat.

Flep lets out a breath as she answers in a giggling jabber of French—meaning nothing to him. Torin laughs.

"What about a box?" Isabelle seems afraid that her father means to leave the rest of their dessert here.

"Run back and grab one for us. They're still cleaning. I told them we've got to dash—you two should be in bed." Torin grins at Flep, tilting his head as he sets Carine down and Isabelle runs off. "Or should I say three?"

Maybe Flep looks as bad as he feels. "How was dinner service?"

Carine chatters over him, telling her father how she beat her sister in a race.

"Never." Torin lifts his eyebrows.

"I did. Watch!" She runs, dodging tables.

Torin turns to Flep. He offers his hand. Flep takes it, familiar with the gesture, and flushes as Torin bends to kiss his knuckles.

"Service was a Slough of Despond compared to finding you all here," Torin says, although Flep had thought he missed the question amid Carine's verbal deluge.

"Funny, I don't feel that uplifting these days." Flep manages a smile as he stands.

"For you." Releasing his hand, standing close enough for Flep to see varied shades of blue in his irises, Torin reaches for his own breast pocket. He plucks free a tiny flower, pink and white, and passes it to Flep. "My apologies for having no mint."

His eyes are sparkling, embarrassing Flep further when Torin does not shift his focus even as Carine bounces off the wall somewhere to his right. He clearly suspects that Flep partook in dessert. Not a stiff drink, but the flower taste will chase away lingering lemon.

Flep drops his gaze, taking the little flower in thumb and forefinger, feeling electricity from Torin's skin. He longs to hug Torin—but feels too self-conscious in the restaurant with Torin's employees in the background.

"Thank you." Flep lifts his eyes to Torin's as Torin turns his head.

"That's how I won!" Carine returns. "Daddy! Were you watching?"

"Of course I was—"

"Watch this time." Off again, undaunted, knocking over a chair.

Isabelle meets them with her bag, telling Torin that Carine ate four puffs, though she was not supposed to have more than two. This leads Carine to calling her a liar, then Torin debating with them as they start for home.

Flep feels bad for Isabelle. Although he grew up an only child, he thinks he understands her efforts at stability. Alert to Torin not providing a carryout box and her little sister's sugar intake, while Torin slides on the responsibility scale.

Flep did not even know Torin had issued Carine with a limit. Isabelle could have told Flep, making him dessert police, but she still has no faith in him.

He hangs back, nibbling off petals, as they walk home. Flep had never eaten a flower until a year ago, surprised to find that, not only do they not taste like perfume, but that he enjoys them. Then again, half of what he eats these days was unknown a year ago. Like stepping from high school Spanish into an immersion program.

He pockets the stem, unsure if it counts as littering to drop it on the sidewalk of Lexington.

Torin, discussing grams and nutritional values for each cream puff with Isabelle, slows until he can walk beside Flep, arm at his back, hand on Flep's far shoulder.

"You only have to know the overall value of the batch of cream and choux dough," Isabelle says, walking ahead and looking around while Carine tries to snatch the bag from her. "Divide all your grams in each batch into the number of puffs you make. How much is—? Ree, stop it!"

"That's smart, Bell." Torin beams. "Give it to me before monkeys pillage it."

"Daddy, I didn't eat four—" Carine starts, following the bag as it is passed.

"Of course you didn't. How many do you want for breakfast?"

"Lots!" She is distracted when they reach their block and races to meet the evening doorman, her unbound hair streaming behind.

Torin pulls Flep's head over to kiss his temple as they follow the girls to the door. "Next time, they're all chocolate."

Flep manages a smile, leaning on Torin in his fatigued haze.

Inside the apartment, Torin puts the girls to bed while Flep almost falls asleep brushing his teeth.

At least Torin is already home. After a quick shower to wash away sweat and grease and food aromas from the kitchen, maybe they can both sleep.

Flep starts awake when Torin climbs into bed beside him, alarmed to realize he had drifted off. He never heard Torin walk into the master bedroom or shower.

He rolls toward Torin, pressing his face into Torin's pillow. "Sorry."

Torin kisses his brow. "What for?" he asks, tone amused. "I was just going to say thanks for getting the girls today. Didn't know you'd done anything wrong." Torin's hair is wet, his skin hot from the shower. He still smells of thyme, browned butter, and red wine.

What did Flep do wrong...? Right now, being a lackluster boyfriend. Occasional babysitting is about as proactive as he has been lately.

They work so much, and on such opposing schedules, that they see little of one another most days. They had more of a sex life together before Flep moved in. Back then—this time last year, last autumn, around the holidays—Flep was sleeping. No nightmares. Certainly not recurring, horrifying ones.

Flep feels disquieted, worrying that Torin will think his dropping into bed night after night and passing out, even when the girls are not staying over, is a sign of disinterest. Worse, that Torin himself could be regretting this choice by now.

"I'm not sure I should have moved—" Flep starts, trying to explain his apology.

"Of course you should have moved in," Torin interrupts, kissing him again, lips lingering on Flep's. "People have sleep problems all the time. It'll pass."

Flep reaches to stroke Torin's jaw, sliding his fingers through wet hair and down Torin's neck. Torin turns his head to kiss Flep's palm.

"Have time for breakfast with us before work tomorrow?" Torin asks.

Always food. It's how Torin interprets the world. Since being with him, Flep finds himself preoccupied more by meals. Even odors and tastes of his dreams remain with him for hours after the visuals fade.

Torin follows his knuckles around and takes Flep's first two fingers into his mouth.

Flep smiles, eyes shut, as Torin's teeth press into his skin. The man is so tactile, so orally curious. He explores the world like a puppy—

mouth first. He can easily open Flep's jeans button and zipper with his teeth. This skill shocked Flep the first time he did it, several months earlier in this same bedroom.

"Doesn't that hurt your teeth?" Flep had asked. "The metal zipper?"

Torin laughed and shoved him back on the bed. "*That's* what you're thinking? Seriously?" Torin followed, straddling him. "Try it."

"I'd hate to waste thousands of years of evolution." Flep had wiggled his thumbs.

So easy back then. They teased and laughed and met for lunch or a walking breakfast in Central Park before Flep went to work. Flep rarely felt awkward walking with Torin, even kissing as they parted. Torin was self-confident enough for them both.

He ached to introduce Torin to his mother, though that time was long gone. She would never see her son settled, never know if he had found the family that they both wanted for him—which both thought unlikely after he came out.

But he could meet Torin's family: the daughters Torin had talked about. Flep longed to feel a connection as fast as he had with their gregarious father. Such anticipation had left him unprepared for their disdain—which, again, involved food.

He had first spent time with the sisters at Carine's sixth birthday party last February at the Park. A guest list comprised of Carine's kindergarten friends and her sister, mother, father, French grandparents on her mother's side, and Flep.

Flep expected pizza and cake. They had a picnic of lobster salad in lettuce cups, walnut quinoa salad, homemade dill pickles, sparkling apple cider, and mini cupcakes—vanilla with strawberry and chocolate with caramel.

Flep knew on that cold, sunny day—watching Isabelle referee younger kids and Carine shout her love of lobster to the world, while half the family spoke French around him—that he was in way over his head. This was no premade family he could knit himself seamlessly into. These children—and their divorced parents—were as remote from his life as if they came from Antarctica.

Of course, moving in was the next logical step.

Which, all things considered, is working out swimmingly. Except for one thing which has nothing to do with Torin or the girls. Nothing to do with food. Nothing to do with moving in at all, as far as Flep can see.

Gently, Flep pulls his fingers from Torin's mouth. "I'm sorry." Breathing words against Torin's lips. "I love you."

"It's okay," Torin whispers, stroking Flep's cheek with the backs of his fingers. "Turn over."

Flep feels hardly conscious enough to comply, but rolls away from Torin and leans into him. Torin reaches across his chest, pressing to Flep's back, kissing his neck, ducking his head to breathe against Flep's T-shirt collar.

Flep is too far away to hear as Torin murmurs something. Maybe about sleep or breakfast. Maybe an endearment. It doesn't matter. Torin's arm around him matters, holding him tight and warm and not letting go. As terrifying as each night is becoming, the thought of waking alone from these nightmares is the only thing that makes Flep feel more afraid. To avoid that, he can live with his own selfishness—can stand to disrupt Torin's life as well. He cannot face this, whatever it is, alone.

Wednesday, June 29

I sat on something damp, leaning on a cold wall. Not a wall. Maybe dirt. But rough and bumpy. Larger, more uneven than bricks.

Dark fog hung around me, metallic on my tongue. I longed to speak to someone. There was a man nearby. It would have been wrong to speak. Or start a fire. There could be no light. We sat alone in the dark on seeping walls of earth or clay or...canvas?

In a mud wall, the back of a shin and heel of a boot jutted out. Underground. Like us. Our grave was open to the frozen night. This dead man with the boot was encased in earth, all besides that foot.

My living companion reached to grab something off the boot. A flask. He took a swig. He rested it back on the boot and went on watching.

Trying not to shiver, trying to be silent, I sat as hours, or days, stretched by.

I woke to a predawn bedroom, feeling more miserable than I had from all the screams or explosions of previous nights.

Still so cold and damp, I want to grab all the towels from the bathroom, all the blankets from the closet, all the coats in the apartment, and wrap up like a mummy. I long for a blazing fire and hot tea. Although I have never lived anywhere with a fireplace and I don't like tea.

Even so, the room feels hot. Torin has the window open, despite an acrid city stench crowding in. A warm breeze shifts the blinds.

Only one sheet over us. Shuddering, I press closer against Torin, trying to keep my illuminated tablet away from his face. I'm sure I already woke him once.

He has said light sleeping is a biological response to being a parent. Waking to an infant's cry could mean life or death. His kids are not exactly infants anymore. Still, parenthood makes a better excuse than caffeine, hyperactivity, or other issues associated with racing minds and an inability to sit still or do only one job at one time.

At 2:00 a.m. Torin abandoned stillness and ran his hand up my freezing arm to my shoulder. "Flep? What're you doing?"

When I said, "Updating my dream journal," he sighed and told me to do it in the morning.

I might as well pull the covers up since he is awake anyway. Or get up for more blankets. And anything else I can think of to stall going back to sleep.

Friday, July 1

So many images. More and more specific sights emerging. Craters of mud, handwritten letters, a strip of pale fabric I lifted in the air.

I'm sitting at the kitchen table in a patch of morning sunlight, shivering while New York City scorches. Over 80°F outside and hardly past sunup.

The girls are in the living room with the TV on. At their mother's place for the past two days, returned last night. She does not have cable, or a TV.

Torin is still in bed. I crept away after the third time waking us both, finally able to see a pink horizon.

He plans to cook them lobster today, launching the weekend, not that he has one. He takes only Mondays "off"—still working from home any way he can, or taking the occasional trip from the city to visit his suppliers. He refers to these as "my farms," and I originally thought he owned property upstate. Not even close.

In these summer months, he gets the girls to go with him. Apparently an effort since they are not impressed by farmyard aromas or ground cover. I wouldn't mind joining them for a day out sometime. Mondays are not so flexible in my book.

They're the ones who are off now. Carine has nothing until starting first grade in September. Isabelle will keep going to ballet all summer, but nothing else. She lives for it. That and cooking.

24

Torin will take them to their grandparents' place—his ex-in-laws—before he leaves for the restaurant. I'll fetch them after my own work. Then Saturday morning for all four of us until their mother is back to collect them for the rest of the weekend.

The poor kids are juggled like beanbags.

They tiptoed from their bedroom for the TV half an hour ago without glancing at me. Now they have the volume low as Carine draws with crayons and Isabelle dances on a half-inch wide ribbon lying across the rug to practice balance.

Dreams. This is supposed to be about dreams.

A glint from something steel. A splash of mud on my face. A man calling for someone. Voice echoing through my skull.

Martha? Was he calling Martha? Or Mary? Or was it Mother?

Snow drifting over my legs. Sitting on dirt. The snow looked so...white. Nothing else was ever white. Only dark and dull. Besides the blood.

That's what happened last night.

Blood in snow. Snow on the field. Not a field. A stone road. Not a road. A...quarry? A pitted, rutted, twisted up place. Holes in the ground the size of trucks, or houses. The surface of the moon if the moon was black and dead. Bright blood ran through ice.

I looked around, tried to call out—knew I was dying. No one there. Only a white and black and red broken world.

Just glanced up from my tablet to see Carine in the kitchen, hunting for breakfast. I should help her, or offer to make something like toast or an egg. Too embarrassing. She finds a banana and slips back to the quiet TV.

I would be more than happy to help them with breakfast. I would love to. But both extremely bright girls regard me as an imbecile—a well-meaning yet pitiably inept character at best. This image is enhanced each time I make an appearance in the kitchen.

Through the windows, across 2nd Avenue toward the East River, the sky is golden, the city silver. Yet I see all through a sheen of scarlet blood.

CHAPTER THREE

Amélie stands just inside the closed door, one foot crossed in front of the other to balance on the toe of her boot. Her iPhone reflects the overhead foyer light as a white glare. She tilts the phone and her head while she reads.

Someone runs from the hall through the living room, then back again down the hall to the small bedroom.

"Ree? Have you seen my workbook?"

"No!"

Another little set of feet darts around in the girls' shared bedroom. A heavier footfall sounds in the kitchen.

Amélie does not look up from her phone.

The stalling grows worse every week. They do it at both homes, yet only when both parents are present. If she tells them to grab their things, they are going to Dad's for the day, both are ready in seconds. If Torin comes to collect them in person, they take half an hour to find everything.

Why? She cannot believe they want their parents face-to-face anymore than Torin and Amélie desire this. Yet here she is, standing in the doorway, reading emails for fifteen minutes. As if they were surprised by her arrival.

Isabelle flits past once more. "Ree! Where is my book?"

"I didn't touch your book!"

Amélie looks up.

Isabelle scowls as she storms past the foyer and her waiting mother.

"Bell? Do you want to stay here tonight?" Amélie asks. "You don't have to come home with me if you don't want to."

"No," Isabelle snaps. "We'll be right there. Ree!" She stalks down the hall.

Amélie objects to her eldest daughter's tone, but says nothing. She understands impatience. And she understands what are good and bad times to discuss these things. Unlike her ex-husband, who will argue anything with anyone at any time for a thrill.

Flep appears from the kitchen, watching Isabelle go. He also seems to be considering saying something, eyes troubled as he sees her march past.

Don't do it. Amélie's gaze goes back to the screen. *Keep your mouth shut, Flep.*

He does. More brains than the girls give him credit for. Polite introverts are so easy to underestimate. She pushes a button to start a response.

"Beautiful boots." Flep is looking at her feet.

Amélie glances down. "Coach. It's the Trudie boot in python." She looks at him. "But I doubt you'll find them in your size."

He smiles. "Very funny."

She returns her attention to her phone. "Would you tell Torin to do something about these lights? Or fix them yourself? Surely you have an eye for soft light."

"It is harsh. He's not much for noticing that kind of thing."

"No...but he's not much for noticing anything besides work, the girls, work, and himself, is he?"

When Flep says nothing, she again looks up.

He stands on the gleaming maple floor in the open space between the kitchen and living room, gazing around at stark bulbs.

"You look like a raccoon," Amélie says. "Still not sleeping?"

He runs a hand through his hair. "Uh...no. Not really. Thanks for the suggestion about the dream journal. I'm trying to write them down."

"Still the same things over and over?"

"And some new details. But it's often all dark. A lot of noise and confusion... Maybe I'll figure it all out if I can keep track of them." Flep shakes his head. "Does that make sense? Figure out a dream? It's just a dream..."

"I would label it sleep deprivation and stress inducing while edging closer to a full-fledged disability every day."

He smiles ruefully. "That makes it sound like a serious medical condition."

"Extreme sleep deprivation is a serious medical condition."

"Bad dreams are not." He will not meet her eyes.

Torin steps through the kitchen behind Flep, buttoning his shirt. It will be covered by a white chef's jacket after he walks to work.

"Did you get the reports from June?" Like Flep, he also does not look at her—though for completely different reasons.

How about a hello, asshole?

Amélie goes back to her phone. She feels tension rise off Flep like steam from a kettle. He must want to say goodbye to Torin and the girls because he does not leave the room, despite the two exes being in close proximity.

And he has never even seen us really going at each other.

"Girls, are you ready?" Torin calls. "Your mother's waiting."

Like they don't know.

"Just a second!" Isabelle shouts back.

"I'm not in any hurry, Torin," Amélie says with her gaze on the phone, thumb still moving.

"Of course you are," he says. "You're always in a hurry."

"No." She looks up. "*You* are always in a hurry. I have my priorities straight."

Flep slinks backward.

"Speaking of priorities—" Torin keeps glancing around for something. Probably his wallet since the keys are where they should be by the door. "I want to take the girls to see the fireworks on Monday."

"They'll enjoy that."

She assumed as much. Torin is not a planner. But the 4th of July is the day after tomorrow. He has made more of an effort to be with the girls since the divorce, cutting a seven-day workweek back to six—or, six and a half—for the first time since the place opened. As owner and executive chef, it's true he needs to be there. Lately, he is finally learning to hand over the reins to his seconds.

"I don't have time to stand on a street corner on the West Side for half the day to keep a spot before the show," Torin goes on. "Can we go to Kate and Aidan's place?"

"They're out of town," Amélie says.

"What?"

"Gone for two weeks. They're in Spain."

"*Shit.*" A whisper. He tries not to swear in front of the kids. "Could we go there anyway?"

"Break in, you mean? They didn't leave me keys to their place. We're not that close."

"Then what the hell are we supposed to do? I don't know anyone else with a view of the Hudson like that."

"Stand in the street with everyone else who the Earth does not orbit?" She returns to her phone.

"I'll keep a spot," Flep says. He has retreated to the far side of the kitchen. "I don't mind waiting out there."

Amélie smiles, almost grimacing. *Why not blow him while you're at it?*

When will Flep learn that accommodation is rarely the way to handle Torin? She cannot excuse people who can't say no, or otherwise don't stand up for themselves. Not even that she dislikes Flep. If she did, she would not care if he groveled.

"You can't do that," Torin says.

Really? It would occur to Torin that Flep has work, a life, friends, and interests and things he needs to get done? Is Flep's amenable approach paying off?

"No one can hold space like that," Torin continues. "The cops won't even let you bring lawn chairs. The crowd just pushes in. We'd never reach you."

Amélie resists a sigh as she finishes her note.

"I could take the girls then," Flep says.

"We'll have to figure out somewhere else. Do you know anyone over there?"

We. Does Flep know the distinction yet?

Just as well exes don't often spend time with the replacement. Flep would think she was being bitchy—or lying—if they had a real heart-to-heart about life with Torin. Hapless Flep must figure out Torin's pitfalls for himself.

"John, my boss at the studio." Flep looks even more uncomfortable. "Not someone I can ask favors from right now."

Isabelle hurries into the foyer with her bags. Carine trails with her own backpack, lower lip sticking out.

"Sorry, Mom. We're ready." Isabelle shoots her little sister a glare. "Finally."

Carine tugs on her shoes without saying anything.

Amélie pockets her phone. "I love your new hairband, Ree. That is so chic on you."

She smiles, but looks around to Torin. "Will you walk us downstairs, Daddy?"

"I can't, sweetheart. Got to find my wallet before I head out."

"Have a good night," Isabelle says. "You're booked, aren't you?"

"Of course." He kisses the top of her head. "Love you. Have a safe ride home. I'll see you on Monday."

"Dad, we don't have to go to the fireworks if there's not a good spot. I don't want to stand on the street all day. They're on TV."

"Sure," he says distractedly, reaching for Carine to kiss her. "We'll see. We might find somewhere. Have a stellar night, Ree. Make me something new for the menu."

She nods, eyes brightening.

Amélie wishes he would not encourage the girls to cook at her place. They love to cook. They do not love to clean up after themselves.

Down the hall, Carine tells Amélie about everything she has eaten lately. Breakfast, lunch, dinner, and snack. Every sauce and drink and spice.

Just a phase? Or is Carine, at six, destined to imitate her father? At this rate, she could be the youngest chef-owner of a restaurant in New York City history.

Amélie wants her children to pursue what they love. To have interests, passions, things they long to learn more about. Yet, she cannot help wishing that they will grow up to be something like dentists or teachers or sidewalk artists. Just so she never has to face Torin after one of his kids earns her first Michelin Star.

Monday, July 4

Snow. So much hot blood stretched away over white, it overwhelmed my eyes.

Then the dark again, and sitting on earth. Chalky dirt above ground level. An earth bench.

Paper in my hands. Maybe always there, but I could not see it before. This time, I remember holding it, feeling a slightly rough texture. I struggled to keep that paper away from blood, determined to protect it.

Snow again. Standing in snow, a man beside me.

Something fell from the sky. Ground shook as I started to move, ducking my head, looking around to my companion. A chunk of steel blazed past like a rocket. Grit powdered over me from the blast. A fine spray of hot liquid splashed my skin.

Lucky. That metal could have killed us. I reached for the man beside me, shaken by the nearness of it, opening my mouth.

He turned. He wobbled, staggered, and twisted on his feet. I saw his face clearly as he moved. But he no longer had one.

Half the man's head was gone. Like a sword had sliced down the middle of his skull to his throat, removing the whole right side. I saw the mass of brain tissue, the glint of white teeth and jawbone, a torn open nose, and half the tongue inside the open half of a mouth. Severed veins in the neck sprayed my face.

I leaped away, screaming, as the man toppled toward me.

Torin shook me awake. He kissed my ear, saying everything was okay.

I could not lie there in the dark, even feeling him beside me.

I got up, splashed water on my face, went for a glass, then stood looking out the window for half an hour.

I write this with Torin back to sleep beside me. While I pray not to join him.

CHAPTER FOUR

Flep sags into his desk chair, rubbing his eyes. He reaches mechanically to switch on the desktop Mac with his free hand, then sits still with his eyes closed, head bowed.

Mud vibrates under his boots. Men scream in his ears. Whistling metal zips past with a speed that hides the flight paths. Blood stretches over snow like a crimson river. Where is the paper? He reaches for paper, its familiar feel—needing that letter so desperately it's terrifying that it is not here.

Flep's eyes snap open. For an instant, he sees the paper clearly: brown and dirty, wet with snow, covered in handwriting, clutched in his freezing fingers. Holding his breath, hands shaking, he squints as he fights to see the words.

He blinks.

Sunlight falls across his work desk in a long rectangle from the small window. The computer awaits his password. Coffee steams in its lidded mug, sending up a wisp of vapor through the spout. A phone rings down the hall—an old-fashioned telephone sound, not a chime. Three or four people are talking in the office next door. The floor beneath his shoes feels solid. Air around him feels warm, even stuffy.

The clock on the wall to his left ticks softly, reminding him to be efficient.

Never waste a minute. You can rush and worry and stress all week and you will never get it back.

His mother's words. She was always trying to catch up. She never did. Flep keeps the clock for white noise in his workspace, reminding him to use every moment.

Yet, here he sits. Motionless and dumb in the busy studio offices.

A car horn honks outside. He is only four floors up and traffic is loud here. No screams though. No bullets or explosions. No snow. No blood.

He presses a hand to his stomach, fighting to swallow, pushing the mug away and turning his head at the same time.

"Boss?"

Flep spins in the swivel chair to face the door. "What?"

Simon steps back. "Sorry, didn't mean to—"

"That's fine," Flep says. "What do you want?"

"I just...have these sketches for you." The young intern holds out several sheets of hot press watercolor paper covered in graphite and ink sketches.

"Thank you." Flep takes them and turns away, avoiding meeting Simon's eyes.

"I can go over the ideas with you..." Simon trails off, addressing Flep's back. "Did you get breakfast? Need anything?"

"We'll talk about these before lunch," Flep says. "I'm leaving early today." He logs into the computer and turns back to Simon, trying to smile. "Happy 4th. Doing anything fun?"

Simon still looks uneasy.

Late attempt at civility not cutting it.

"Seeing friends tonight," the young man says. "We're trying to catch some fireworks."

"Good luck in that crowd."

"Thanks. They know their way around better than I do." Simon only came to Manhattan three months ago to start his internship with Time Marks. "Well..." He nods, smiling weakly. "I'll talk to you about those later."

"Give me a couple hours. I'll get back to you."

Light from Flep's office window catches Simon's Ray-Ban glasses as he glances down to the papers he handed Flep. He opens his mouth, nods, puts his hands behind his back, lets them hang at his sides, then hurries away.

Flep rubs his eyes again. *Heartless bastard.* That kid was probably up half the night doing these drawings. Now Flep is treating him like a prop?

He turns his attention to the screen. He'll make it up to Simon. Take him to lunch tomorrow with Tanya, the other art department intern, and talk over their progress. The two of them can brainstorm. Flep only has to encourage them and act like they have good ideas. They *do* have good ideas. Two smart kids and both superb artists.

"Flep!"

Half crouching away from the voice, he looks around. "John?"

"Do you have those concepts to show the producers?"

Friday, damn him. John first asked for them on *Friday*. The day before a weekend and major national holiday when half the team wasn't going to be here. But John Case, West Side, river front resident, does not believe in putting off until tomorrow what someone could have done for him yesterday.

"We're working on it," Flep says. "I'll have something ready tomorrow and get a meeting on Wednesday."

"Tomorrow? You've got four people on this. Good God." John shakes his head and turns away. "Well, whatever it takes."

As John stomps off, Flep exhales a slow breath, wishing he could also walk out.

CHAPTER FIVE

They catch a bus up 42nd Street, walk to Lincoln Highway, and look for a spot in the already thousands-strong crowd.

Isabelle glares through the masses toward the waterfront. Hours before sunset and the show. This is what compromise looks like.

She does not mind crowds, loves performances at her dance school, and mostly only gets nervous for auditions before she goes on stage. But, if she is going to bother doing something, she wants to do it right. If you're waiting a few hours for fireworks, you might as well wait six and have an amazing view. Otherwise, stay home and see them on TV.

Flep had to work most of the day—longer than he said he would—though he was not the reason for their late arrival. That was planned by her dad, who decided compromise was the only way.

He worked all morning from home, where he could shout at people over the phone instead of in person and update orders from upstate farms.

They fixed a picnic dinner. Each took a small bag since the cops wouldn't allow even a backpack. Flep carried a towel and bottle of water, Ree had a coloring book and water, and her father and herself split the food between them. Isabelle also carried her camera and antique iPod. The thing won't even get online. Only good for audio books and dance drills.

When will they let her get a real phone that can do more than make a call? Then she wouldn't need the old iPod.

Piers and park space have long been staked out. The four of them find a decent square of pavement with a curb to sit on.

Isabelle stands on one foot, trying to see the Hudson River through the crowd.

Ree is already pulling on Isabelle's foldaway grocery bag, telling everyone she is starving. She ate two goat cheese and apple tarts and three spears of white asparagus when they were packing.

Isabelle ignores her.

Dad stands behind them, muttering about their location and his best guess of fireworks placement.

"*Bell.*" Ree's voice rises as she yanks Isabelle's bag.

Isabelle is seized with a desire to kick her. She keeps it to herself. Ree hates being ignored. Still, Isabelle wishes her father would say something to stop her little sister from being such a pest.

"Carine?" Flep says beside her. "Could you help me spread the blanket?"

"I want a tart." She hardly looks at him.

"We can't eat before we're settled. Don't you want to sit?" He unfolds the towel.

Ree turns to him.

Thank you. Isabelle shifts to fourth position, biting her lip. She glances at Flep. She shouldn't be so hard on him. He's okay. The problem is not even his fault. So there is nothing he can do to fix it.

He smiles at Ree, holding out the towel, asking where she wants it.

Flep is always asking. *What would you like to do? How are you? Did you have a good day at kindergarten? Do you like the new dance instructor?*

Her parents are tellers. Not askers.

Maybe that is one reason they can never get along. *Do this, do that. That's wrong—fix it. Don't be late. Don't mess up.* Two tellers in one relationship.

Tabitha, at dance school, has parents who divorced and have not seen each other since: mother in New York City, father in Chicago. Tabitha flies back and forth for visits with her dad twice a year. She told Isabelle her parents will not speak to one another, not even to answer the phone on her behalf when one calls the other's place.

Tabitha thinks Isabelle is lucky.

Sometimes, Isabelle thinks Tabitha is lucky. Not only do Isabelle's parents still see each other and argue regularly, they even work together to an extent.

Her mom wanted her dad to buy her out of the restaurant. They compromised instead. Exactly what all that entailed, Isabelle does not know. But she knows compromise is always a bad thing.

She changes to third position. She shouldn't envy Tabitha. It would be horrible to only see either for two visits a year. She is lucky in so many ways with both of them. Still...

"Aren't we fine here? We'll be able to see..." Flep says, trying to convince her dad that he does not need to keep looking.

"We could get closer to the water. There might be a spot on a pier."

"Doesn't everything look crowded already, Torin?"

Isabelle looks again at Flep. He seems anxious—exacerbated by the dark circles under his eyes and his ruffled appearance.

She whirls to her dad in a light spin, shifting into first position. "No. We're fine here. We'd get smothered on a pier, even if we could find a spot."

"I'm starving," Ree wails again.

Does Ree know she is intervening, the way she has hidden things when one parent is coming to fetch them? Or does she really just want to eat?

"I'm hungry too," Isabelle says. "We'll stay here."

"Okay," her dad says, though he keeps looking around for something better.

Beside him, kneeling with Ree on the towel, Flep lets out a breath.

You're welcome. Back to fourth position. *Now we're even.*

Ree sits beside Flep on the curb while Isabelle stands by her dad on the street, facing them. They split up tarts, grilled asparagus, and bamboo skewers of cherry tomatos, fresh mozzarella, and basil.

Aromas of grilling meat and fried food fill the air as people buy and sell hotdogs, hamburgers, and other American fare to celebrate Independence Day.

Red, white, and blue hats, shirts, and flags bob everywhere. Her own family is not so festive. Flep has on khakis and Ree wears a yellow and blue skort with the "I Heart Lobster" shirt that their mom got her. Isabelle and her dad are in jeans, him in a black T-shirt and her in a sleeveless white blouse with navy detailing. That's white and blue enough.

He has extra shirts for both girls folded in the bottom of his food bag. So hot now, it's hard to imagine wanting them.

She does a half *battement tendu* as she eats.

"You put on sunscreen, right?" Dad asks her while he holds skewers out to the others.

She sighs. "Dad, you saw me put on sunscreen."

"Did you get your calls done this morning?" Flep asks him.

Isabelle watches him as they discuss her dad's farm suppliers and prices of produce and grass-fed beef this summer. He really does look bad. They talk about Chaleur for half an hour before her dad finally asks Flep about his own workday.

Ree starts coloring after Dad passes around homemade truffles: raspberry with dark chocolate, and Key lime with white chocolate and toasted coconut.

Grown-ups are surprised that he cooks so much at home. They think it will be a case of the cobbler's children. In fact, he uses the home kitchen as a test kitchen for the restaurant. Isabelle and Ree are the first to try possible dishes. And, used to be, Mom would too. Now Flep. But Flep isn't good with tastings like her.

She has an eye for flavors and a discerning palette that Dad still compliments. She knows all there is to know about French food, as far as Isabelle is concerned. Mom traveled between the south of France and New York City growing up. Dad only visited France with them to see relatives.

Flep does not have a discerning palette. He does not know the difference between Gouda and Gorgonzola. He gets things like bruschetta and prosciutto mixed up. He thinks roux is slang for a kangaroo.

Isabelle puts in earbuds as people push around them—greeting others, eating, talking on phones. Kids and parents sit along their curb.

Flep offers her his spot. She only shakes her head. It's good for her legs and back to have this upright stretching time. He looks so pale and haggard anyway, he probably should be sitting down. She can trade later.

Dad holds his arm out for her and Isabelle uses him as her barre while she listens to audio drills, trying not to bump anyone around them.

Everything is fine, if tedious, until the show finally starts after sunset. And Flep vanishes.

Tuesday, July 5

What was I thinking? No true nightmares to report. Only waking ones.

We waited over three hours for fireworks in a crowd that made my skin crawl. I had to sit down with Carine when we found a place, nauseated. I have never been able to handle crowds, even groups of ten. One reason I always wanted to work backstage.

Torin would have taken the girls alone, but they mean too much to me to refuse participating in the first big holiday all four of us have shared.

Torin had a long argument with Isabelle about learning pointe and bone development. Apparently, she is old enough to learn and get her first pointe shoes, but she is so small for her age that her teachers are reluctant. Not a happy conversation when it comes up: rubbing it in to an eleven-year-old that she looks two years younger.

Then he brainstormed with Carine for new appetizers. She wants everything to include lobster, though duck is the specialty at Chaleur. He has customers from upstate, Connecticut, New Jersey, and Pennsylvania coming just for the duck.

In the three hours, I almost forgot the crowd—helped by both girls talking to me like I was a real person. Torin seemed only slightly irritated by having to exercise his meager store of patience. Spending time with his children softened the situation for him as well.

By the time darkness fell, cheering and yelling spread. Hundreds waved flags for news cameras.

Torin picked up Carine. She waved both hands at a camera taking in miles of tightly packed people. Isabelle stood on her toes on the curb, looking into the sky.

I felt choked by hundreds of thousands of people who all seemed close enough to shake my hand. My stomach churned and I flinched against Torin and Carine as a flag-waver nearly caught me in the head with his elbow.

Stupid. Why not hang out in Times Square on New Year's Eve?

No way out. I would have had to fight through thousands of people to reach an open block where I could catch my breath. All over soon. Once the fireworks began, there would be something distant to focus on.

I closed my eyes and tried to take long breaths through my nose, afraid to open my mouth.

A cheer burst from the crowd closer to the waterfront. Music stopped. New music started. I opened my eyes.

First colors lit the sky over the Hudson. Then a series of explosive pops and cracks rose to thundering booms.

I stepped back, my heart leaping like a trapped bird. I couldn't breathe, tripping into people behind us. Beer fumes filled my nose, followed by smoke as more rockets burst over the water. A rattling, breaking crescendo of fire blazed through darkness as the mass of humanity subsided to watch.

Broken ground stretched away for miles. Snow glowed the soft orange and lavender hue of a watercolor painting.

I stood on a crude wooden ladder, frozen and slick beneath my boots. Posts, metal stakes, and scraps of shattered trees stuck up across the landscape. Dark, twisting bunches of wire crisscrossed snow.

My breath fogged, freezing condensation to my mustache. My hands shook, one on the ladder rung, one on a revolver attached to a cord. Nonstop explosions—*boom, boom, boom*—rumbled through the ground, the ladder, my bones. Fragments of frozen mud sprinkled my helmet, clattering like nails.

I freed a hand to feel for the letter in my breast pocket. Tears filled my stinging eyes. My heart beat faster as fear chilled my lungs and left my head spinning.

A sense of doom took hold of me, nearly making me retch. I fought for outward calm but that made me feel worse. I wanted to scream, sob, run away, fall to my knees. Home. I needed to be home.

Then I was falling back, staggering. I shoved through a dark crowd of a million, fighting for fresh air as I pushed past police and noise and trash bags and drunks, ran into an alleyway, and vomited in a drain.

I fell against a building, reaching for my face, looking down at my feet. I had no mustache. No heavy boots. No revolver. Of course.

I ran on, my own senses still tricking me as explosions burst through the summer night, ground vibrating. So terrified, so certain I was about to die, I could think of nothing but getting away.

CHAPTER SIX

Torin stretches under the sheet, arching backward and extending his arms. Avoiding the headboard, he hears his shoulders pop. He hopes the headache is only a waking one.

Flep lies on his back, staring at the white ceiling lit by July sun reflecting off Manhattan windows. How long has he been awake?

They were home before midnight. Flep had gone at once to shower while Torin sent the girls to bed and read a chapter of *The Trumpet of the Swan*. Amélie has read to them in French since Bell was a toddler. Torin reads in English, his own French shaky and mostly concerning food.

Torin relaxes from his stretch and leans over to kiss Flep.

"I'm sorry about last night," Flep says. "Running out on you."

"You were sick. Not your fault." Torin pushes his left hand through Flep's hair. He feels as if they've had this exchange a lot lately. Why does Flep apologize for everything?

Flep closes his eyes. "If I was 'sick,' you'd think I'd be able to find treatment."

"Have you really looked? What about sleep specialists? Anyone who studies REM sleep?"

Flep nods, his eyes still shut.

Torin and the girls were only able to find him last night after Torin texted to ask where he was. They met all the way out at 10th Avenue and West 42nd in front of MiMA.

Flep had looked ghostly in the streetlights, trembling. Torin took his icy hands, asking if he was okay and what had happened. His lips felt as cold as his fingers. His mouth tasted acidic, making Torin wonder if he'd been vomiting. He did not ask in front of the girls.

Flep only apologized and said he was fine: he had grown dizzy and just needed to get out of the crowd.

The night had stayed so warm that Torin never bothered getting the girls' extra shirts out of his bag. Yet Flep was unable to warm up until he got home to a hot shower. Even then, he heaped extra blankets on the bed that Torin could not stay under himself.

Flep said he saw things from those nightmares in the fireworks and crowds. And he had felt sick. Torin recommended he see a doctor, but could think of no other solutions.

"If I didn't know better, I'd say what you're describing sounds like post-traumatic stress," Torin had said at last, his face against Flep's shoulder in the dark room.

Flep took a slow breath. "If I didn't know better, that's what I'd say also."

"Sure you don't have repressed memories of childhood...uh, warfare?"

Finally, Flep had laughed. "Ridiculous, isn't it? I don't know what to think." He rolled onto his side to face Torin. "I'm sorry it's affecting you and the girls. I hate being the world's worst party date."

Torin had tasted his wintergreen toothpaste and smiled. Only dreams. He could not get too worked up about the symptoms when his mind raced with price lists, orders to place, menus, staff changes, taxes, budgeting, school and stories and kids' schedules and new clothes to replace ones outgrown. Even if he tried, what could he do to help someone with such an abstract ailment?

Now the bedroom is bright—no one pulled the blinds last night—and it's easy to return to morning routines.

Torin sits up, dragging a hand over his short hair. "Breakfast before you go?"

Flep looks at the digital clock and nods.

"What do you want?"

"Protein. Eggs, I guess, with crumpets."

"Excuse me?" Torin stares at him.

Flep blinks, looking confused. "What did I say?"

"You said you want crumpets."

"What are crumpets?" Flep appears bewildered, even alarmed.

"A kind of British biscuit served at breakfast or with tea, like English muffins, full of holes from extra baking soda."

"I've never heard of them...I don't think." Flep also sits up. "That was..." He trails off without finding a sufficient word.

"I'll be glad to make you some, but they're a yeast bread. We're not having them this morning unless you can delay going into work by about two hours."

Flep smiles weakly. "That would go over well."

Torin leans in to kiss his temple. His body temperature seems normal, though he kept those extra blankets all night.

"You get ready for work, I'll fix breakfast. We'll turn on NPR if we want news. Sounds like the TV is already monopolized."

Breakfast. This he can do. He is not sure where the money will come from for Ree's new private school on top of Bell's school and dance. He does not know how to help Flep. His own brain feels fogged by months of diminishing sleep. But he can take care of his family as he was once taken care of by meals.

He has hardly cracked an egg before Ree is in the kitchen to help.

By the time the oven has preheated, Bell glides in, twirling on hardwood, asking what they are making.

As Torin grabs plates, Flep joins them, dressed for work, listening attentively while Ree rattles off the menu to him.

They sit down together: all four spaces filled.

Torin smiles, headache gone. Nothing so bad after all. Nothing they cannot overcome at a table.

Leaving the girls with the dishes, Torin walks Flep to the elevator as he starts out half an hour later.

"Any better?" Torin asks, pushing the elevator button and watching Flep in the empty hall.

"I'm okay." Flep will not meet his eyes. "Thanks for breakfast."

"How about one at the Park tomorrow? The girls will be with Amélie, and I can go in late for lunch service."

Flep looks up. Only a hint of a smile reaches his eyes, which he seems hardly able to keep open. "That would be great. It's been a couple months."

"Maybe we'll have crumpets." Torin smiles as the elevator pings and the doors slide open.

"Looking forward to the Park." Flep leans forward to kiss him.

"Don't fall asleep at work."

"Not sure I can make promises about that at this point."

The last Torin sees of Flep as the doors close, he is stifling a yawn.

Wednesday, July 6

A hot day this time. Sun seared across the wings of black and green flies. The pungency of death made me feel like I was chewing decaying meat.

I looked down at the letter in my hands, balanced on a scrap of board. Writing it, not reading it. I wanted to finish, but lost my train of thought as my stomach turned over. Flies swarmed on every exposed thread of skin.

I glanced up again to earth stretching away at eye level. Flies rose, blacking out patches of horizon, as something moved, disturbing the stillness of the stinking quagmire.

Leaning forward, I clutched board and letter in my right hand, reaching with my left. I pressed my face to a tube—a periscope—scouring the quarry or field.

Another cloud of flies. There: not just one animal. Several lean, shuffling creatures on short legs with large ears and apparently no tails. Shapeless bodies like skinny potatoes.

Hogs. Half a dozen stray pigs. There must have once been farms out here. Now pigs were out scattering flies, looking for food. No, they had food.

They stopped at decomposing human bodies, biting and nosing to turn over faces stiff with black blood. Brief squabbles erupted as each jockeyed for the best spot into the skull cavities, pushing with strong snouts. The winning pig ate out the dead man's brain before moving on to the next corpse.

When Torin woke me from whatever I was doing in my sleep, I rushed for the shower, not glancing at the clock.

I still don't care what time it is. I only sit at the kitchen table, heart pounding, until the apartment glows with dawn light. Now I can get ready for work. Torin wants to share breakfast at the Park on our way. Which, yesterday, seemed like a nice idea.

CHAPTER SEVEN

Not exactly dinner and a show, though it's as close as they get to a date these days. It has been several weeks since Torin took Flep to the Park for breakfast before work: a walk on quiet trails with freshly prepared panini or leftovers from dinner.

Even longer since they really did go to dinner and a show. After they met last spring, Flep kept inviting Torin to musicals—his favorite activity—and Torin took a couple of days off work.

Torin could never get behind anything that involved passive observation on the part of the participant. Still, he liked that Flep liked them. Flep got tickets—*Chicago* and *Wicked*—and Torin took him to some of the best restaurants in town, none of which Flep had ever set foot in.

When, the year before, Torin learned it was Flep's birthday in June, he took Flep to Strip House for the twenty-four-layer chocolate cake. This, Torin was sure, sparked a revelation wherein Flep decided he could give the wider culinary world a chance.

A solid ten months now since they've had a whole day and evening set aside for the two of them.

On Wednesday morning, Torin gets up early, finding Flep at the table, never having returned to bed after his latest nightmare.

Torin puts together a ham and Brie panino for himself and—at Flep's request for a vegetarian option—a spinach, sun-dried tomato, and Brie version. He brews coffee, rinses organic grapes for dessert, and pours the coffee into two thermal mugs. As much as he loves his panini press and ice cream maker, it's the coffee maker that may be his favorite home kitchen purchase.

He packs a paper bag while Flep grabs his messenger bag.

A stunning July day and the perfect breakfast partner to share it with. Haggard as he perpetually looks these days, Flep smiles, thanking Torin as they start up 2nd Avenue, cutting over toward 5th.

Only joggers, walking or biking commuters, and a few dog walkers frequent the Park at 8:00 in the morning, their shadows long. Noise fades as they walk up from the south end. The smells are rich with grass and coffee rather than urine and exhaust fumes.

They make a ragged loop to what Torin refers to as "the dog"—a regular stop with the girls. For once, no children climb on Balto. They take a left at the bronze monument to walk under the bridge and start west. Flep is already checking his phone for time.

Torin wishes they had more mornings like this, gratified to see Flep relax as they walk side by side. They talk about food, the girls' schools, their jobs, and upcoming musicals or plays Flep intends to see.

"Want to plan a Saturday off next month, and I'll take you all to a show?" Flep asks, passing back the paper bag with grapes. *"The Lion King?"*

"Later in the year." Torin smiles, watching Flep's dark hair glow in morning sun. "I've been too late and too early a lot lately. You're welcome to take the girls to something if you want to."

"It would feel like a bribe for just the three of us to go." He looks sideways at Torin, squinting as they walk south, passing long greenbelts. "What do you mean late and early? You haven't had a complete day off since the New Year. Not even Carine's birthday or when—I mean, I didn't need you to take a day off when I moved. I told you that. Just saying, you're not exactly missing a lot of work."

"I'm supposed to set an example, not only run things. Going in late and leaving early *is* a day off in this business."

Flep looks away, pressing his lips together. Torin wonders if he wants to say something about it being a shitty business then. Not something Flep would say out loud. Maybe just wanting to say, *What about us?*

Torin reaches to touch the back of his neck, bag and mug in his left hand, walking so close their shoulders touch. He slides his fingers up into Flep's hair.

"There's so much going on just now," Torin says.

56

Flep nods.

"I need to get out to my farms in the next weeks and 'drag'—as they see it—Bell and Ree along. You're always welcome to step out of the City with us on a Monday."

Flep starts to speak, but his slightly pained expression rushes ahead of him.

"Or," Torin hurries on, "free after work this Monday for something less time-consuming?"

A wry smile. "As long as I'm awake."

"Meet us at Bethesda Fountain. We'll have a summer picnic by the Lake and still get everyone to bed at a reasonable time."

"Sounds perfect." Flep's expression remains drawn as he looks forward. "Sorry, Torin, I'm—"

"You know, I think I'm getting used to it."

When Flep gives him a look, Torin goes on.

"Really, you're improving my ability to sleep on airplanes and that kind of—"

Laughing now. "Such a silver lining."

Torin grins. "Just worry about sorting this out for yourself. Don't worry about me."

"Isn't that usually meant sarcastically?"

"I'm never sarcastic." Torin loves seeing him laugh. Watching Flep's face, hand still at his neck, Torin adds, "Let's find a restroom."

Flep laughs at that as well. "I'm late for work. Though that has nothing to do with a firm *no,* of course."

"If you're so uncomfortable, come back home with—"

"Aren't you supposed to be in at nine today also?"

"A few minutes more or less..." Torin shrugs.

"You are such a hypocrite." Nearing a south exit, Flep checks the time again. "I've got to go. Sorry." He stops, tugging Torin's hand away from his neck while several bicyclists pass them. "Instead of everyone being so late, why don't you come home early tonight?"

"And put off until tonight what we could have right now?"

"First, because I really have to go, Torin. Second, because 'right now' is a misnomer. There are laws against public indecency in this city."

"Which are often ignored." Torin beams at him, now catching Flep's hand in his.

"Lunatic." Flep pulls back. "I'll be expecting you home early." He steps in to kiss Torin. Their lips have hardly met when he turns, running for 59th Street.

"You'll be asleep," Torin shouts after him. "Even if I'm there before sunset!"

"Worth the risk or not?" Flep calls over his shoulder.

Damn. Flep has him on that one. He cannot keep leaving early. He was never in the habit of this before. On the other hand, maybe that's why it is okay now. Just a few more times.

CHAPTER EIGHT

He had longed to be a set designer since he was twelve and performed in his first school play. Acting in front of a crowd made him queasy. Remembering lines made him panic. But the stage itself—backdrops and props, colors, layers, lights, and energy—he never wanted to leave.

His first crush was Evan, the ninth-grader who supervised set construction along with Mr. Omdal. Evan had not begged for the job, but his father was a carpenter, and Evan worked efficiently through construction and painting backdrops of a forest, castle, and dungeon.

Flep still remembers those green eyes and red-blond hair shining under the stage lights as Evan worked with plywood and Styrofoam. He didn't think Evan ever noticed him watching when Flep was supposed to be running lines. He was quite sure, really, that Evan never knew his name. The two never exchanged a word in the three months they worked on the Arthurian play.

Next time there was a school production, Flep had begged his way onto the set crew. It never occurred to him that he would be anything besides a Hollywood set designer after that. Leaving frozen Connecticut to rush around Southern California, working with big names on location, gathering set dressings, collaborating with other artists and designers for the next hotel room or office in which Meryl Streep or George Clooney would be seen.

But he, like Simon and Tanya, landed an internship in New York City straight out of college. He has worked for Time Marks, a small Manhattan production company, for fourteen years now—been their chief set designer for eighteen months. And he has still never been to Hollywood.

There have been major motion pictures and high profile TV shows over the years, but, mostly, Flep comes up with sets for vodka commercials and furniture still shoots. Time Marks does not specialize in George Clooney's hotel rooms. It specializes in selling a night at the hotel.

His mind wanders over nostalgia and visions of snow, blood, and pigs while Simon and Tanya argue about lampshades around plates of sushi. Even past soy sauce and wasabi, Flep cannot clear the odor of sulfur from his nose. Ever since the fireworks.

Tanya's concept of a gothic look over Simon's more rustic take fits Flep's own vision of the project. Her impassioned defense of her ideas makes it easy for Flep to focus on her without ever having to put down Simon's work.

He wishes Craig were here. Craig, Flep's second-in-command, currently in the position Flep held for years, is out sick. Craig is a renaissance man, a dynamic personality, a go-getter. He would have Flep's job by now if he didn't also clash with John, the studio's head producer. Flep was promoted because John did not want a dynamo heading the art department. He wanted a yes-man. And everyone knew it.

Craig bears Flep no ill will over the situation. That is the other thing about Craig: a nice guy who loves his work, eager to collaborate. He also drinks like a fish. Mondays and days after holidays are not the best times to get work from him.

Sometimes too eager. Like these interns.

Flep feels so extraordinarily tired.

He should not have spent the energy to walk with Torin this morning. But that was something he wanted to do. No...this is what he wishes he could skip.

"She's right," Flep interrupts after increasingly tense moments.

The interns look up from their sketchbooks, a glint in Tanya's eyes, hurt in Simon's.

"But we can't go black," Flep continues, turning wooden chopsticks in his fingers. "The lighting department needs all the help they can get since Savannah went on maternity leave. Gothic doesn't just mean black drapes and gargoyles. What's gothic that's A) subtle, and B) easy to light, making the actors look good?"

"Copper," Tanya says at once, leaning forward in her seat.

Flep smiles. Wonderful when they come out with something he would never say himself. He wishes Craig with his energy, and Tanya and Simon with their skinny pants and unlaced hipster boots, would do his job for a month. So he can sleep.

"Copper the color? The metal? Do tell." Flep sets down the sticks, hoping he looks thoughtful rather than like he's dozing.

Simon is soon on board with the subtler approach to a gothic aesthetic. By the time they return to the studio offices, Flep feels ready for the encounter with John Case. If only he can stay awake.

Following an afternoon of meetings and sketches, explanations and changes, budget analysis, and more than a few moments of grinding teeth, Flep walks to his station in a daze. In the subway, he feels so exhausted his knees shake, his vision blurring. Normally, he never bothers trying to sit. Now it's worth squeezing between an admirable set of dreadlocks and a bulging suit to avoid the risk of collapsing in the crowd.

The final walk home takes longer than usual, familiar streets and storefronts smudging into a wash of color.

Still phosphorus or...something in his nose. And rotten flesh.

Did they like the ideas? Are they ready to move forward to set construction?

He can't remember. It seems like they did, mostly. The kids did good. Had he thanked them for all their work on this? And for toiling right through the holiday? He will send each an email telling them they did a good job.

When he was an intern, the head of the department was an asshole who thought no more of thanking someone like Flep than thanking his keyboard for making letters. Those kids deserved support. Hardly earning anything, struggling to pay insane rents.

Flep pauses on a curb, leaning against the pole of a traffic light. He cannot read the street signs. Only green smears. This seems...odd...

He must be on 2nd Avenue by now. Yes, there is the Spanish restaurant across the street. How strange that it did not register.

Those pigs...where did they come from? Why?

Cigarette smoke. The other thing he keeps smelling. Not just now, but at home—in bed, while eating, while shaving. He ventured to ask Torin several weeks ago if he thought someone was smoking in their building, next door or below. Torin's confusion led Flep to second-guess much of what he smells these days—especially if unable to pair it with a visual cue like a cup of coffee.

This time...there goes a man who is smoking on the sidewalk. There... Man...

Real smoke. Or is the man himself only in Flep's mind?

Men in his mind wear uniforms and helmets. Not black leather.

There were no savage hogs in his mind until today though. Something new appears all the time. Horses and maggots... Half a man's head...

If the smoke is real, as well as the walking man in leather, is the smell of an abandoned butcher's shop also real?

Flep looks around, almost losing his balance as he shifts. A light turns green. Men and women talk loudly around him. Not to one another. They seem to be speaking into their own hands. So fast. Everything here is fast. All day. All night. New York City...impossibly fast. That is where he is. Downtown.

He sees no bodies. Real smoke. Only an illusion of putrefaction.

Didn't he just decide he was on 2nd Avenue? Standing right here. Right...here.

He walks a straight line to the doors of their building only by staring at his own feet—one of the few things that appear clear.

"Evening, Mr. Andries."

Flep blinks to see Martin holding the door for him, touching his hat. So old-fashioned. Flep likes the doorman tremendously.

"Are you all right, sir?"

Sir. Someone else called him that.

Or was it only a dream? It can't be in a dream because no one ever talks to him. Did they? The man with the paper, jabbing a finger at it, trying to make him listen?

Flep feels he should say something, explain to Martin. Tell him something important about...

"Did you get my letters?" Flep asks.

Martin glances in the direction of mailboxes in the lobby behind him. "I'm sorry, Mr. Andries. I wasn't aware you were expecting a delivery. Is it oversized?"

"What?" Flep shakes his head.

What is he talking about? Flep isn't expecting anything. He only needs to know...about the last letter. But the letter is with him. He shifts his shoulder bag and reaches with his free hand for his breast pocket.

The fabric is soft and smooth: pocketless. He glances down, a surge of fear making his heart beat fast, mouth dry as he tries to take it in. No pocket. No letter. He is not even wearing his wool tunic. Where's the tunic?

Heart in his throat, the doorway spins around him like a car on black ice.

"Mr. Andries?" A man catches his arm. Martin, brows furrowed. "Why don't you sit down? You don't look well."

Leaning on the hand, dizzy. But why? What letter? What is wrong with him? There's no letter. No tunic. What is he thinking?

He wears a dress shirt and jeans with a nice belt Torin gave him.

"I'm just...really tired, I think. Sorry, Martin." Flep has to take a step to regain his center of gravity and keep from leaning on Martin. "No letter. It's nothing. Thank you."

He walks past neighbors checking their mailboxes. Alone in the elevator, he leans against the wall, fumbling for his door key in the inside pouch of his messenger bag.

He just needs to lie down for a minute after running on momentum all day. All week. Lie down, maybe watch TV. Think of something other than dreams or work or letters.

Inside, he pulls off his shoes, washes his hands, splashes water over his face, then sits on the foot of the bed.

"Flep? Flep?"

He opens his eyes.

Torin stands beside the bed.

Flep struggles to sit up. "What's wrong?"

"Wrong?" Torin tilts his head. "You tell me."

"I mean, what are you doing home? Shouldn't you be at work?"

"I was at work." Torin sits on the bed by him. His expression is uncharacteristically concerned.

Flep can smell grease, smoke, and sweet and savory aromas that always cling to Torin at the end of his work night: a mix of garlic, onion, fish, and butter.

Noticing that lamps are on, Flep turns to see the blinds have been drawn over dark windows. "What time is it?" He rubs his eyes.

"Nearly midnight." Torin makes a face. "Didn't get home as early as I planned."

"What? But I just walked in..."

"No, *I* just walked in. You were asleep on top of the covers at the foot of the bed with all your clothes on."

"That doesn't make sense. I don't..." He shakes his head, frowning. "I don't remember falling asleep. I don't even remember lying down."

"Maybe 'passed out' would be a better description."

"Are the girls at Amélie's place?" Looking around, Flep still cannot get his bearings.

"For the next three days. Do you want something to eat?"

"Uh, no...thanks. I guess...I'll go to bed for real." Why did Torin plan to come home early? Flep has only the vaguest memory of a previous conversation about tonight.

Torin pulls his head over to kiss his temple. Flep closes his eyes, leaning against Torin, but his stomach rumbles as he inhales restaurant aromas.

"Maybe just a snack?"

Torin chuckles. "How about toasted crumpets with shrimp salad and watercress? Then one drizzled in chocolate honey for dessert?"

Flep sits back to look at him. "You really made crumpets?"

"Between lunch and dinner."

"You didn't have to do that." Flep shakes his head, almost laughing at the same time. "Thank you. And for the chocolate honey. Both sound wonderful. Though I'm still not sure what a crumpet is."

Torin stands, offering his hand. "A perfect midnight snack."

Throughout sitting at the kitchen island, watching Torin prepare the shrimp, trying his first taste of a chewy crumpet, asking Torin how dinner service went...the room seems clear and solid. Real.

This is real. His job and the interns and this family he is now a part of. All real.

The other stuff—blood in snow, pigs and smoke, panicking over a pocketed letter in an outfit he has never seen or worn or touched in his life—must go. He has to focus, has to stop it. This, here—Torin grinning at his rapture over a crumpet with homemade chocolate honey, and a comfortable kitchen thirty-one stories up...this is what matters.

He must only figure out a way to keep this at the forefront of his world—waking or otherwise.

STAGE TWO

CHAPTER NINE

Amélie sits up in her desk chair, scanning the list of names and emails on her laptop. A gold bracelet digs into her wrist as she rests her hand on her desk. She reaches to undo the clasp, still watching the screen.

She has forgotten someone. Or has she? She always gets that feeling.

She closes her eyes, runs through the list in her mind, and looks over the screen again. RSVPs mostly in. Only a few unable to make it, a few unresponsive.

The party is a tradition, ongoing since Isabelle was a toddler. An end of summer, back to school, Labor Day affair. This will only be the second year she has had the party without Torin catering. She had to resort to real, highly recommended caterers. Still, no one can cook quite like him.

Last year, her friends were enthusiastic about the switch, saying that the food was wonderful and Amélie looked amazing. So the divorce didn't come with compromises after all? Improved mental health, less stress, and overall well-being—perhaps a fair trade for the loss of homemade meals and a sex life. But no compromises? Not exactly.

The clock on the computer screen turns over to 10:50 a.m. She picks the girls up at noon on most Saturdays, when Torin goes in for the dinner shift. She has learned not to be early. They will have been out at the Park or Chelsea Market all morning.

Amélie keeps running over the list in her mind as she gets ready to leave. Too late now. The party is tonight, even if she is forgetting a guest.

She waits only seconds while her doorman hails a cab, then gazes out the window on the slow ride, thinking of food, wine, and guest lists. Everything ready.

Martin has standing instructions from Torin to send her in. His eyes sweep her down and up ever so briefly as she approaches. A smile leaps to his face.

"Afternoon, Miss."

"Good afternoon, Martin. Do you know if the girls are home?"

"Just got in."

Always predictable.

"Thank you." Posture impeccable, ruffled silk blouse fluttering about her, Amélie sweeps past. Her boots click across the granite foyer. She loves the fashion permitting high boots all season. She would have a pair for every day of the year if she had a large enough closet and bottomless checking account.

Amélie strides along the upstairs hallway and knocks on the door at noon.

Flep opens it, smiling as if he honestly likes her. She cannot imagine why he would.

"Come in. They're still packing up."

"No problem." She smiles back to share that she does not mind waiting, but expects it.

The dark circles and puffy eyes have faded. He looks younger, more relaxed than the last time she saw him...what, three or four weeks ago? Part of it may be his replacing the entryway light bulbs to create a natural glow rather than a spotlight. She was startled when he did this in July not long after she mentioned it.

"You're looking better than a month ago," she adds as Flep shuts the door behind her.

He rubs his neck as if embarrassed. "Not sure what to say to that. I can't honestly return the...compliment since you look like Jennifer Garner with a perpetually perfect hair day. I've never seen you better or worse than you are."

He apparently thinks she backhanded him.

"I didn't mean it as a dig, Flep."

"Would you like to sit down? I have no idea how long they'll be."

"Where's Torin?"

"Bedroom. On the phone with the designer."

An ever-changing menu means website and print updates take a slice of the monthly budget. The designer is polished, professional, and fast, but at a price.

"I'm surprised he hasn't roped you into doing that yet."

"He's still trying," Flep says, looking away. "I have a full-time job already. Can I get you anything? A drink? Lunch? Canapés?"

Amélie chuckles as she sits on the red couch, legs crossed. "What's fresh?"

"Vol-au-vent. He made them this morning with the girls. Smoked salmon, mushrooms and spinach in white wine cream sauce, or mango and kiwi."

Hard not to say yes, to not sweep through the kitchen and inhale anything Torin has cooked. Perhaps if Isabelle and Carine offered, begged her to try their work, she could have. But eat his food on his couch in his apartment with his boyfriend and risk him walking into the room?

Never. She has her pride.

"Thank you." She smiles at Flep, hoping it comes across as genuine. "Water with lime if you have that."

He takes the accent chair by the window when he brings her water, chewing a mango and kiwi vol-au-vent—she can smell the fruit—and carrying a glass of water for himself.

He looks flushed from being out in the sun. His plain T-shirt and slightly too large jeans send the whole room spiraling several states west. Will it be flannel and fleece for the winter?

"Are you back to sleeping?" she asks, lifting her glass.

Before he can answer, Carine races through the kitchen.

"Hi, Mommy!" She zooms past the counter, reaching up as she goes to snatch vol-au-vents from serving plates, then dashes back to her room.

"Mom?" Isabelle passes her sister in the short hall, coming to see what Carine was shouting about. "*Desolée qu'on est en retard, je ne savais pas que t'étais déjà là.* We'll be ready in just a minute."

"*Pas de problème. Prends ton temps.*"

Isabelle grabs a pastry and hurries back to their room.

Amélie returns her attention to Flep, who smiles after the girls.

"They're lucky. It's a special opportunity to grow up with two languages." His expression is so sweet, so sincere…she longs to slap him.

She had not liked Torin asking his new boyfriend to move in—after they had known each other for eight months—when Amélie herself had never even met him. The girls lived with their father half the time. Add a strange man to that half?

When she had told Torin she didn't want them there if the boyfriend was moving in, Torin had been bizarrely accommodating. He eased the transition along slowly for all their sakes save his own. Always supremely confident in his own decisions, Torin usually saw no reason to drag his feet once his mind was made up.

Instead, he asked her to meet Flep, spend time with him if she liked, and let her instincts decide. Amélie's intuition was something of a family legend, having saved her life on at least one occasion and creating the ruling factor in her own choices. She had often driven Torin to arm crossing and eye rolling by taking one look at a potential chef or server and telling him no way was she willing to make the hire. Later, she sometimes heard from the place that had hired him or her about the drug problem, or endless sick days, or otherwise low integrity.

When the boyfriend situation arose, she wanted to tell Torin no—if for no other reason than to spite Torin's smugness and self-confidence. She planned to say that this new man creeped her out, and she didn't want him around her children. Also for Torin to stay away from him if he had any sense. The bitterness remained strong at that time.

Even with that bitterness, she couldn't do it.

Torin introduced them before the holidays last year, leaving them to have lunch together while he headed to work, the girls in school.

And it was all good. All white light and smooth, warm feelings making her want to hold his hand, damn him. Even with that light, only her own sense of fair play compelled her to admit to Torin that she approved of Flep—since doing so meant endorsing Torin's choices in the matter.

Flep, who clearly adored Torin—hard as that was for her to imagine by then—had moved in around the 1st of March. Now it's the start of September, and he watches the girls run through the kitchen with the soft, gentle admiration of a proud parent. With love. He has fallen for them as well. Do they even know it?

By now, their attitudes toward Flep have been softening. Just last week, Isabelle confided to Amélie that Flep was doing better, as if to get Amélie to like him, give him a chance.

Amélie vividly remembers Carine in tears as she gave her mother a report of that first disastrous outing Flep had with the girls. He was supposed to pick them up from school, take them for something to eat, and bring them home for the evening.

"Everything was mushy!" Carine had howled.

Her sister shook her head, lip curled in disgust. "Mom, he tried to take us to McDonald's. *McDonald's*. We wouldn't go."

These days, Isabelle feels the need to defend him. Carine, who early on dropped all expectations of Flep as far as meals, also admitted to her mother that he is funny, and he helps with her reading. She shares her crayons with him, and they draw pictures of animals from the TV.

Still, Amélie does not think they guess how much he has started caring about them.

Flep looks away from the hall, back to Amélie, apparently recalling her question about sleep before being interrupted.

"I have been managing a few hours here and there." He seems upset, almost grimacing.

"You make it sound like you'd rather go back to skipping sleep," Amélie says, one eyebrow raised.

"Almost. I went to see someone a month ago. Now I'm...on sleeping pills."

"Lovely."

"I know." He blows out his cheeks. "But I couldn't work. I almost fell asleep walking home on a couple of days. I've never been tired like that. There was at least a full week in July when I don't think I slept more than eight or nine hours."

"And the dreams?"

"Oh, they're still around. Just...not so distinct. I'm trying not to think about them. Haven't been keeping up the journal, but they're mostly the same each night anyway."

"I'm sorry to hear that. Glad you're getting some rest though. You do look better."

So what is he planning to do? Stay on a prescription? The underlying problem needs to be resolved, not only the surface medicated.

"What are you doing with the rest of your Saturday?" she asks.

Flep shrugs. "Homework, reading, catching up on emails."

"My annual end of summer party is tonight. Would you like to come?"

He looks confused. "Uh...why?"

"Why?" She sits back, listening to Isabelle and Carine argue over some object in the bedroom. "For fun. It's not a business meeting. Just friends, colleagues, a few kids there with the girls. Dinner is catered and it's a chance to catch up with people we seldom see over the summer, or meet new friends."

He still appears unsure. "I guess I meant, 'why me?'"

Amélie fixes him with a stern, unblinking gaze. Obviously, she cannot tell him she feels sorry for him.

Flep squirms. "Uh, yes, thank you. I'll be glad to."

She can't figure it out—his connection with Torin. A sweet, kind, soft-spoken, hard-working man—but where is the backbone?

All of her life she has been attracted to strong personalities—to men who can, at the very least, keep up with her. And look how that worked out with Torin...

Is that the point? After living fourteen years with a tigress, Torin is turned on by a koala?

Even an opposite personality wasn't enough of a new start, although the gender swap was not as unexpected. Since culinary school, when Amélie first met him, Torin was clear to anyone interested—and to many others—that he is bisexual. As much then as now, he loved an argument. He often found one defending his own sexuality and condemning both straight and gay communities for being biphobic.

To her surprise, as someone who never thought much about sexual orientations—what difference does it make with whom a stranger, or even a friend, sleeps?—Torin ended up being right. Both "sides" of the spectrum often seem to take issue with the bisexual identity. From the queer community he is closeted, pretending to be a "breeder" to live the lifestyle when he knows he is gay. From the "breeder" community, he is a slut.

The world, even the world of Manhattan, turned out to be a much less welcoming place than she had imagined as a liberal and sheltered twenty-year-old.

Torin will still deride bigots, questioning what makes the other party morally superior for finding only a potential half of the population sexually attractive. But he has mellowed in the past years through the awakening of fatherhood, the challenges of running a thriving business, and even the divorce. He does not go out of his way to start arguments any longer—which, for Torin, is a milestone.

Amélie lifts her water glass, dropping her eyes from Flep. It is surprisingly satisfying to wither the man with her gaze. If only her court appearances were so straightforward.

"Six tonight. But anytime is fine. Before or after. I'll introduce you to my sister."

Flep's look of alarm increases. She reads his face like a sandwich board. *God, no, two of them?*

"I thought she lives in France...?"

"Paris. Just visiting. Staying with my parents in Greenwich Village."

"Ah, well, that sounds...great. I look forward to it."

The master bedroom door bangs open. Torin stalks into the kitchen, muttering and dropping his phone on the counter.

"Two thousand." Torin drums his fingers on the counter, then turns to look out at the City.

Facing these windows is nearly the same as touching them. The apartment is tiny. Living room, eat-in kitchen, mini bedroom and bath for the girls to share, small master suite. But nice: great windows, wood floors, and a real kitchen, all stainless steel.

Having any kitchen at all in the City is a big deal, especially beyond a galley. Torin is the only chef she knows who constantly cooks at home. The man has no other interests outside of his family. He doesn't go to movies or read novels. He doesn't do yoga or watch birds. He doesn't collect figurines or study astronomy.

Nor, like so many addicts, does he think of himself as having a problem.

Torin lucked out with the place when they split and both went on renting—him only a few blocks from his darling Chaleur, while Amélie went to the Upper West Side across town, near the Park and her own work at the firm.

She was in the restaurant business with him so long that she is still working back to a good place with Adams & Greenberg. At least she had remained there part-time through the years. Now she needs junior partner. Costs with the girls will grow, the City itself always exorbitant. She needs to buy something, not keep paying someone else's mortgage in the form of rent. She needs security. To get it, she must focus on her career and goals. Not her ex-husband's goals.

She has been telling Torin for three years that she is done with the restaurant. She gets that he cannot afford to buy her out of the business outright. She does not get why he seems to prefer stringing her along rather than settling *some* terms—hopefully reasonable to both parties—in a clear split.

Haggling and negotiating and "Why don't you just...?" worked to a point. But this is the point. They are never working together again. For her, the restaurant is dead. Time to sign off on the body.

Torin addresses Flep. "Really, if you ever want to give up the studio work—"

"Uh-huh." Flep looks out the windows.

"I'm serious. Two thousand dollars we owe her, and for what? You could be doing the design, the site, interiors of both places. Start from scratch with the new one. You have all that experience and you're arranging flowers on sets for air freshener commercials."

"Yeah, that's pretty much what I do all day." Flep sighs.

"And we can pay you. I mean, God, two thousand for tweaking a damn website? You'd make your own hours with us, be your own creative director. Anything you need, I'll make it happen."

Flep finally looks at him. "I like working on sets, Torin. I worked really hard to get where I am now in my job. Despite all the signals I'm sure I've been sending to the contrary, I honestly have never had the slightest interest in working in a restaurant."

Torin is not listening, stepping around the corner to the hall. "Girls? Your mother's waiting. Aren't you ready to go?"

Flep leans back, thumb and forefinger against his eyes.

Amélie smiles at him, unable to suppress her own affectionate feelings. He looks up and catches her eye. He also smiles then, slightly, and she is glad to think he knows there is one other person in the world who understands how he feels right now.

Torin returns, grabbing a vol-au-vent and popping it in his mouth. He walks to the living room windows to glare at the river and glittering glass of other skyscrapers.

"How's your airline case going?" he asks after swallowing.

Trying to make conversation or fishing to see if she has bonuses coming in? Of course, her income has *nothing* to do with what she is owed from a legally co-owned business.

"It's over," Amélie says. "We won."

"Congratulations."

He has no idea. A case against an international corporation? *Congratulations.*

"You didn't answer my last email," she says. "Are you coming in to sign paperwork?"

"More paperwork?" Torin asks.

Really, like he doesn't know? So juvenile.

"Come into the office on Wednesday morning," Amélie says. "We'll finish everything there and save us both time. I'll email you to confirm."

Torin opens his mouth.

Is Flep actually holding his breath?

Isabelle and Carine trundle into the room with their bags and shoes, the latter veering off for the kitchen.

Torin shuts his mouth, looking away.

Miracle.

Flep leaps to his feet to help Carine with her shoes. She does not need help with Velcro, though her hands are full of creamy pastries. And, unlike her independent sister, she has always had a royalist streak, with a need to be pampered.

She plunks herself down in the second chair, munching while Flep slides on her shoes like a studious footman.

"Mommy?"

"Yes, Ree?"

"Do you know what we had for lunch yesterday?"

"What did you have?"

"Lobster!" Carine almost screams the word, kicking her little feet out of Flep's hands in her enthusiasm. He dodges to avoid a bloody nose. "Lobster, lobster, lobster!"

"That's wonderful," Amélie says. "I'm proud of you, sweetheart."

Carine laughs. "There was supposed to be lobster left to make vol-au-vent. But! Guess what happened?"

"Don't tell me someone ate it all up?" Amélie lifts her eyebrows.

"Yes! Someone did. Ate it up so there's *none* in our vol-au-vent."

Isabelle clears her throat. Torin's whole manner has changed. He grins while he watches Carine. Flep bites his lip as he catches her foot.

"I don't suppose you know who ate all the lobster, do you, Ree?" Amélie asks.

Carine presses the tip of her forefinger to her pursed lips, gaze on the ceiling. "Bell," she proclaims, finger pointing at her sister. "Bell ate the lobster so we didn't have any today."

Isabelle snorts. Flep chuckles, releasing the foot.

"That's just dreadful," Amélie says. "I don't think girls who gobble up lobster like candy should go to a party tonight, do you?"

"Party!" Leaping to her feet. "Party tonight!"

As she starts away with the girls down the hall, Amélie feels inexplicably better than she had when she came the other way.

Torin found little chance to argue. Both girls are in good spirits, looking forward to seeing Aunt Marcelle. And she, Amélie, no longer has to consider that guest list. She hasn't forgotten anyone.

CHAPTER TEN

Isabelle sits on a spindly wooden stool at the kitchen bar. Her mom likes delicate things. This stool seems a bit much. What good is it if people can hardly use it? Her dad has stainless steel and leather barstools at the island that you could rest a pony on.

No, it's not fair. No comparisons between the two. She frowns as she points one leg and toes. No "he said, she said." No "that's better, that's worse."

They are different. Their new apartments are different. She can't help thinking of each as new despite it being two years since the final split and move. No one better. No one winning. Just not the same.

Just split.

Isabelle points her other foot, concentrating on the motion, feeling her leg stretch to be as long and smooth as the leg of the delicate stool.

"Are you the little bartender tonight? Checking IDs and setting limits?"

Isabelle looks around to find Mr. Barry leering at her. Cheeks red, teeth stained from too many years of red wine. Maybe he even smokes. Disgusting.

And "little bartender"? Every terrible word she is never supposed to say races through her mind.

"Let's see it then," Isabelle says instead, holding out her hand as if expecting him to offer his ID.

As if the great, sweating, red walrus can be younger than a grandfather. He works in Mom's law firm. *Most* of the people at the end of summer/Labor Day party are here because her mom wishes to see them. But there are always that bunch invited out of necessity.

Mr. Barry throws back his head and lets out a bark of laughter that makes her ears ring. "I can just see you refusing me!"

Isabelle narrows her eyes—that bit about the "little" still stabbing. She already knows she is small for her age.

"In a New York minute," she says in barely more than a whisper.

This further delights him. He actually wipes a tear from his beady eye.

The caterer on drinks has popped up beside the counter with a fresh glass for the walrus. As he pours and mixes, Mr. Barry slips a tightly folded stick of paper from his breast pocket and holds it out to Isabelle.

He winks. "For you, madam—for making my evening. A back to school gift."

Is he really offering her money? How incredibly creepy is that? *Sleaze bag.* She would rather spit on him than take it, but even her dad wouldn't do that.

She plucks the folded bill from his fingers. "Glad to oblige." *Gag.* They say that stuff in old books everyone calls "classics"—otherwise known as "hard to read."

She should thank him. He is giving her a gift, total creep-out or not. But she can't bring herself to do it. That's going too far.

He laughs again, apparently satisfied with her reaction, then takes his drink and waddles into the crowd around the buffet and living room.

The young and gorgeous caterer steps out with a fresh tray. The son of the lady who runs the company. Mike. Or Nick. Something like that. Ten years older than Isabelle. And gay. She feels more and more that all the men she knows are gay. Or bi. Too much time at a dance school and Chaleur's kitchen. How is she ever going to date?

Isabelle closes her hand around the bill and goes back to her stretches. She should have learned pointe by now.

Up, down, out: she stretches until it almost hurts.

"Too little" for pointe. Too old to watch *My Little Pony: Friendship is Magic* on Mom's bed with Ree and the other little kids. Too young to be a real guest of the party. Just small, young, old, not-quite-right Isabelle—split down the middle.

Split.

"Hey, are you all right?"

She looks up.

Flep stands beside her, between the window and bar. He looks worried, brows knit and hazel eyes anxious. At least he has black hair, even if his eyes cannot decide what they want to be. The hair is no-nonsense.

Her own eyes are dark brown, piercing, like her mom's. She wishes she got her dad's. Ree got the blue eyes.

She likes having her mom's auburn hair, but she would trade the darker hair for the lighter eyes.

What were Flep's parents' colors? One with green and one brown, and hazel is the result? Does that happen?

He has told her that his mother's family was originally Dutch, implying that either she skipped taking her husband's name, or his parents were never married. Flep has her last name. But aren't the Dutch usually light? His father must have been the dark one. Or maybe his mom and dad were both blue-eyed blondes, and Flep is the black-haired, medium-eyed, pale-skinned freak of the family.

Isabelle has never met anyone from his family.

"*You* don't look all right," she says to avoid his question.

Flep's frown deepens. "You and your mother keep commenting on my appearance today. Did I miss something?"

For some reason, she feels bad, like she did something mean to him. She hasn't, has she? She doesn't know what Mom said to him.

Isabelle shakes her head. "It's nothing. I'm fine."

"I thought you were all watching a movie?"

"The babies are watching TV shows," she mutters.

He leans toward her in the noisy room. "Who?"

"No one. Nothing. I just...thought I'd come see the party."

"Do you want something to eat?" Flep asks.

"I already ate a bunch of the cheese skewers and vegetable dip." Something prickles her palm. She opens her hand to see the crumpled bill.

"What's that?"

Is he trying to talk to her to avoid the rest of the party? Or is he genuinely interested in her sitting here alone, feeling sorry for herself? *Is* she feeling sorry for herself?

If so, she has justification. And, if he is avoiding the crowd, she has no help for him. Her mom has already introduced him to a dozen people, including Isabelle's aunt, but she can't handhold him all night. He must mingle on his own if he plans to attend these things.

Come to think of it, why is he here?

And how does her mom introduce him? "Sonya, I'd like you to meet the strangely named Flep. Flep is my ex-husband's boyfriend and he's here as my special guest."

That just...doesn't make sense. In so many ways.

Isabelle sighs, unrolling the bill. "Twenty bucks."

Flep glances at the bar. "I'm pretty sure they're on the house."

She narrows her eyes at him. He appears serious, regarding her with that same worried expression.

She smiles. "Good one."

He smiles too, much to her surprise. "But, really, are you needing to buy something?"

"An old man just gave this to me. I wasn't carrying it around."

He blinks. "Excuse me?"

"That old man in Mom's firm, Mr. Barry, gave it to me."

"Seriously?" Now Flep looks positively alarmed. "Isabelle, that's not okay. What did he say to you? Did you tell your mother?" He looks around as if trying to catch Mom's eye. Or searching for a phone to call 911.

"She already knows he's a creepy, old man."

"Has he done this before?"

"Given me money, or been a creepy, old man?"

"The former."

"It's only because he's drunk, and he thought I was funny." She shrugs. "He said it was a back to school gift."

Flep pulls his gaze from the crowd to look at her, all concern. "You need to say something to your mom about him. And stay away from him. It's not okay—"

"Yeah, I know. I'm not the one who's six. But a twenty's a twenty. I can put it in my savings account."

He still seems bent on saying more about it so she cuts him off. "And no, he didn't say anything inappropriate, and we're not going to start texting or chatting later. I've lived my whole life in one of the most densely populated places on the planet with two overprotective parents who would hardly even let us have a babysitter because they're so paranoid. We've heard the Creepy Adults lecture before."

She waves the bill at him. "And this is perfectly good cash that I'm not giving back. All I had to do to earn it was have a smart mouth."

"Your mom might feel differently about giving it back. It's not—"

"That's up to her," she snaps. "Not you."

Flep falls silent. They both look away.

Isabelle bites her lip. Stupid. She never meant to get testy about it. She should apologize for saying that. But for what? Speaking the truth? For hurting his feelings...

She glances at him, looks away again.

Flep looks out the dark windows, genuinely concerned about it. She understands why, in a way. But he is not her parent. Not even close. He's what her friend, Tabitha, calls a "live-in." Just a live-in. A live-in who cares.

"I'm going to tell her about it," she says after a long pause. "If she wants to take it back and tell him to go to hell, I'm sure that's what she'll do. But he's been drinking, and it's not like I ever normally see him. He doesn't even know my name."

Flep nods, still not looking at her. She has seen him do the same thing with her dad. He doesn't necessarily agree, but any argument more intense than who will pick up the tip sends him scurrying for cover.

Now she has even lost him for company.

Isabelle tells him she is sorry in her mind since she cannot get words to her lips.

"Is that him?" Flep asks.

She follows his gaze. "Yeah. The one with the red and yellow tie."

"He looks like a walrus."

She looks at Flep until he meets her eyes. "That's just what I thought. He has big, yellow teeth and walrus jowls."

"Like *Alice in Wonderland*."

She nods. "I just read the book."

"Have you seen the movies? The animated one helped inspire me to become a set designer."

"But it's not real. No one designed a set for it."

"Sure they did. How do you think design starts? With ideas, imagination, art. That's one of my favorite films."

"Even though it's for kids?" She laughs a little.

"*Dora the Explorer* is for kids." One side of his mouth turns up. "Movies like *Alice in Wonderland* and *An American Tail* are suitable for kids. Not the same thing. *Lady and the Tramp* is about class and social differences, prejudice, acceptance, love, loyalty, what it means to be part of a family... I have rarely seen such sophistication in an R-rated film."

What does she have to look forward to in entertainment with an adult telling her that cartoon movies are the best? She feels both let down and intrigued, almost grateful somehow that he thinks family movies are cool—right when she was starting to feel too old for them.

Isabelle can think of no answer, but asks, "Why don't you work in movies if that's what you wanted to do?"

"I fell in love with New York and my job here. I wouldn't have said no to being a Broadway star—if I could have handled the crowds. And could sing." Flep smiles. He has seen every show performed on Broadway in the past decade. "But I enjoy what I do."

"I hope I can be like that one day." Isabelle flushes as soon as the words are out, trying to stop them. She looks quickly away.

"What do you want to do?"

"Dance. But ballet's not a job unless you're in the one percent. Even then, not for more than a few years."

"Then cherish every moment. That's no reason not to do something."

She glances at him. Her parents would never say anything like that. Mom and Dad are too practical.

"Where are your parents?" she asks impulsively.

"They're dead." Flep looks back to the tall windows. "My mom died while I was still in college. My dad, just a few years ago, though we weren't close. I was raised by my mom. I'm an orphan."

"You're too old to be an orphan."

"No..." He lets out his breath, looking into the window, watching reflections of the party. "You're never too old to be an orphan."

Isabelle feels bad for him, wishing she hadn't asked.

"My dad and my grandfather don't talk," she says. "He left them for a woman twenty years younger than my grandmother and started a new family in Miami when my dad was a teenager."

"Which," Flep sighs, "was for the best, by all accounts."

Isabelle nods. Her grandfather on her dad's side was an alcoholic. She's not sure if he still is, but he was when her dad was growing up. And her grandmother took pills until she died before Isabelle was born. Something doctors gave her—not hard street drugs.

Isabelle doesn't know if her grandmother meant to kill herself, or just took too much. Only that her dad blames prescriptions and doctors. Flep being on prescription sleeping pills has been making her think of her grandmother lately. She gets a worried flutter in her chest every time she does.

"How long do you have to take pills to sleep?" She tries to make it sound like a casual change of subject.

He looks at her, head cocked. "Your grandmother had a problem, Bell. I'm not going to keep taking that stuff long-term."

She nods again, gazing down at the bill she has rolled in her fingers.

He seems about to say something else.

"Flep?"

They both look around.

Isabelle's mom is leading over a redhead with cropped hair, dangling amber earrings, and an upturned nose. Small, like Isabelle, but probably in her twenties. Isabelle has never seen her before. The daughter of one of her mom's friends?

"I'd like you to meet someone. Natalie, this is Flep, who I was telling you about. Flep, Natalie is in her second year of psychology. We've just been talking about dreams."

"Pleased to meet you." Natalie smiles broadly at Flep, her voice low and mellow, though Isabelle was expecting a chirp. "It's nothing but dream analysis since the new term started. Way more interesting than you'd think—studying the distinct stages of sleep and analyzing dreams.

Amélie mentioned that you're having dream dilemmas. I'd be super interested if you want to talk. No pressure though." The smile becomes a grin. "I know that sounds totally weird, right?"

"No, uh, sure. I don't mind." Flep looks confused, glancing anxiously at Mom. Why is he scared of her? She never did anything to him. "If you're interested...?" He somehow makes this sound like both question and apology.

"Absolutely."

"What are you doing, Bell?" Mom asks, shifting her attention.

Taking money from creeps. "Nothing," Isabelle says. "I'm just sick of TV."

Her mom gives her a narrow look, but guests take priority.

Isabelle exhales as she is left alone with Flep and the mysterious student. Natalie has on bright red shoes and an adorable cotton blouse made with a dozen colors. Isabelle envies her confidence. Definitely not from the business set.

Isabelle folds the bill into origami at the bar, pretending not to be listening.

Before he starts on his nightmare problem, Natalie asks Flep about his name. Even Isabelle can spot flirting. And he's way too old for her—maybe fifteen years older.

He tells his name story even more apologetically, like it's some inconvenience to Natalie.

"It was my great-grandfather. My mom's favorite person in the world. Papa Filippus—the Dutch form of Philip. He was 'Flep' with family and friends. That's how she remembered him and she wanted to name her son for him, though I think she would have used it regardless, girl or boy."

"That's super cool." Natalie still beams, gesturing with her hands as she speaks. "How many people have a unique name like that? Did you know him?"

He shakes his head. "So...tell me about your dream studies. Is it really that compelling?"

"You'd be surprised. I can give you great resources. We're learning so much."

She talks about dreams and her professors while Flep nods for a few minutes, then she asks about his experiences.

Isabelle unfolds her bill and starts over, listening more intently.

"It started...last February."

"What was happening in your life then?" Natalie asks.

"Oh...a lot. It was just before I moved. I was still adjusting to a promotion with a lot of responsibilities. But the dreams aren't about... I don't know what they're about."

He describes sitting on frozen earth, his feet and hands being frozen, mud coating his clothes, smells of gunpowder and rotten flesh, sounds of explosions, and people being killed. All while he tries to find a letter.

"I'm always waiting for someone, or rushing for someone. Always this consuming sense of urgency. I need to get somewhere... Always afraid. And this letter..." He shakes his head.

"Have you ever served?"

"I'm an art director at a local studio."

"Then it could be from the past."

"Believe me, I would remember. I've never been through anything like it."

"No." Natalie smiles again. "Far in the past, you know."

"Nat! There you are. I want to introduce you to the Callaways. Here." An older woman, also red-haired, steps in, taking Natalie's elbow, whisking her away while Flep still has his mouth open for more questions.

He watches Natalie go in silence. Does he really dream about corpses and bombs every night?

Isabelle smooths the paper, keeping her attention on it.

"Excuse me," Flep murmurs at last before he hurries away.

Chapter Eleven

Amongst missing produce and a new chef to break in, Roberto has cut his thumb prepping ducks, Brent has not showed up, first covers in half an hour, and now Zade is calling Torin's personal number. He has had worse Saturdays. Though rarely before the place has opened.

She better be calling on her way here. But, since she was expected an hour ago, and is now using this number, it's hard to imagine she has a joyful message.

Torin snaps the phone up to his ear. "Zade? Where the hell are you?"

"Torin?" The station chef is gasping, voice shaking. "I'm really sorry. I'm at the vet's office. I'm not going to make it in tonight." Unable to get her breath.

Torin realizes she is speaking through tears. The image feels incongruous as he pictures her spiked hair and eyebrow rings. What is she talking about? Veterans? Did a family member die?

"Zade, what happened?"

Chefs Dominique and Ava turn to look at him as he raises his voice over the kitchen racket and Zade's own noise.

"I always take Jasper out before coming in. To the Tribeca Dog Run—I don't know—it was all so fast—" Gasping and sniffling. "He got away. He's never done anything like this. A cab got him—oh, God." Sobbing. "I'm sorry. I've got to stay here. They're working on him now. I can't leave him."

Huh. Torin stands motionless at the stainless steel counter for a solid five seconds while she cries on the phone. Right. Scratch Zade also. He nearly hangs up. Nothing else to say and he must start more triage in the kitchen.

He catches himself. "Hope he's okay." It is a "he," right?

"Thanks—" Still crying.

"Good luck. We'll see you...let us know."

"I will. I'm sorry."

Ten minutes later, clock speeding toward zero hour, Torin addresses the kitchen at large, all eyes turning to him.

"Zade's not coming—"

"What happened, chef?" As a friend of Zade's, Ava is all concern.

"Her dog was hit by a car."

Ava gasps, but so do many others. Torin hadn't even realized Zade had a dog.

"Anyway, we're out a roast station chef and out a roundsman for—"

"I'm fine, chef," Roberto says, cutting Torin off.

Torin is taken aback. "What are you doing here?"

"I can stay—"

"The fuck you can. I see blood through your glove from here. Get out of this kitchen until that's properly—"

"It's covered, chef." Roberto raises his voice and his hand, showing the glove.

Torin moves down the counter to approach Roberto, shoulders squared like a bull. Men and women draw away as if he has palpable horns.

"Go home and get that wrapped properly. Now. Or you are not coming back."

Roberto breathes fast, chest rising and falling, smooth olive skin growing a shade darker. Many eyes flicker toward him—some with pity, some with exasperation.

"Yes, chef," the young man says at last and turns away.

Torin faces his people once more, addressing the new guy, Tai, a Chinese-American who has already racked up years in less fashionable establishments and came with dazzling references.

"Chef Tai, how would you feel about being our roast chef in addition to roundsman this evening rather than continuing with your training?"

"It will be my privilege, chef." The man stands up straight.

Torin loves finding a new guy who actually has the right attitude.

"We've got this." He turns to the doors and his servers. "Push meats tonight if asked. We're missing a quarter of the produce that was

90

expected today."

Many eyebrows jump. Vic and Mason exchange a glance. Mason, twenty-four years old on paper, but looking fourteen, swallows.

"Where is Brent?" Dominique asks, frowning and glancing around from Torin to others in case anyone knows.

Chef Brent—the new sous chef as of six months ago—being absent is not the same as Zade calling in. Missing Zade would be like missing one nurse for open heart surgery. Missing the sous chef is like missing the surgeon. Torin, the overseeing cardiologist, will be both himself and Brent for the evening.

"Doesn't matter," Torin tells Dominique. "We're moving on."

More sidelong looks at one another. Could they have thought Brent would be given another chance after a Saturday night no-show?

And it's not as if Brent hasn't turned in a variety of other bullshit in the past six months either. The only excusable reason for him to not be here—and never call—would be something like being hit by a bus, or devoured by zombies on his way to work. In which case, Brent will also not be coming back.

So many people think things are far more complex than they are.

"Any other good news we should know about?" Torin glances around.

Silence.

"Then get back to work."

Hardly work. Not this part. Beyond practicalities, the business, inventory, prep, being the boss, there remains occasional cooking—much more when his sous chef doesn't show up.

Each hour passes as a minute, each minute like a high from drugs, alcohol, or sex—only better, more complex. The richest, most exhilarating parts of life compressed into a knife and a plate. An obsession not only legal, but celebrated, and even paid.

Forty-five minutes into service, Roberto walks back in, lifting a pristinely gloved hand.

"One hundred percent, chef," Roberto bellows in the noisy kitchen with flames leaping in his face and Ava rushing past him.

"Get to the roast station." Torin does no more than look up to make sure of the covered hand.

"Chef—?" Roberto starts.

Torin goes on, "Chef Tai, learn as you go on roundsman for the rest of service."

"Yes, chef!" Tai shouts back.

Roberto hurries to Zade's roast station and Tai gives him a quick debriefing.

Running late, vegetables slipping away. Desserts leaving the kitchen: clafouti, pistachio dacquoise, and two crème brûlée flavors with which Dominique is experimenting. He must get her to make chocolate marquise or mousse again this week so he has a treat to take to Flep. Though Flep might also like the crème brûlée. Been a while since they offered a chocolate one.

The thought sends an extra ripple of pleasure up his spine, like a fresh hit while already high. The only thing better than the kitchen is merging it with his three favorite people.

Flep went to Amélie's party tonight. Though surprised that he accepted the invitation, Torin hopes he had a good time. Other than the food. He hopes the food was terrible.

Despite having lived in the City most of his adult life, Flep seems to have no social life. If not at work, he reads or goes to shows with art colleagues, or, these days, stays in with the girls. He seems content like this, in fact has insisted to Torin that he could not handle a social life beyond work because work drains him.

He must be honestly unable to compartmentalize. To Torin, work is to socializing what a shoebox is to a lamppost.

Flep will be asleep by the time Torin gets home. He can look forward only to breakfast. Still, Sunday morning is worth looking forward to— the only time of the week in which they can spend more than an hour alone with one another while awake.

Flep needs another cooking lesson, though he resists them, pointing out that he never tries to teach Torin to draw. Again, unrelated. Very few people need to know how to draw. Cooking is a life skill. But, when Flep said Torin could cook and Flep would eat, he had a point.

The rest of Torin's family is so jaded, so opinionated. Amélie never hesitated to tell him if he overcooked a fillet of fish by seconds. Even Ree will turn up her nose at a sauce she disapproves of.

Not Flep, a food virgin being coaxed from darkness, wooed and indulged. Torin loves it. Everything he makes is not only appreciated by this man, but thought of as an almost mystical skill. Torin has never had a complaint from him. It takes Torin back to when he first began learning to cook. To his teacher who was all praise and all love, the only completely benevolent adult he has ever had in his life—until Flep, that is.

He started cooking as a boy, at Isabelle's age, after most of a summer spent with his grandparents in Templeton, Pennsylvania—a town so small, it wasn't even a town.

His two older brothers, Cillian and Rory, hated the sticks, feeling that they were being punished by staying for a month in the Dutch Colonial farmhouse with its creaking floors and its chickens and goats. Not that Torin liked gathering eggs either. But Cillian and Rory were old enough to spend the summer and weekends at home in Pittsburgh out with friends, playing sports, or trying drugs—anything to get out of the house.

While his brothers were out, Torin stayed home, answering calls and making excuses for his mother when she was passed out from taking too many pills that day. Or explaining to the neighbors that they had a party the night before—didn't they hear it?—when they noticed his father's six dozen beer cans in a trash bag.

That first August in Templeton, Torin said he was not going home. He told Nan and Old Tom he would take care of the house and animals, and do all the chores if he could only stay. She gave him an envelope of dollar bills, saying he could get buses to Kittanning from Pittsburgh, and that Old Tom, as he was universally known, could pick Torin up and bring him home for weekend visits—if it was okay with his parents.

Torin's parents were never coherent on weekends. Torin had gotten on a bus the next Saturday morning without mentioning it. And the next. Repeated for most weekends, or whole summers, for six years.

With Nan, he made fondue, and found a better use for beer. He made beef stew and learned how to be patient. He washed vegetables straight out of the dirt and washed away smells and sights and bitter tastes he thought he could never escape.

He fried chicken and learned to be careful with fire. He rolled pie crust and learned to be gentle with his hands. He stewed squash and butchered fish. He boiled eggs and baked cakes. He learned about small farming, milked goats, and made yogurt and cheese by Nan's side.

He kneaded bread until his muscles ached and tears came to his eyes and Nan said that was okay. "We all have to get the poison out somehow."

They never talked about his parents, or what lay back home. They just worked side by side, year after year.

He found a tiny community of human beings brought together around tables of good food and love, forming their own family, a chicken casserole and a bowl of green beans at its heart.

Because the poison never went into the food. The poison evaporated while the food came together, which brought people together—which saved his life.

With Cillian away at college, Rory shooting up with friends in the basement, his father with the new woman, and his mother at the kitchen table, watching him through a haze of cigarette smoke, Torin started cooking at home.

He made chicken parmesan and homemade pizza, Thai coconut curry and chili rice noodles, Greek salads and gyros, apple pie and angel food cake.

And he ate alone. Until the weekend.

Everything slid apart practically at the same time, all within a year.

His father left Pennsylvania for Florida with the other woman. Nan died. Torin dropped out before finishing high school and applied to culinary school with the money she willed him to pay for it.

Until his mother and Old Tom died, Torin only went back a few times to Pittsburgh and Templeton. He scarcely stayed in touch with his brothers through the past ten years. Not at all with his father, though he knows the man still lives in Miami from Rory—who gets clean for a few months at a time, then calls Torin out of the blue.

He built a new family. He filled an empty space in his soul, opened doors, started a business, married, had children, and earned a living—all because of cooking.

Even his instructors thought he was gifted, a protégé, and they were some of the worst cynics he ever met.

He was leaning toward French style when he met Amélie, confirming his opinion that there was no sexier cuisine. By the time he left school, he could cook a meal and his people would rally. His wife, his first boss, his first employees, all of New York opened their arms, asking where he'd been all this time. Like Templeton on acid.

But tensions built with Amélie. As the business took off, Bell grew, and they both worked, his efforts for those same healing family meals fell flat. He had no time. She had no patience, and a too little, too late attitude which made anything he did futile. They were hanging by a thread by the time Ree was born—keeping all together for much longer than they should have.

He hadn't minded it being over with Amélie. Only felt bad for the girls. What Torin had minded—what made him pace at home and lose his temper more at work and lie awake at night—was feeling that he was losing a family all over again.

The girls always rallied for a meal. They could be enough family. Just a matter of taking a day off each week and spending more time with them. Yet he felt haunted by that empty spot at the table.

He had been open to anyone. Moving in food circles, he could have met someone who was even more of a foodie than Amélie. Maybe another chef. But he'd had a free evening for a date perhaps once or twice a year, and two children who came first.

In time, pacing at night, Torin finally wondered if he shouldn't have tried to work things out with Amélie. This while he deliberated how he—in his late-thirties, working days and evenings, with two girls to protect—was going to meet someone who fit into this picture.

As Nan would say, "That's what we call pigs flying out of hell after the freeze."

The kitchen has quieted, cleanup underway. Last entrées have been sent out, most of the dining room empty. The servers have apologized for running out of certain dishes. Sous chef Brent never showed, never called. Roberto didn't do an exactly stellar job on the roast station. The kitchen staff kept wondering about Zade's dog. There was a minor accident with a blowtorch at the pastry chefs' station. Service ran slowly all evening.

What else?

As a last dessert order is going out the door, Renard steps into the kitchen.

"Mr. Cleary." Renard inclines his head to Torin. "Someone here to see you."

CHAPTER TWELVE

Flep should be home long before 11:00 p.m.—exhausted from a solid day and night of people, his mind still on the redheaded student who spoke of the past as if he would understand—but he pauses at Lexington and turns back. It makes no sense. He should be glad to go home and slip into bed alone, relieved to take the prescription and not have to deal with the racing thoughts anymore. Instead, he walks to Chaleur.

Renard lets him in although they are no longer seating.

"Mr. Andries." Renard bows. "Always a pleasure. Would you like to sit down? I will let Mr. Cleary know you are here."

"Thanks, Renard. I don't need to sit. I just wanted to speak to Torin."

"No, no, of course you must sit." He ushers Flep along to a quiet table for two, no longer set for dinner. Close to the kitchen. "I am sure he will be right out."

Flep cannot hear Torin shouting at any of his chefs or servers in the back. It must have been a good evening.

"May I bring you a drink, Mr. Andries?" Renard does not normally deal with such matters.

"I'm fine, really. Thank you."

The immaculate host bows himself away, turning to intercept an alarmed young server—Mason? Though the restaurant is only a quarter full now, Flep cannot make out Renard's hushed words, apparently explaining the special circumstances before hurrying to the back to tell Torin.

The place feels so stark. With some diners still present, the white tablecloths remain in place. Black and white everywhere, soft lighting setting a romantic tone.

Flep imagines warm light fixtures, red napkins, tiny candles, a touch of whimsy, maybe a graphic that ties the theme of the name together. *Chaleur* means heat. So where is it?

What are they known for? Seasonal fare, daily variety, impeccable French inspired cooking, and duck. Unify. A graphic of a duck's feather turning into a flame. Show the clientele how much pride the proprietor takes in sourcing from regional farms. This is not a warehouse.

Flep understands the black-tie look. Not that the place lacks taste. It's just not representative. Warmth. Charm. Sophistication. Damn good food. Those are the messages Torin needs. Chaleur is so much more than just classic French.

Flep can mention none of this to Torin, of course. Torin would be over the moon to "let" Flep redo it. Not just a slippery slope. An oil spill.

He opens emails on his phone, though he cannot see them. Distracted by the vibrant living room at Amélie's party, he sees Natalie's face as he had tracked her down, having to interrupt just to speak to her for thirty more seconds.

"I'm sorry. I wondered—I don't understand... These dreams aren't from my past. I grew up in Connecticut. There were no wars. Besides ones between landlords and tenants."

"No, I meant a lifetime." She had smiled, though clearly trying not to leave her new conversation for him. "Another life. Don't tell my professors I said this, okay? This is just me. Recurring dreams like that, crazy setting, same stuff repeatedly? It's totally a past life. You should be able to figure it out with some research. You know? Where and when?"

"Right...yeah..."

He did not tell her that what she was saying still made no sense. He couldn't ask what would make her say something like that when it was clearly unrelated to what she was being taught in college.

He had retreated and never got another chance to talk before departing.

What kind of thing was that to toss out? He knows that some people believe in that stuff—past lives, reincarnation. But a stranger casually telling him his dreams are...hauntings?

Crazy. He never should have talked to her. So why does he wish he still were?

Torin bursts from the kitchen. He sweeps to Flep's table—his executive chef coat somehow nearly clean—with the air of a king stepping out among the common people.

He always looks taller, more formidable, and more intense than his at-home self in the black slacks and white, double-breasted jacket with the stiff collar. He exudes the kind of presence many men cannot even pull off in a tux. As far as Flep has ever observed, only Torin's daughters and his ex fail to be at least a little intimidated by that figure bearing down on them.

As he approaches Flep at the table, Torin grins, spoiling his royal effect.

"What are you doing here?" His hand reaching around to the back of Flep's head, Torin leans down to kiss him. "Want something to eat? Everything okay?"

"I'm fine. Just wanted to see you. You didn't have to rush out here."

Torin shakes his head, batting the comment away. "You look dashing. Had a good time at the party?" He slides into the chair opposite Flep, arms crossed on the white tablecloth as he leans forward, gazing into Flep's eyes—apparently with no other obligations to his time.

A man of such opposites, such extremes. He still surprises Flep each day.

"It was okay," Flep says. "Had a couple strange encounters. I just..." He trails off, feeling that he must present a reason for being here, when he honestly does only want to see Torin. "Is the kitchen closed? I'll walk you home."

"Don't you want something? Was it bad food?"

Flep smiles. "The food was fine."

"What would you like? Wine? Dinner? Dessert?"

"Only the company. Why don't you finish closing? I'll wait for you."

"We're almost done." Torin leans farther forward, eyes glinting. "Would you try a Grand Marnier crème brûlée for me?"

"It's a little late for me to be drinking."

"Orange, not lemon. I'd love your opinion."

Oh, God, he would? Or is he just saying that? He must know by now that Flep's food opinions are unhelpful. It does sound good. He had nothing sweet at the party.

"I'll try one." Flep rubs the back of his own neck, looking away.

"One moment." Torin springs up toward the kitchen.

He is gone for a few minutes while Flep avoids meeting the eyes of the staff still busy with the last diners.

From the past. Another life.

As if he should understand.

Torin returns with a rectangular white plate and the scent of oranges and lavender. In the center rests a rectangular ramekin. A garnish of candied orange peel is laid out in double rows at its long sides, like train tracks, to form two more rectangles. Down the center of each track run three fresh lavender blossoms. Inside the ramekin itself is a glistening amber sheen hiding the custard below. Above this golden blanket, orange, yellow, and blue flames twirl like modern dancers.

Torin rests the plate in the center of the table. The flames have turned almost pure blue, only the top edges tinted with shimmering yellow gold. The sugar and Grand Marnier beneath them glow like dark honey.

The smells of burning citrus and a breeze of lavender like a spring day hit him first—then vanilla, sugar, the pure orange of the candied peel, and the rich scent of buttery cream.

Torin places a white linen napkin on the table before Flep and a silver spoon on top. Once more sitting down across from him, Torin watches him watch the fire until the blue flames fade to the surface of the caramel.

"I recommend you let that rest for about five minutes," Torin says, though Flep has made no move to pick up his spoon. "And don't touch the ramekin."

Flep looks up. "It's like a living painting."

"Thank you." Torin raises one eyebrow.

Flep smiles. Repeatedly Torin has told him that you eat with your nose and eyes first, and only with your mouth after both have already made the important decisions.

"You didn't have to bring me anything."

"I would like your opinion," Torin repeats. "I'm no fan of the whole orange lavender additions for something like crème brûlée. I'm such a purist, you know. But we just thought we'd try them as an end of summer option for a week while we still have good lavender. Dominique pushed for flavors and people do seem to like them."

"When you distract them with fire, they'd probably go for anything."

"That could be it. Nothing to do with quality of the custard?" Torin grins.

He gets like this after work—solicitous, charming. It makes Flep wish he himself were not usually in bed by the time Torin comes home.

Torin is a night person—more at ease, more undiluted at this time. Showing all his best qualities, wearing his heart on his sleeve.

Now, just for Flep. If one of his staff interrupted for any reason, Flep feels sure Torin would bite his or her head off. Fortunately, he has no chance to witness such bloodshed. Torin's people have the good sense to keep away when the boss's boyfriend shows up.

"I missed you tonight..." Flep hesitates. Not that he wishes Torin had been at the party. Awkward enough for Flep being there alone. He still cannot fathom why Amélie invited him. Or why she seems to like him at all when she generally looks at him like something stuck to her shoe.

He glances down at the custard, back to Torin to finish what he was saying. "I love you."

"And you haven't even tasted it yet. This is going well." Torin cocks his head. Those clear blue eyes dance like the recently absent blue flames.

Flep chuckles and tries a candied orange peel while he waits on the cooling. "I spent half the evening watching other people's families. I guess I was feeling too sentimental and sorry for myself to go home alone. I'm sorry we don't have time to do more together. Just the two of us. And four of us. I enjoyed going to the Park with you all this morning."

Torin's look of amusement fades as Flep speaks. By the time Flep pauses, picking up the spoon, Torin is frowning slightly.

"I didn't realize you still felt like you don't have family here."

"I'm not..." Flep wishes he said nothing, wishes he asked Torin a question rather than trying to share. Always easier to get Torin talking than attempting it himself.

"The past few years have been long ones," Flep goes on. "I didn't mean it like that. I'm not complaining. I'm grateful for you and the girls and everyone I know here. We only...feel like ships passing in the night. You work late. I work early. The girls are only there half the time..."

"I told you from the start—"

"I know you did, Torin. It's not your fault, and I'm not fishing for a solution. It's the nature of your work. I just miss you. Even so. Even understanding. That's all."

Torin watches him and Flep cannot meet his eyes, feeling tension from Torin now, but unsure of its exact form.

"You know, if you worked some with the restaurant yourself—"

"I'm not doing your website. I'm not a web developer."

When Torin says nothing, Flep looks up.

Torin is smiling.

Flep lets out his breath, almost laughs.

"Want to take a sick day on Monday?" Torin asks. Pushing him about Mondays again. And yet, if Flep brings up Torin taking a weekend day off, Torin invariably shoots that idea down.

Flep taps the amber crust of the custard to crack it and lifts a small spoonful of cream. "I've got enough points against me there right now."

"A day at the Park? It'll be ice skating season before you know it."

Torin does not skate, but Flep does. He promised to teach Carine, even though he himself is only a fair skater, having learned after coming to the City as a new college graduate. Isabelle will not risk hurting her ankles, but she used to skate with her mother when she was younger, according to Torin.

Flep lets custard dissolve in his mouth. Sweet, rich, and biting with the burnt sugar and tangy orange.

"I would love to go with you all," Flep says. "But I can't lie for a sick day. Can it wait until 6:00? You need to spend time with them yourself. Not just with me attached."

"Why do you say that like an apology? When I get a day, or a morning, or an hour, with any of you, it's a gift. All three of you, that's bliss."

Another bite of cream, then of lavender buds. "Not this place?"

"This place is the needle, the bottle, the cliff." Torin still smiles as he watches Flep. "You're the parachute."

"What happened tonight?"

"Happened?" Torin rests his chin on interlaced fingers, elbows on the table.

"During dinner service. You're in a good mood."

"I get to see you here at the end of it. That makes it perfect, no matter what else happened."

Maybe he is buzzed. Unlikely, but Flep cannot account for all the soppiness—even from Torin at his most flirtatious.

He goes on eating while Torin tells him there is a single serving of duck left over if he needs a real dinner, and did he meet Amélie's sister, Marcelle, and did the girls have a good time?

Flep thinks of mentioning Natalie. Instead, he tells Torin the sister greeted him in French, talked to Amélie and the girls in French, and that was the extent of Flep's conversation with her.

Torin is smug over any slight when it comes to his ex, be it less than perfect catered food or a rude relative. Flep also forgoes mention of the man with the twenty dollars. Torin is in too good humor for that.

Talking to him now, Flep is reminded with a bittersweet pang how much he loves spending time with this agreeable Torin.

They had met, of all places, in a club on a Monday night, bonding at once over the fact that friends had brought each of them out—they never did this kind of thing, had no time for it, and would rather be at Chaleur or curled up on the couch with a movie.

One of Torin's chef friends knew Flep's coworker, Craig, who had dragged Flep out for "fun" after hours. Following introductions, there seemed to be little to do unless you enjoyed stiff drinks and invasions upon personal space.

With the other men in conversation, Torin pulled Flep aside, asking if he wanted to get high.

Flep said he didn't have the luxury of doing drugs, or drinking beyond a rare beer or a glass of wine. He worked way too much and had way too many social anxieties for such indulgences, having enough worries over saying the wrong thing when stone cold sober.

Torin was delighted with him, telling him that was a test, and he, Torin, didn't do anything, even pot.

"Sometimes I feel like ninety percent of my industry is, or was, an addict of some kind." Torin had to shout over the music and crowd in the dark bar. "It's a fucking high-stress business. I made a really conscious choice about staying out of it."

"The business? And look what happened."

"The substances." Torin laughed.

Of course, Flep learned later that both Torin's parents were also addicts.

That night in the bar, Flep hadn't been sure if he could take the ubiquitous handsome stranger at face value. But he was prepared to give it a try.

"So you're the only substance-free chef you know?"

"I draw the line at giving up caffeine," Torin said.

"Then you're a man after my own heart."

"Glad to hear it."

"So, what's with the bottle in your hand?"

"Keeping up appearances. Want some?" Torin grinned as he passed over the beer bottle.

Suspiciously, Flep took a swig. He almost spit it out, choking.

"What the hell?" He pushed it back at Torin.

"Grapefruit juice. Straight up. It's packed with vitamin C." Torin took a drink.

"That's living on the edge. So what kept you in the ten percent?"

"These days, being a parent," Torin called back. "It destroys and rebuilds your whole world in a blink."

"You...what...?"

"I'm divorced. Don't look at me like that." He was laughing again. "Guys in gay clubs can't have kids now?"

Flep knew plenty of people with kids in his and Torin's age-group. More lesbians than the guys, but it wasn't an unknown concept to him. Still...

"You're just...really playing those numbers," Flep called back, leaning closer as the music roared. "A chef without a substance problem? A gay guy with kids? What else?"

"Bi, actually."

"Of course. Sorry."

Torin was laughing. "What would you be watching at home?"

"What?"

"You said you'd be home with a movie now if you could."

"Hell if I care. I'd rather see *Titanic* than be in here shouting introductions."

"What's your favorite food?"

"What?"

"You just said that. Food! What's your favorite food?"

"Chocolate ice cream. Anything chocolate. And pecans."

"Come on, then." Torin jerked his head.

"Come on, what?"

"Come on, let's watch the movie, and I'll make you ice cream."

"You'll what?"

"We've got to get out of this fucking place. I keep hearing you say the same thing. It's the noise. Go on."

They had said—shouted—goodbye to Craig and Torin's friends.

On the street, Torin repeated his invitation: couch, movie, ice cream.

"No, thank you," Flep said. "I don't go home with guys on a first date."

Even downtown, the spring air felt crisp and refreshing after the stifling club scene. Neon lights blazed, cabs rolled past dozens of pedestrians. The sidewalk and streets shimmered after the evening's rain.

"I'll remember that." Torin grinned. "When we get to the first date. Over to 2nd Avenue, then north."

To his own bewilderment, he had followed Torin home. And, even crazier, they really did watch *Titanic* and eat homemade chocolate ice cream.

When Torin started streaming the movie, Flep was horrified.

"I said, 'I'd rather'—as in, this would be almost as bad. I'm not watching that."

"How come? It's some great cinematic whatever of the nineties, isn't it?"

"You've never seen it?"

Torin shook his head.

"It's shit. It's one of those...you know. It's...*Titanic*."

"It sinks?"

"Yeah."

"Are you one of those people who needs a happy ending where no one dies and even the dog's okay?"

"Especially the dog. What is up with dead dogs in kids' books anyway?"

"Look." Torin pointed at the screen. "We could watch *Brokeback Mountain*."

"*Jesus—*" Flep recoiled. "Just put on *Titanic*." A college friend had dragged him to *Brokeback Mountain* in the theater. Flep had never quite gotten over it.

Within an hour, Torin served him dark chocolate ice cream along with homemade pecan shortbread straight from the oven and decaf coffee.

Flep felt bemused by the treatment and his own giddy lightheadedness. Two small drinks at the bar had not made him that dazed hours later. There was something wrong. Something crazy. Because Flep—unlike Torin, he soon discovered—did not believe in love at first sight.

Since Torin skipped forward through huge chunks of the movie when he found anything dull, the three and a half hour runtime flew past. After this and the ridiculous treats—not overly sweet, just rich and decadent and perfect—Flep had thanked his host, wished him good night, and returned his kiss in the doorway before hurrying to the elevator.

Flep had to remind himself that it was a Monday night.

But Christ, Torin was gorgeous. Part of it might have been his skill with the ice cream machine, but he had been gorgeous in the dark club, in the glossy street on the way here, and all evening. Crystal blue eyes, disheveled light brown hair—intense and energetic in all his motions. Leonardo DiCaprio had nothing on this ten percent chef.

He let the elevator reach the lobby before pushing "31."

Back at the door, Flep's heart was hammering, his palms damp with sweat. He tried to compose some pretense, something forgotten, or a question. They had already exchanged numbers.

Torin, quick to size up any situation and take action, relieved his discomfort at once. He yanked open the door, grabbed Flep's face, and pulled him inside, his mouth over Flep's.

Flep followed him without worrying again about what to say. He had Torin's shirt off by the time they reached the kitchen island, then his own at the windows, kicking off his shoes at the same time.

Tongue in Flep's mouth, Torin had pulled him to the bed by his waistband.

Screw Tuesday—2nd Avenue was convenient. He could figure it out the following morning.

Now, Flep is glad he did, tasting orange and vanilla and listening to Torin talk about plans for the rest of the weekend and Monday with the girls.

Maybe Flep can start taking Mondays off. At least now and then. Make up extra hours elsewhere. Probably not.

Torin looks over his shoulder at a commotion from the kitchen.

"Still want to walk me home?" he asks Flep.

"I'll wait. Go finish up. And I like the orange and lavender, Torin. For what it's worth. You don't have to be such a purist."

"Hmm..." Torin glances at the plate. "Thanks." Standing, he leans over to kiss Flep, lips tasting of salty sweat and coffee in contrast to the sweet custard. "I'll be right out."

"Take your time." Flep watches him go, hearing the words again. *Another past. Another life.* Absurd.

And why is that damn gunpowder smell stinging his nose again? He is sure it's not from the flambéed dessert. Just as certain it is not from a past life.

Sunday, September 4

I skipped the sleeping pill. Home late with Torin after Amélie's Labor Day party.

Mixed feelings with the girls gone. I miss them the minute they're out of the place. It's so quiet, so empty, when I'm alone in the evenings here when Torin is at work and the girls are with their mom. But Sunday is the only day of the week I'm at home, the girls are away, and Torin sometimes doesn't go to work until noon.

I didn't want to ruin spending time with him by taking something with a "do not drive or operate machinery" label at 3:00 a.m.

Now it's 6:00 a.m. Torin is asleep beside me. I slept for forty minutes in the past twenty-four hours. Smart: not taking a pill to avoid being tired on Sunday.

How many times did I almost drift off, only to snap awake as the nightmares began? Six? Seven? Ten?

I was always running. Shouting, calling for someone, terrified. As I went, I tripped over ground strewn with hundreds of human bodies, falling on white and black ice splattered with blood.

Again and again. Every time I shut my eyes.

Godawful smells still fill my nose. Still an urgent sense of trying to protect something I held. Hands sticky and hot with blood, dripping down my sleeves, staining my trousers. Where does a word like that come from? I don't wear "trousers." I wear pants and jeans, sometimes khakis. And I don't have anything on at the moment besides a cotton sheet and Torin's arm across my waist.

Stupid. Next time, just take the damn thing.

But it's not worse now just because I didn't take it.

At the party last night there was a young woman, a college student Amélie knows. She said stuff about dreams—it doesn't matter. Only more dreams again now because I talked to her about them.

My throat is tight, bile below the surface. Pressure in my head, inside my ears—

I just grabbed at my own chest for the pocket, for the letter. Insane.

I desperately want to wake Torin. He deserves sleep also. Never to bed until after 1:00 a.m.

If I hadn't talked to Natalie, the student, I wouldn't feel now like I will explode.

Shit. I just drifted back to sleep.

In the bathroom now after retching over the toilet—washing my hands and rinsing my mouth over and over before I realized there was no blood. Nothing to wash away.

Now Torin is up. Still only 7:00 and I woke him after all.

Shit.

CHAPTER THIRTEEN

On Monday morning, Flep wakes with Natalie visible before him, as if he was dreaming about her rather than a black field littered with dead men.

At least he slept. And feels relatively clearheaded compared to yesterday. He looks forward to getting back to work. Away from the death field.

But Natalie, that girl at the party, why does he keep wishing he could see her again? Seeing her in the first place caused this violent relapse of nightmares.

Can he see her again, even if he wants to? He would have to ask Amélie. The girls' school schedule is changing now, and he is not even sure when he will next see Amélie. He cannot call her up and ask. Too...awkward.

Flep shaves and dries slowly from the shower, rubbing the towel across his hair, eyes shut. He wishes Torin had joined him. He must be making breakfast, shaping croissants after their final rise in the refrigerator overnight. The pastry chef side of Torin's cooking comes from his grandmother's influence, little from school. Nostalgia—never business.

Towel draped around him, Flep leans against the bathroom counter, imagining Torin beside him. Torin complains about the excessively hot water that Flep uses when he joins Flep in the shower. Flep finds it therapeutic.

His mind skips back to Natalie, her words buzzing like flies trapped in a jar. A sharp smell of rotten flesh and copper blood fills his nose. He jumps as if pinched.

Stop it.

He pulls on briefs and slacks and hangs up the towel, hoping Torin has put the pastries in the oven.

In the kitchen, Torin is listening to NPR, singing under his breath—nonsense tunes unrelated to the radio news updates—as he turns dough deftly in his fingers. Also shirtless, he wears jeans from the day before.

"Breakfast in thirty minutes. Do you always work on Labor Day?" He does not look around as Flep walks up behind him.

Flep slides his arms around Torin's chest, kissing the back of his neck, looking past his shoulder to the baking sheet of shaped dough.

"What'd I do?" Torin sounds amused.

"Nothing."

"Last time you left the shower half-dressed to hug me while fixing breakfast, you broke the news that my using the bed as a drafting table for scheduling staff shifts was driving you up the wall."

"I appreciate that you stopped doing that. But it wasn't on my mind." Flep kisses down from his hair to his spine and shoulder blades.

Torin shifts his attention to a basting brush. "You'll delay your breakfast."

From the past. From another life.

Why won't she leave him alone? Just as bad as the dreams themselves. He deserves an occasional moment with his lover.

He doesn't resent the girls. He doesn't resent the work schedules. But he is damn sure resenting Natalie and her casual observations about his life.

"I've got your beverage steeping," Torin says, still teasing, as Flep glides his fingertips in an X across Torin's naked abs.

Flep presses his face to the back of Torin's neck, almost laughing. "You have? I didn't mean for you to get that stuff."

"Worth a try." Torin turns his head as far as he can, brush in his hand, until Flep meets his lips for a kiss. "You liked the crumpets and jam. Not to mention the cream. We'll have you turned into an English country gentleman before you know it."

Flep had finally mentioned his newfound interest in black tea to Torin several days ago. He never meant for Torin to buy some and brew it.

Torin also brought back honeycomb and homemade clotted cream from his visit with the girls to one of his farms last Monday. Flep found the honey delightful on chocolate chip scones or toast, and the cream amazing on absolutely everything. He put it on scones, skillet potatoes, ham and mushroom quiche, grilled chicken, roasted vegetables... Somehow, it already seems to be gone.

More than for tea, or extra clotted cream, Flep wishes he could have taken Monday off in advance and accompanied them. Torin springs so many plans on him that Flep has no chance to get a day off. He had only found out about the last New Jersey farm trip at 7:00 a.m. on Monday morning when Torin invited him along.

According to Isabelle, he missed nothing. On Monday night, she said she had to burn her shoes. This made Torin roll his eyes—did she really think the streets of Manhattan were cleaner than a farmyard on an organic family farm? But Carine had been cheerful, with armloads of fresh cheeses and produce in canvas bags.

Torin is also clearly thinking of the vanished cream as he mentions tea to Flep this morning.

"You're not a closet Jane Austen or Dickens fan, are you?" Torin asks, finishing shaping the last croissants.

"If I were a closet fan, why would I admit it? I told you, I didn't even know what a crumpet was." Palm flat against Torin's stomach, Flep runs his hand inside Torin's jeans, skin and denim providing tight pressure. "And you don't need to start making me tea. I've had tea. That's how I know I don't like it."

"Tastes change." Torin leans forward against the counter edge, mashing Flep's wrist. "You're the one who brought it up."

"You're such a control freak," Flep says in his ear, breath short with pain.

"And you are trying to make your breakfast late, darling. I'm doing this for you."

"That's what it feels like." He pushes his left hand backward through Torin's untidy hair. When Torin showers at night and goes to bed with wet hair, it always looks peculiar in the morning.

Torin drops the brush in the sink and grabs the full baking sheet, ready to open the oven. His motions free Flep's right hand, and he reaches down a few more inches.

"*Fuck*," Torin whispers, amusement gone. "Let me put these in."

"Go ahead. I don't have you in a straitjacket." Flep kisses his neck, leaning into him, stroking the backs of his left fingers over Torin's bicep, down his arm.

"Bullshit—get the oven door."

"I have plenty of time." But Flep obliges, and Torin shoves the tray into the oven.

Torin turns, forcing Flep to release him. Flep holds Torin's hips as Torin shoves him into the kitchen island. His mouth still tastes of toothpaste before his morning coffee, hot cinnamon caressing Flep's tongue. His pulse quickens while Torin's hands slide over his chest, up to his neck, holding his face. Heat floods him as their bodies press together.

He stood in a doorway, his arms around another, kissing...her. A woman who smelled of lavender and fresh bread and black tea. Her skin felt soft, comforting, yet he tasted salt as he kissed her. Hot tears ran down her cheeks—from her eyes or his own, he was not sure.

Ridiculous. Flep has never kissed a woman on the lips. Then where is she from? He has never dreamed of her either. Never in his life. In *this* life. Impossible.

The pressure from Torin is as painful as it is arousing, the counter digging in, Torin's teeth on his throat, hands running down his hips.

Where is the lavender? The kitchen here and now smells of yeast and tea, cinnamon and coffee. The dessert plate on Saturday night...

She dropped her head against his chest, hugging him, holding on.

He could not breathe.

Torin's lips again meet his, and he takes in the full intensity of the kiss. Torin's body, his firm hands, rapid breaths, stubble of his jaw, smell of his sweat, taste of his tongue. Torin's fingers unzip his fly. Flep pushes into the pressure.

Her eyes were ocean blue, yet red with crying. The lump in his own throat nearly choked him, wanting to tell her he did not have to go. But he did have to. He must leave her. And the girl. The little girl with bright blue eyes looking into his own.

Flep gasps as if dowsed with ice water. His heart hammers, breathing fast. Torin has both their pants open. Flep cannot sort out which feelings are which. His skin is coated in sweat while chills race up his spine.

Crazy. That other part. It isn't real. He never dreamed any of it before. Not that dreaming it would make it real, but... *Stop.*

Another life.

This is real. Torin, here, real and more than worth focusing upon. Impossible not to focus now, the way he touches Flep. Impossible to ignore. *Keep it that way, please.*

As if to answer him, Torin drops to his knees. Flep seizes Torin's hair, now so in the moment no other sight or smell or feeling can intrude.

Torin keeps him here, in this particular kitchen, even after the oven timer goes off.

Still here, in the moment, for breakfast while Flep laughs at Torin's story of the first time he attempted making homemade croissants with his grandmother. He thought he could take shortcuts with the dozen steps and ended up with flat patties of butter dough.

Right up until the tea, his mind moving ahead to dressing and leaving for work. While Torin gets a refill of coffee for himself, Flep finally tastes his own drink. And almost sobs—without any idea why.

CHAPTER FOURTEEN

"Service! Vic, get that Camembert out. Mason! Your sole's up! Were you taking a fucking coffee break?"

"No, chef!" Mason answers as he dashes through the swing doors toward Torin, a plate already in his hand.

Torin meets him around the dividing half-wall of warming plates. No one brings a full dish back into his kitchen.

"What the hell are—?"

"A complaint, chef." Mason stands rigid. "Undercooked."

"Are they after a free meal? No one can undercook scallops."

Mason holds out the plate. "Sorry, chef."

"It's bullshit—" Torin grabs a knife. The Gruyère on top is golden, so the scallop must be cooked—even these giant king scallops. He cuts in as half a dozen other servers and chefs rush around them. Translucent. The thing isn't even room temperature in the middle. "Jesus Christ and—who made this?"

Carnage again: chefs at unusual stations, Zade in, Brent out, people moving and filling in.

"Here, chef," Ava calls.

"Do you know how to make Coquilles Saint Jacques?"

"Yes, chef." She can only half face him from her station, mincing steak tartare.

From scallops to tartare? What is happening to his station chefs? Torin knows he needs to do less cooking and more supervising than ever, but this is ridiculous.

He takes the dish to Ava. "Then what the fuck were you going for here?"

"Chef—?"

"Did you think table seven also wanted a tartare? It's raw! You really have to work at it to serve raw scallops in a hot dish. Start a new one! And I want to see it before it goes out since you need a goddamned babysitter!"

"Yes, chef."

"Mason, get that sole out of here. Now!"

What is wrong with these people? It shouldn't matter if there are upsets at stations, if they must stretch themselves. Everyone here should be capable when called on, no matter their assignment on paper. He does not *want* to micromanage them. But what is he supposed to do when they can't cook better than his six-year-old?

And he imagined he could delegate more, working toward another location. As it is, he is not here enough. Should be in all day for Mondays, and for all lunch services, not just some.

A year ago, Chef Keon, the best sous chef Torin ever had, left to open his own place. Or two years ago? A long time either way. Nothing has been right since then. Torin is beginning to wonder if anything ever will be again.

Executive pastry chef Dominique, experienced in savory cuisine and possessing superb leadership skills, has helped close gaps over the past years while Torin tests new hires, but it's not her job.

He had just been feeling that things could get back to normal with Chef Jackson on lunch and Chef Brent on dinner. Now, no more Brent.

No-show Brent had not, after all, been consumed by zombies. He had arrived the day after his Saturday disappearance, trying to explain his absence to Torin. Torin made no effort to follow what he said. Final pay for Brent was owed. End of story. Though Torin eventually had to tell the man to get out of his kitchen since Brent seemed to think he could return to work.

Why has turnover been high since Keon? Chaleur has not usually had this problem. As if perfect Keon left a jinx for future sous chefs.

Now, with chefs at the wrong stations and raw scallops being served, Torin and Dominique have themselves spread like rice paper.

So, a new hire on the way. Another headache. Amélie used to handle much of the hiring and interviewing process, but she was gone even before Keon.

"Chef, lemon sauce?" Chef Dominique offers him a tasting spoon.

Why exactly is she making a savory sauce? Torin does not ask.

Pure lemon hit on top. Below, butter and tempered egg, hints of thyme and dill, white pepper spice, and salt. Rich and comforting.

"Perfect, Chef Dominique. Excellent."

"Thank you, chef."

So much more than a pigeonholed pastry chef, Dominique is the food equivalent of bisexual. Doesn't matter. He needs her in her own job. Still another hire to face.

He must get this kitchen into shape—beyond reproach—before he can be serious about the second location.

"Chef Ava, where are my scallops?"

"Coming, chef!"

Torin soon snatches the plate from her hands. He wipes the edge of the dish with a towel, tests a couple of the hot scallops with pressure from a fork, and whisks them from the kitchen himself.

Every table is full. Chaleur is booked weeks out for dinner. First come, first serve at their few lunches. The new place, whenever it opens, will offer brunch. Multiple colleagues tell him they do as many covers at brunch as dinner. Make Chaleur exclusively dinner, move Jackson to the new place, which Jackson wants. Keep it lighter, more family-friendly. If only Flep would do the interior...

Two couples in their sixties at table seven, finished with their other appetizer, which must have been cooked, and the damn plate still on their table. Not so old as to be hopeless cases. The very old ones are nearly always the rudest.

Torin bows and presents the dish, taking the empty plate. He apologizes, asks if they need refills, and assures them their appetizers are on him. The two ladies are all nods and smiles, the men softening at the gift and offer of wine.

Easy—no bad reviews. But, God, he can't afford to do this all the time.

Three more hours, and they can start closing, sending out last dishes.

Tai is doing well. If he sticks, he'll be one to promote. Zade doesn't have her head in the game, worried that her dog may lose its leg. Mason drops a dessert tray, but only because Vic ran into him. Torin does not get involved, doesn't even shout from across the kitchen. At the end of the evening, his throat hurts.

He is looking forward to home tonight.

Walking through the September midnight, he thinks of the girls. A swap-over night. Their French grandparents picked them up from school and dance, then Flep got them after dinner from Greenwich Village and brought them home.

They, or Flep, would have made sure the girls attended to their homework. Just starting for Ree. She already seems enchanted by her limited school experiences, so Torin isn't worried about her.

Then they would have watched a movie or Food Network until Flep sent Ree to bed and asked Bell to switch to a book, working on his own design homework for whatever the ad project is this week.

Now, all asleep. He must wait to see the girls until morning, but it soothes away the carnage of the evening just to think of them being home.

He can get all three ready for their days on Thursday and Friday, not just cook breakfast for Flep. Then all of Saturday morning together.

Home at 1:00 a.m., he opens the door quietly to discover Flep sitting at the table with his laptop.

"What are you doing up?" Torin asks in a whisper, delighted. He passes the kitchen island to kiss Flep.

"One guess." Flep smiles, also speaking in a whisper.

"You should have taken something."

"I did. I don't like to take another past midnight."

He has no lights on in here, just a lamp filtering from the master bedroom and city lights creeping through the living room windows. His laptop screen is missing the usual digital sketches or diagrams or photographs. He does not even have his drawing tablet attached. Instead...

"Are you reading about Nazis?"

"World War Two in general," Flep says. "Just curious. It's amazing how little I know about history once I start to think about it."

"You know a lot about *Phantom of the Opera, Les Mis',* and *Shuffle Along*—"

Flep chuckles, closing his laptop. "Bed."

"Don't forget *Mary Poppins.* Is that where the tea and crumpet thing came from?"

"Not that I recall."

"I had a great uncle who was SS in the War."

Flep squints up at him. "Honestly? Your father's people were Irish."

"On my mother's side. And my grandfather on her side was technically Jewish. Didn't count because it wasn't the maternal line."

"That's why you're not circumcised?"

"Everything happens for a reason. Too bad I'm not in touch with anyone who would know the family history these days. I just know her side was very involved in the War."

"I feel debriefed after a few Wikipedia articles anyway." Flep sighs.

Torin sheds his jacket and shoes. Laundry in the morning, which reminds him...

"How'd it go with the girls tonight? And you should ask Amélie's parents about it. They were born in France around then."

"The girls were great. Ree read me two easy readers, has a new loose tooth, and explained that 'the quick brown fox jumps over the lazy dog' has all the letters in it. Bell wants me to help her get on your case about doing pointe."

Torin grins, cocking his head. "Any plans to?"

"I really don't know anything about ballet or childhood bone development. But she is small. I'm not sure I'll be much help to her. Maybe next year?"

Torin turns, remembering to replace keys and wallet by the door. Before he can, he sees Ree, just padding into the kitchen on bare feet, smiling up at him. She looks tiny in her pink nightgown—a frilly sack in comparison to her big sister's preferred practical pajamas. Her hair is a tangle around her face after a few hours of sleeping on it.

She gazes benevolently up at him, holding out both of her little hands. How can she already be in school? How can she be turning seven in five more months? Every time he blinks, a season changes.

"What are you doing up?" Torin rests keys and wallet on the island and obliges her, reaching to pick her up under the arms and kiss her forehead.

"Now you have to put me to bed," Ree says groggily, tucking her head against his chest as he shifts his hands to hold her.

"Is that so? I heard you have a loose tooth."

"Uh-huh." She yawns. "You smell like lobster."

"We had a lot of seafood tonight. Do you need a story, sweetheart?"

"Flep read us a story. We started *The Cricket in Times Square*. Three chapters, plus one more because of the cat. The cricket comes to New York from Connecticut, just like Flep."

Torin smiles around at Flep, surprised to see him looking uncomfortable, even embarrassed.

"We better put you to bed then," Torin says to his daughter.

She nods, already drifting off.

He carries her to the girls' room, resting her in place on the lower bunk and pulling the blanket over her.

"Dad?" Bell stirs.

He stands to look past the rail at her.

"Did you bring anything home?"

"Not tonight. Want pizza for dinner tomorrow? I'll make your crusts in the morning. You can put them together with Flep after school."

"Yes, please." She smiles, eyes shut.

She does not even say anything about placing toppings on a pizza crust being a culinary stretch for Flep.

Torin kisses them both good night and retreats to the master bedroom.

Flep has left the kitchen for the bathroom. Still with only the lamp on by the bed, he stands over the sink, splashing warm water on his face and rubbing it around to the back of his neck with a washcloth.

He wrings it out as Torin steps up behind him to put his arms around Flep.

"Thank you for looking after them." Torin kisses his ear, turning his head and resting his face against Flep's shoulder. "What's wrong?"

"Nothing."

"About bedtime stories? You don't have to read to them."

"Oh. No, it's not that. I like reading to them. Ree doesn't even interrupt anymore, so I guess I'm doing something right, even if I'm not reading in French. I just don't want to be...usurping...taking your place..."

"Don't be crazy." Torin holds him tighter. "I love you so much. Ree saying she's satisfied that you read to her—you don't know how that makes me feel, what a gift you are to us. You didn't need to have anything to do with them. Even seeing me. You didn't have to move in."

"I wanted to. I love kids." Flep twists away to face him, nose-to-nose in the dim bathroom. "I never thought I'd have an opportunity like this. I love being around them. Even when they think I'm a moron..."

"That's my point." Torin holds his face with both hands. "You didn't have to. You're here anyway."

Flep appears more embarrassed than ever, flushed, biting his lip. "Why is your staff scared of you?"

Torin kisses him. "I have no idea."

Thursday, September 8

Sickly smell. Something across my face, sharp and numerous. A million fire ants. A weight pressing down.

I opened my mouth to shout. Claws and a length of thick, hairless tail dropped onto my tongue. I thrashed, yelling. Rats everywhere in darkness. They launched themselves off me, crashing to the earth floor, running down my arms and legs, straight up the wall, springing off my head.

Then more and more, piling on top of me instead of fleeing. Slick, heavy bodies, bloated from gorging on human corpses. They covered me, forcing me back, snapping for my face.

Sharp pain in my hands. Not from a bite. From hitting something. My hands were grabbed and slammed...into the headboard.

I lurched awake. Torin straddled me. He held both my wrists against the headboard. Crushing me. He swore while his own breath sounded ragged.

He wasn't the one telling me everything was okay now. I had to tell him, relaxing under him, before he would let go. Then he sat back on me, right hand going to his face.

"What the fuck?" he whispered, shaking his head.

I still felt them: claws on my skin, a tail in my mouth. Heard them, smelled them, tasted the putrid blast of rotten flesh about them.

I struggled to reach the bedside lamp. Torin would not shift his weight off me.

When I flipped the switch, I was horrified to see crimson on Torin's hand and face. Blinking, fighting dark images, it took me a moment to understand I was not hallucinating. Torin's face really was bloody.

"Are you okay?" He stared down at me, hand over his bleeding nose. Shirtless, shivering with adrenaline.

"Are you? Torin..." I tried to sit up, reaching for his face.

Torin climbed from bed to avoid me, covering nose and mouth as he walked to the bathroom.

"I'm sorry—God, did I hit you?" Following him, I found my legs too weak to carry me. I sat on the foot of the bed and leaned forward with my elbows on my knees, battling for my own breath. "I'm so sorry, Torin."

He had his face under the sink faucet.

"I thought you were a pack of rats." I ventured again to follow, managing to lean on the bathroom counter and offer a towel as he turned off the tap. "Are you all right?"

He wiped hands and face, gingerly feeling his nose.

I longed to hug him, continue apologizing, to touch him. Torin did not appear to be in a hugging mood.

"It's okay," he said through his towel. "It'll stop with pressure."

"Torin—"

"Wasn't your fault. Just go back to bed."

Now my skin crawls and my teeth are on edge. I don't want to be in bed, or keeping a record, or here, living. Not like this.

CHAPTER FIFTEEN

"Cucumbers, cucumbers, cucumbers!" Ree shrieks as she races past the island, around the couch, down the short hall to her and Isabelle's bedroom, then back the other way.

"Did she get sugar for lunch today?" Flep asks Isabelle anxiously as Ree flies past them in the kitchen. "Or espresso shots?"

She leaps onto the master bed, runs across it, jumps off, and streaks back to the couch.

"Cucumbers, cucumbers, cucumbers!"

Isabelle shrugs. "I think she was born that way. She's better behaved when she's upset than when she's happy."

"One thing she and your dad don't have in common." Flep winces as Ree dashes around the island, almost knocking into him when she slides in her socks. "Ree, do you think—?"

She is already gone.

"You can't just ask people questions all the time." Irritated, Isabelle turns to him. "You're the grown-up."

"That doesn't mean if I tell her to sit down and stop screaming she will."

"Give her a cucumber." Isabelle opens the refrigerator.

"Your dad put them in the salad—"

"Here's one. Ree!" Isabelle holds it out.

Ree runs through the kitchen and the cucumber disappears.

Flep's eyebrows jump. "Aren't you supposed to...clean it? Peel it?"

"Cucumber!" Ree lands on the couch, already biting like a dog on a bone. She reaches for the remote control.

Isabelle gives Flep a look. "It's organic. She'll live. Let's start the pizzas before she's back in here. I'm starving."

"*Chopped* is starting!" Ree shouts from the living room, then crams her mouth with another bite.

"I never knew a child who liked vegetables and seafood so much." Flep helps her get ingredients out of the refrigerator, including the proofed dough made that morning. "Don't your grandparents feed you anything after school?"

"Cucumber is a fruit. And they're strict about 'mealtimes.'" Isabelle puts on a high, severe voice. *"Ne mange pas avant de dîner, Isabelle!"*

"Uh..."

"Mémé doesn't believe in eating between meals."

"Kind of harsh for a six-year-old."

"She wants us to do homework there since she thinks no one else will remind us. Do you know how hard it is to do homework in English when you're getting advice in French and your sister, who has no homework, yammers about cucumbers and pizza that we're not eating until we get home?"

"I thought you like going to your grandparents' place." He looks hopelessly around at the cheese, tomatoes, mushrooms, fresh basil, dough, and other ingredients that Isabelle piles on the counter.

"I do. When it's only ballet in summer. It's crazy now."

"Sometimes I can leave work earlier. Or your dad could go in late. We could probably work it out for you to come straight here on Thursdays and Fridays..." His brows are drawn, clearly at a loss as to what to do with all these whole ingredients. "He didn't make sauce, did he?"

"I'm sure he thought we could handle it. There's everything for pesto. I like pesto and fresh tomato on a pizza."

"Also a fruit," Flep says under his breath.

"It doesn't matter about going to Mémé and Pépé in the afternoon. I just wish I could come home on my own. I'm almost twelve—old enough to stay alone for a couple hours."

"Not old enough to also be responsible for Ree and travel around Manhattan on your own. I'm trying to change my schedule to have some Mondays off and work some weekends. While I'm at it, I'll see what I can do about Fridays, okay? I'd only have to leave a few hours early to pick you both up and I could go in early."

Isabelle drops her gaze to the pizza toppings. She wishes he were not so nice, so concerned. Then it would be easier to maintain a bad attitude about him.

"Thanks," she says, still not looking at him.

"When's your birthday?" Flep smiles. "I didn't know it was coming up."

No big surprises being planned by her parents then.

"October 23rd."

"What do you want for it?"

"One home again."

Stupid, stupid thing to say. This is what happens when she spends too much time with him. Him and all his niceness and questions. All of his *What do you want?* instead of *This is what we're doing.*

Stay around people like him too much and you start to let your guard down.

"Sorry," she says at once. "That was dumb. It doesn't matter. I don't want my parents back together like Ree. She doesn't remember how awful it was. They couldn't talk without arguing, and neither will ever, *ever,* back down because they're both always right. So I don't want that. I just..."

She sorts the toppings to one side of the maple cutting board as she goes on. "It's better...but it's worse. That's all. It's hard to have two beds and three places you could be going after school or ballet on any given day. But...just how it is." Babbling because she feels guilty and he hasn't even said anything—only watches her and looks really sad, making her feel worse.

"Yeah," Flep says softly. "I know. After my dad stopped paying child support, my mom and I moved a lot when I was a kid. She couldn't keep up on bills, or there was an abusive landlord, or the rental was being flipped. Once, our apartment building was condemned. We had to move out with a dozen other families. It's scary...not knowing your place in the world... "

He looks up from the food around them. "You have so many people here who love you, Bell. You're going to be juggling homes for a long time. What can we do to make that less stressful for you both?"

Isabelle cannot look at him. She feels a lump in her throat, chewing her lip, wishing she were not acting like a little kid.

She should not be having this conversation with him. Maybe with her mom or dad, if anyone. No one, really. Why does he talk to her and listen like she is a grown-up? Why not her dad?

"Being an only child was a lot of responsibility," Flep says when Isabelle has no ready answer. "You've got to get it right. Not just grades or chores—everything." He lifts mushrooms from a small paper bag, lining them up beside the cutting board. "Maybe being the oldest can be like that also. Maybe even more responsibility."

Isabelle still says nothing, watching the row of mushrooms.

"Sometimes, you get so busy doing a good job at playing your part in the family, you forget what you need back. Or know, but can't say it. Or no one will listen." He removes the last mushroom and folds the bag, looking at her. "If you could ask and everyone would agree, with no one thinking less of you, what would you ask for?"

She swallows and glances toward the living room where Ree is watching TV.

"I just wish..." She looks at Flep's mushroom row: a perfect line beside her neatly sorted tomatoes, onion, olives, basil, soppressata, and cheeses. "I wish we could stay in one place for longer. I wish everything was set up better. Some days, I don't know who's going to be at school or the studio. I just wait and Mom or Dad or Pépé or you show up, while I'm the last to know. Even a friend's place maybe, if it's not a ballet day and Mom's coming after work. Sometimes it's the same. But...even then..." She has to swallow again.

"We go where it's convenient for the adults to send us that day and that moment." She speaks fast now. "Two days later—or one day—we're moving on. If we just...knew. And stayed longer. I don't mind one week and one week. We used to do that."

"Do you want to go back to every other week?" he asks. "And a set schedule?"

"We can't."

"But do you want to?"

She blinks and chews her lip more, still looking at the mushrooms.

"Of course, but my mom's working more and more and Dad's wanting to open a new place and they have stuff changing each day."

"That's not your business, Bell. You're right. You're shifted around for the convenience of the adults. You shouldn't have to change beds every day or two. I'm almost always free in the evenings. Your grandparents are usually home during the day. I don't see why you can't stay for a solid week at your mom's and a solid week here and always know what's coming."

She can't answer, but nods.

"I'll talk to your parents about it, okay?"

He will? Even her mom?

She looks at him, then away, her throat in pain. "You don't have to..."

"I want to. You shouldn't live in chaos just because one of us can't be bothered to get on the train for ten minutes and bring you home for the night."

She nods again.

"I'm sorry," he adds.

Ree runs back into the kitchen during a commercial. "Where's my pizza?" She has polished off the cucumber and pokes a lump of dough.

"Stop it, Ree." Isabelle sniffs, hoping Flep doesn't notice. "We've hardly started."

"I need a mozzarella ball!"

"No," Flep says, surprising Isabelle. "You can have a taste, and we'll call you when it's time to put on toppings." He slices off a bite of fresh mozzarella with a butter knife, and Ree is content to run back to the couch.

Isabelle looks around at their assembly line. "We...um...have to use the food processor for pesto. And clean and chop everything else we want."

"I'll do the chopping if you want to put pesto together. I'm not even sure what's in it."

She nods a third time, managing a "Thanks."

He smiles, although he still looks sad. "Anytime."

They stretch dough, build toppings, and preheat the oven.

131

Flep makes her nervous, the way he handles knives like a toddler even though her dad has tried to show him how to slice vegetables properly. She feels too grateful to Flep now to sound disagreeable. She does, gently as she can, mention that a serrated knife works best for tomatoes.

Still, he's better than when she met him last winter. Even if he does pick half the produce up to cut it as if he cannot find a good angle on the board.

"Do you want a tomato sauce base, or do you like pesto?" Isabelle asks, carefully removing the blade from the food processor and scraping green paste back into the vessel with a silicon spatula.

"Uhh...?"

"Want to taste it?"

"Thanks."

She hands him a tasting spoon, pretending it is perfectly normal that a thirty-whatever-year-old living in New York City doesn't know if he likes pesto on a pizza.

"Sure. That's great, Bell. Good job." He sounds surprised.

"Can you put the pizza stone in the oven to warm up? It's too heavy for me. I'll spread pesto so Ree doesn't make a mess and we'll all do our own toppings."

She is covering the last of the three crusts, deftly swirling the back of the spoon in a circle, about to call Ree in, and half-listening to dessert judging on the TV, when she hears Flep say something that makes her look up.

"Damn." In a low undertone. That's it. The one word. Not exactly an appalling eruption of temper, but Isabelle is still startled.

She has never heard Flep swear before, even when he didn't know she was around—whereas she has heard her own father use extraordinary vocabulary in such moments. It has led her to the impression that Flep just doesn't curse at all. Apparently not true.

There is a split second after her looking up to see what is wrong in which she wonders what provoked the...outburst.

Flep looks at his own left hand, where he holds an heirloom tomato he was just slicing. Why is he holding it in his left and the knife upright in his right rather than keeping both on the board?

Then she realizes that what she thought was a strip of tomato skin across the side of his hand is expanding. In a flash, it goes from a red line to a waterfall.

Isabelle catches her breath. She hurries around the corner of the island, leaving her spoon.

"Flep? Are you okay? Put your hand under the faucet."

He does not move or look at her, knife and tomato still in his hands as blood drips onto the cutting board.

Is he in shock? Doesn't that take a few seconds? She knows that some people just can't stand the sight of blood.

"Flep?" She pulls the razor-sharp blade from his hand, then the tomato.

Still, he does not turn for the sink.

Isabelle grabs a clean dishtowel, trying to stop the bleeding. He cut across the side and palm, evenly between his little finger and wrist. Not much force is needed to make a deep slit with that knife. Why did she tell him to switch to serrated? She should have asked him to do the pesto.

Scared now—her heart beating fast, not because of the cut, but because of his reaction—Isabelle presses the white towel around his hand. Almost at once, bright blood is visible through cloth.

Flep is still staring at his hand. Yet, as she looks up into his face, his eyes are vacant, unseeing, a million miles away.

"Flep, it's okay. Why don't you sit down?"

He will neither move toward a barstool or chair, nor take the towel to hold the pressure himself. He reaches blindly for his own chest, groping as if for a zipper, though his shirt has none. No, a pocket. Like he is reaching into a breast pocket for something. But there is no pocket. Nothing to reach for.

Isabelle looks around desperately. No one to help them. She should call her dad. He could run home, even with dinner service underway. He would drop service and come home if they had a real emergency, which is more and more how this is looking. But he would never hear the call.

Her mom would answer, but her mom is across town. She wouldn't be here in less than half an hour even if she ran out her door right now.

Isabelle only knows a few people in the building. Martin, downstairs, would help them. She could send Ree running to get him if she needed to, and, in the meantime, call her parents.

"I'm sorry, Mary. I'll be right there."

"What?" Isabelle looks up at Flep.

He still will not move, won't even look at her. Who is he talking to? Who is Mary? She doesn't know a Mary. Religious kind of Mary? She didn't even think Flep was Christian.

"Tell her I'm sorry," his voice breaks. "I'll be home soon. I'll see you soon."

"Who are you talking to?" Terrified, Isabelle leans away. "Flep?"

He blinks down at the bloody cloth, her hands around his, and steps back against the counter—the first time he has moved.

"Come sit—"

Her words are cut off when Flep drops to the wood floor as if shot, unconscious.

CHAPTER SIXTEEN

Amélie thanks the last EMT at the door before turning to her daughters. Both hover at the end of the short hall leading to their bedroom.

She kneels and Carine rushes forward to hug her. Amélie kisses her soft hair.

"I called them, Mommy. Bell told me, and I did."

"I know you did, sweetheart. You're a brave girl. I'm so impressed with both of you. You are two mature, smart people."

"I didn't know what else to do." Isabelle walks up and Amélie hugs her also.

"You did just right, Bell. I'm proud of you. If it's a false alarm, you can apologize later. You were right to call 911 and right to call your parents."

"I don't even know if Dad's got the message yet."

"Don't worry about it. I'm sure he'll be home as soon as he can. I'll stay until he gets back."

Isabelle nods. Her hands shake and her skin looks like parchment, tears in her eyes.

Carine, on the other hand, is more curious than anything now: comforted by her mother's praise, fascinated by the commotion of minutes before.

"You never had dinner, did you?" Amélie asks, stroking Isabelle's hair.

She shakes her head. "Is Flep okay?"

"I'm sure he's fine. Why don't you let me talk to him for a minute and figure out what happened. Go sit down, take a deep breath. Then we'll all get something to eat."

Isabelle pulls Carine by the hand back to their room.

In the living room, Flep is sitting on the red couch. He's leaning forward, elbows resting on his knees and hands at the back of his head—the left one bandaged by the EMTs.

Amélie starts to take the accent chair to face him. She thinks better of it and sits beside him, an arm's reach away. He is so sensitive to confrontational situations, even at the best of times.

"Christ, I'm sorry," he whispers, lowering his hands, looking at the wrapped one.

"For what?"

"Traumatizing your children." He rubs the bridge of his nose with his good hand.

"*C'est comme ça*," Amélie says with a shrug.

He looks at her, eyes weary, whole aspect haggard.

"Shit happens," she adds.

He goes on staring at her for a moment, then smiles, just a little.

"I'm not worried about them," she says. *Him* on the other hand? "They're intuitive. They're smart. When they see you're okay, they'll be okay. How do you feel?"

"Dizzy, shaky. Like I've had a low blood sugar attack. Headache from the fall and hitting my head. That's about it. Ethan—or something with an E—told me to go to the hospital first thing in the morning in case I need a stitch or two."

She waits a moment, looking at the dark windows opening to the glowing city and river beyond. He says no more.

"What happened?" she asks.

Flep does not look at her or move for several seconds.

"I...hallucinated. Something about the sight of blood. Why this and not last night...I don't know..."

"Last night?"

"Oh, I..." He shakes his head, color returning to his cheeks. "Torin couldn't get me to wake up, and I...seem to have punched him in the nose."

Amélie forces the corners of her mouth down to keep a straight face. How many times has she longed to punch Torin in the nose?

"I've never blacked out, or fainted, or anything like that in my life," Flep continues. "I have no idea... I wasn't there, wasn't in the kitchen. I wasn't even me." He shakes his head again, repeating, "I'm sorry."

She wants to tell him to stop doing that. Or put her arm around him—he looks so miserable.

"The same as the dreams?" she asks. "They never stopped, did they?"

"No, but it's not that. It's this past week. Something changed. They've been getting..." He looks vaguely around, as if just waking. "The girls need something to eat. They haven't even had a snack since school. Besides a cucumber." Barring the one smile, he has not met her eyes since she sat.

"We'll finish dinner," Amélie says. "Do you want to lie down?"

"I can sit at the table. It's just a cut."

He does not look like he should be sitting up, but she shares his desire to demonstrate to the girls that he is fine, not keep making a big deal out of this for their sakes. She nods and goes to clean the kitchen.

Only a couple of tomatoes were contaminated. With the blood cleaned from counter and floor with rubbing alcohol, and all other signs of combat erased, Amélie turns the oven back on and fetches the girls from their room.

Flep sits at the small kitchen table, though he still looks ill.

Even Carine is subdued, keeping her voice soft as she builds her pizza, standing on a chair to reach. She says nothing to Flep, though frequently glances at him.

Amélie talks to him instead—about pizza toppings and the right way to slice tomatoes. Isabelle asks him how he feels as Amélie slides her and Carine's pizzas onto the hot pizza stone.

He assures her he is fine, apologizing for scaring her and for his culinary inadequacies.

While Carine tells Amélie about her loose tooth, and all she did at school today, Amélie finishes Flep's pizza with extra soppressata. He looks like he needs the protein and it is the only meat on hand. Isabelle prefers veggie pizzas mounded in basil. Carine is all about the cheese.

"Dad made us a cucumber salad to go with them." Isabelle grabs a bowl from the refrigerator.

The four of them sit around the table with plates ready for pizza and pass around the salad. Tart and sweet with balsamic and olive oil, the salad lifts her buried longing for homemade food like this every day.

At her daughter's insistence, Amélie promises Carine she will try a slice of her pizza to keep her happy. Amélie does not need to be eating cheese-smothered pizza after her own dinner. Unfortunately, Carine's kindergarten was big on teaching sharing and interpersonal skills to impulsive five-year-olds. She earned a gold star every time she shared, which corrupted her into becoming a sharing maniac who grows distraught if the recipient of her generosity does not wish to accept. She shares outgrown toys with her sister, her hairbrush with Amélie, her art supplies with Flep, and, of course, food with anyone she can find.

One small slice only. And the cucumber salad won't hurt anything.

In French, Isabelle asks Amélie if Flep is really okay—that he got super weird when he cut his hand.

Amélie tells her not to be rude. "There's your timer, Bell."

Carine leaps up. "Pizza!"

They are all still at the table, eating and talking about pizza combinations and the best pizzas in Manhattan, when Torin hurries in. Two hours before closing. Four before he would normally be home.

Handsome as he is, particularly in the fitted white chef's jacket and black pants, she cannot help feeling let down to see him. Just his appearance, his voice, his presence, kills her budding benevolence. Too much baggage. Too much of seeing what a single-minded asshole he can be to comfort herself with how doting he is on the girls.

As he walks in and Carine runs to him, thrilled by his early arrival and offering her last slices, Amélie feels regret for the interruption. Feels almost sorry for Flep. For her own conflicted feelings toward him in the past and the breaking up of their moment.

Not that she could ever wish to steal Torin's gay boyfriend. Still...it's absurd, but she is beginning to understand the appeal of a koala.

"What happened? What's going on?" Torin looks even more alarmed by the sight of Amélie there. He lifts Carine into his arms, crossing quickly past the island to join them, looking from Isabelle to Flep. "Everyone okay?"

"Fine," Flep says. "I cut my hand slicing tomatoes. No other casualties."

"I'm sorry to call," Isabelle starts.

"No, don't hesitate to call me if there's ever anything wrong, Bell. You know that. Sorry I didn't pick up your message until fifteen minutes ago."

Always the hypocrite. If one of his staff ran from the kitchen for an emergency—never mind if someone died—he would probably fire them. Their families are clearly not as important as Torin's.

He sits in Carine's chair with her on his knee, though she has grown too big for such a perch. At close range, Amélie notices his nose looks perfectly healthy—not even a bruise. Flep needs to work on his swing.

"We're fine, really." Flep looks down. "You can go back to your service. Neither of you need to stay."

"It's okay," Torin says. "I've got Renard on front of house and Dominique in charge in the back. She'll keep everything under control."

Amélie cannot help a small smirk. Dominique was her hire from a few years ago.

"She has turned out good, hasn't she?" Amélie asks. "Taste and leadership."

"I've been working with her since she came on," Torin speaks hotly, eager for the argument.

Taking all the credit then, of course. Amélie says nothing. Torin hates that more than any other move one can make. He would rather be shouted down and insulted than given the silent treatment to which he can build nothing back.

Carine happily gets him to accept her last slice, though Isabelle looks as tense as Flep to have the two of them together at the table.

Maybe it was never both girls at all. Maybe it's only Carine who invents all the stalling to keep her parents in the same place at the same time, waiting for them to all go back to sharing a living space. *Poor Ree.*

"I'm glad everything's all right." Amélie smiles at Flep and Isabelle. "I'll see you on Saturday. Unless you need me before then. Just call."

Isabelle nods. "Thanks for coming out."

"You did great, Bell. Have a good night." She gathers her bag and phone from the island, then her jacket from the door, Isabelle seeing her out.

Flep and Carine bid her good night.

Amélie squeezes Isabelle's shoulder and tells her she loves her before starting down the hall.

She is waiting for the elevator, a long way from the door, when she hears her name and steps back to the main hall.

Flep, still pale and looking like he should not be on his feet, but no longer shaky after the meal, has followed her out.

"Amélie, I wondered—I'm sorry... You introduced me to a young lady, a college student, at the Labor Day party..."

"Natalie Trumbauer?" Amélie cocks her head. "The dream student. She's the daughter of a colleague of mine."

"Do you think—I don't know how well you know her—that...I could get in touch with her? Is that inappropriate? She said stuff I wanted to follow up on."

"Of course. It's fine. I'll ask her mother for her email, or give her yours to pass along."

"Thank you. I appreciate it. And thanks...for coming out late."

"It's no problem, Flep. It's just being a parent."

He nods. "Lovely boots."

"Jimmy Choo." She starts to say good night and turn away, but stops. "Do you mind if I ask what she said to you? About the dreams?"

He looks up from her boots, still tense and uncomfortable. "She said my dreams are from a past life."

"Do you think they are?"

"I think that's impossible, of course."

"But you want to talk to her again?"

Flep says nothing.

"Have you done any research?"

"Into dreams?"

"Into past lives."

He only looks bewildered. "You think there is such a thing?"

"My personal ignorance inspires me to research. Not scratch my head and grope about in darkness. If someone told me I had lived before—and that experience was trashing my current life—I'd be at the library the next day, literally or figuratively. There are entire cultures and religions that believe in reincarnation." She arches one eyebrow. "Have you told Torin about this?"

Flep shakes his head. "It doesn't make sense."

"Neither do strawberries and balsamic. So who are we to judge in ignorance?"

"Do you think I'm dreaming—and hallucinating—about the past?"

The elevator dings and the door slides open.

She looks back at him. "I don't know. But I wish you would do something about it. Conventional or otherwise."

Monday, September 12

Lying on snow. Frozen to earth. Reaching and unmoving. Calling out and silent. Praying and alone.

Mary, Mary, Mary, I called to her. Words that never left my stiff, frozen lips.

What is happening to me? I thought they were fading. I thought the sleeping pills kept them under control. Like a vicious dog with a muzzle. No less vicious. Only more...safe.

Since Labor Day...

Now, since Thursday night, when I saw her through the blood: not even a pretense of safety any more.

Why?

I sent Natalie an email over the weekend. Aiming to sound both casual and professional. Anything but desperate and creepy.

No answer.

Tuesday, September 13

Walking through mud, turning corner after corner in the dark. Rain on my skin through layers of heavy clothing. It ran down my collar, down my trousers, filled my boots.

I had to post a letter. First, I had to check on...something.

Checking at night. Routine. Dark and cold. Cold from rain, wet feet, oppressive darkness.

I turned a corner. Again and again. Never seeming to get anywhere. Never finding anything. What was I looking for? What was I out here in the rain to do? Another corner, another. Left, right, left, right.

I looked up. The outline of a young man I knew was visible before me in the dark. A flash and explosion from the rifle he held illuminated

143

his face at the same time I saw him.

I jumped at the deafening crack of the weapon in my ears and the sight of it going off three feet in front of me. I would have fallen from bed if Torin had not already been trying to wake me, holding both my arms.

I could not stay in bed.

Out on the couch now, bedroom door closed and all the kitchen and living room lights on.

I have coffee dripping. TV on mute for something to look at. Skin crawling. Pacing, hands shaking. My heart hammers as if someone is marching me around these small rooms with a gun against my skull.

Still, the image remains sharp. As if seconds of film are plastered to my eyes.

Walk around the corner, two steps, look up just as the boy in uniform pulls the trigger.

He had the butt of the rifle against the ground, sitting on an earth ledge above the weapon, holding the barrel under his jawbone, angling toward the back of his skull. He struggled to reach, to maneuver a much too large weapon to match his intentions. Found the right spot and leverage as I stepped out. Burst of sparking light in the dark. Report from the rifle as the boy's head snapped back and soft tissue burst into the rain. Hot spray through a cold downpour.

I don't see him topple over. I don't see the heavy rifle crash to the mud below his boots. Just that. Step out; explosion. Step out; explosion. For the rest of the night. Though I'm not letting my eyes shut again for more than a blink, waiting for dawn.

The eastern sky has lightened several shades by the time I open my laptop at the table and see I have an email from Natalie.

CHAPTER SEVENTEEN

Flep resists twisting his fingers together in his lap. He looks at the door, the table, and back. Hands relaxed, his left still wrapped to protect the two stitches in the mostly healed cut, he waits.

He sits in the Bubby's on Hudson, packed with other New Yorkers on lunch breaks—a place Isabelle and Carine introduced him to. For them, this is fast food.

Lunchtime aromas mingle with ever-present scents of breakfast—eggs, bacon, coffee, and pastries. Burgers, fried chicken, lobster rolls, and green salads pass Flep while he waits. He can pronounce every item on the menu. One of his favorite places from the girls' choices. Still, he does not feel hungry today.

Turkey club with the arugula side salad, maybe. He offered to buy her lunch and cannot just sit and watch her eat. If she shows up.

Flep sips from his water glass, feeling guilty about holding up a table. He checks his phone. Not that she is late—it's only him getting here early.

She arrives on time, looking around the noisy restaurant. Young Natalie Trumbauer: the daughter of Amélie's colleague, the redhead with vintage clothes and a quick smile.

Flep stands to shake her hand and thank her for coming. He cannot waste time, mouth dry. She already knows why he wanted to meet. He lets her decide what to get first, telling her his own favorite salads and sandwiches.

The moment they place their orders, Flep starts, first thanking her again for meeting him.

"I did some research, but I'm at a loss. Those dreams got worse after I met you. I thought you might give me ideas or referrals for someone to talk to about...dreams or..." He swallows.

Yes, he did read some in the weeks since they first met. He found works of Edgar Cayce and Ian Stevenson, startled to discover not only sound scientific evidence of reincarnation, but what some would call proof. Still, he hesitates.

"Or about past lives?" Natalie smiles, apparently relaxed in the hubbub. "What a fun place. I can't believe I've never been in here. And I'm happy to help. Is it still the same?"

"Battlefields and a letter... The biggest problem, though, after Labor Day, I started...seeing things. While I was awake."

"Really?" She looks intrigued, encouraging him to continue.

"I did once before, on the 4th of July. But it was all confusion. Now it's happened three times this month. First, I was in a doorway, saying goodbye to a woman I had never seen or dreamed about. In the next, I was...dying."

Flep holds up his left hand, showing her the bandage. "I accidentally cut my hand. Seeing the blood triggered a...vision. I was in snow and blood and was dying. Blood filled my mouth. I had to get back to that woman. Her name was Mary, but I don't know how I knew. And the little girl. There was a girl with Carine's eyes—that's Amélie's daughter."

Natalie nods. "She's adorable. I met her at the party. What about the last one?"

"Recently, I saw Mary again. It was morning. We were at home in a dim room. I don't know where or how. I just know I was home and saying goodbye. It seemed like the same day as the other vision, but before the doorway, like watching a movie out of order."

"What were you doing when you saw the woman both times? There must have been a trigger, like fireworks and blood?"

"I..." Face hot, breathless from trying to rush everything out, Flep swallows again. "I was...with my boyfriend..."

A waitress brings Natalie's hot tea.

"If you have the triggers," she goes on to Flep, "you could recreate them to remember more. Maybe not the cut, but even something on a screen could be a trigger, like watching a war movie. Have you tried anything like that?"

It sounds like a terrible idea. He wants them to stop. Not keep endangering his sanity or even his life. This chipper young woman seems to think the whole thing is just a fun mystery.

"I don't want to keep hallucinating. It's not exactly pleasant. I did research into World War Two after I saw you, but it wasn't like..." He shrugs helplessly.

"Like it rang a bell?"

"Yeah."

"History's full of wars. Maybe that's what you really need." She pauses, apparently considering her words. "That might be stupid about deliberately creating triggers. But you still want to figure out what's going on. More historical research?"

"So you honestly think these are...?" Deep breath. "Memories?"

"What else would it be?"

"Schizophrenia?"

She laughs and lifts her mug. "Take notes about your dreams and everything you do remember. Before you know it, you'll be able to figure out when this was."

"I've mostly given that up, they're all so similar." Or too stressful to keep writing down.

"Have you read...?" Natalie trails off, smile slipping as she watches his face. "You know, you shouldn't take my word for this. I'm not exactly giving you a professional opinion. If this is super weird for you...? Have you seen an accredited psychologist or psychiatrist?"

"They're only dreams. I didn't want to make a big deal of..." Flep also hesitates, feeling wretched, looking around the packed space as if for inspiration. "I was in the middle of so many transitions when this started. A new relationship and a move. A recent promotion that I didn't particularly..." He stops, yet every sentence makes him feel even more that he must justify his actions.

Why hasn't he done something? Seven months and he only got prescription sleeping pills?

She appears so...interested. Nodding, looking at him. Someone apart from his life. Someone who might know something.

"I should have done more," Flep continues. "I didn't because I didn't want to be...perceived...I didn't want to be the crazy guy who everyone regretted promoting or committing to."

"Who, at work, would even have known if you saw someone about nightmares?"

Flep drops his gaze. "It's not them. I'm the one who has trouble...dealing with..."

"Imperfections?"

He blinks, looks at her.

She tilts her head, her sweet smile returned. "Are you an eldest child?"

Flep feels a shiver at the back of his neck.

"What's wrong?"

"Nothing. Déjà vu. No, I'm an only child. Single mom."

"Going to see someone doesn't mean you're failing at anything. You're not letting anyone down by taking care of yourself. If you don't look out for yourself, how can you be your best for everyone you're trying to be perfect for?"

He says nothing, feeling worse and worse, like he ate something toxic.

"What's your Myers Briggs?" Natalie asks, still relaxed.

"I...don't know. That's a personality test, isn't it?"

"No worries. Listen, I totally got carried away about the past life stuff. That's what it sounds like to me. But, if you take a case of the flu to a brain surgeon, you've got a brain tumor, right? I can give you referrals through the school if you want to talk to someone who's actually accredited."

Why is she backtracking? She's all he has.

Flep shakes his head. "I'm sorry, no, I don't mean to be, uh...noncommittal. I don't believe in—I'm not into—but, when you said that at the party, I couldn't get it out of my head." He takes a deep breath. "How do you know about this? It's not what they're teaching in psychology these days, is it?"

She wrinkles her nose. "I said you can't tell my professors. It's a personal fascination. My whole family's into it. My mom's a lawyer working with Amélie, but she's been saying for ten years that one day she'll have a mid life crisis and start a metaphysical bookstore. My dad's a theologian—totally into Eastern religions. Growing up, we went to India for family vacations."

Flep returns her smile. Maybe she's a natural, or maybe it's her new training, but her ability to put him at ease is working.

He takes a drink, glad of a moment to collect his thoughts as their lunches arrive.

"Studying psychology didn't lead me to an interest in reincarnation," Natalie continues. "More the other way around. Things happen for a reason."

He meets her eyes for a moment, thinking of these past weeks, starting with Amélie's inexplicable invitation. Didn't Torin recently say something like that to him? Even teasing, even unrelated, maybe he should have been paying more attention.

"You were going to ask me something," Flep says. "About reading? I truly want to know what you think. Even if it's...weird. Even if I only have the flu."

Natalie grins. "I was going to ask if you've read Brian Weiss. *If* you want to look into this possibility, he'd be a good place to start. And there's a book called *Soul Survivor*. It's been years since I read it, but it would be relevant. It was World War Two related." Not yet starting on her lentil and veggie burger, she takes a tiny notepad from her purse to write down the name and title.

"Thank you. Go ahead and eat."

She drums her pen thoughtfully on the notepad. "The biggest thing, of course, is knowing what you're dealing with. You said you're always on mud? Sitting in dirt, freezing? Sounds like trench warfare. The Civil War or World War One. I'm totally old-fashioned, but you'll find the best stuff in books, not online. Go to the library and browse the biggest pictorial history books you can find. Watch documentaries. Figure out when and where."

She looks up from the pen tapping. "Best thing you could do, if you really do want my advice: go for a regression." Another grin. "Right now, I believe more than ever that nothing happens by chance."

"Why is that?"

"I just finished a book by a New York psychiatrist who *has* been

149

studying past lives. Gregory Kulmala on the Upper East Side. I was so excited to find he was in practice and taking appointments here, I tried to get one myself, before he's as famous as Ian Stevenson." She makes a face. "Turns out 'taking appointments' is a stretch. He's not seeing new patients unless by referral."

How does one even get a referral for a past life regression?

Natalie goes on, "If you call, or email, and explain what's happening, I'd be surprised if he didn't take you. He's going to be interested in your story. Here's the book." She adds another title to the page and rips it free. "And the website for his practice. You'll still be lucky to get in anytime soon, I'd guess. But you should try."

"Thank you." Flep takes the page and sits back, finally feeling hungry after all.

"I'd love to know what happens." She lifts her burger.

"Me too."

CHAPTER EIGHTEEN

Flep runs back to work after lunch, ears buzzing, yet lighter. He feels freer, ready to take action, even if he needs to get through his workday and wait until Saturday to hit the library. Today is Friday. He must pick the girls up from Greenwich Village after work.

Research. Should he recreate triggers? No. Just the thought makes him shiver. Something to ask Dr. Kulmala about, at most.

The girls are staying over tonight, but their mother will collect them in the morning. They are shifting to a constant one-week schedule. Ree, the free spirit, is put out, as is Torin. Yet Flep is sure it will be better for both girls. He, Amélie, and Isabelle pushed the change through.

Tonight, send Dr. Kulmala an email, explain what is happening, and hope it is enough to get an appointment. Also tonight, he'll tell Torin. He never even admitted to Torin what had really happened when he cut himself.

Torin laughed about it after the fact. "I had no idea you were so sensitive to blood. Makes me feel better about spiders."

Flep had rescued all three of them from spiders on two occasions. Once, Isabelle walked into a web at the Park, sending her into a screaming panic. Another time, Flep ran into the living room in answer to shrieks and found both girls on the back of the couch. Their father stayed behind the kitchen island. The cause: a tiny house spider dashing across the living room rug.

Flep had been incredulous—even more so when he tried to pick it up and all three shouted at him to kill it, not save it. The girls were bloodthirsty, advising shoes or books to pummel the arachnid to dust.

And Torin had laughed at him for blacking out.

"It wasn't the blood," Flep tried to explain at the time. "I saw things from those dreams. Like on the 4th."

"Be more consistent with the pills. You got them to stop in August." After having rushed home early from work that night and found everyone essentially well, Torin had turned his attention to cleaning the kitchen with the girls, then putting Carine to bed.

Flep has said nothing else about it, or corrected Torin's thinking everything was good in August. Nor has Torin bothered to ask.

Flep pretends to himself he does not care. Both are busy. Both have a lot on their plates. Yet, as he practices silence, waiting, needing Torin to ask about any developments, Torin never does. Flep is finally beginning to realize that if he does not bring something up, Torin never will.

As the evening encroaches, Flep wraps up work, catches a bus— though the tight space is nauseating— and picks up Isabelle and Carine from their grandparents. He takes the girls to Artisanal Fromagerie Bistro for a fondue dinner on the way home. He says it is just for fun— though really a goodbye until next week.

Through prickly autumn air, they take the long way home, walking out to 6th Avenue to "shop" before winding their way north and west back toward 2nd.

Shopping involves roaming in and out of tourist-filled department stores, enjoying Halloween window displays with Isabelle taking pictures, and pretending to pick out things like new furniture and exotic outfits.

Flep has never been a gift giver to them. A conscious decision on his part. It would be so easy—especially would have been at the beginning— to bring them stuffed animals or art supplies. And he would love to take them to *Annie* or *Finding Neverland*.

Flep has taken the girls to a couple of movies and several meals, and they regularly shop for groceries with Isabelle making the decisions. But he will not be the stepparent who buys his way in. Special occasions— Isabelle's birthday only weeks away—and no more.

He feels glad of it now. Neither girl is accustomed to being handed the pretty things they see in stores. Even impulsive Carine knows window-shopping means admiring only, like the Central Park Zoo. Much harder to get her to give up a desired prize at Gotham West Market or Whole Foods than in a toy store, where expectations run low.

So he is unsure why he stops at a display of Betta fish when they stroll through a bright, bustling pet store to admire reptiles, white mice, and dog toys. Carine terribly wants a dog or cat. Isabelle is too practical to indulge in such fantasies.

Flep flinches at sight of the mice, catching his breath, his stomach lurching. He looks quickly away from bald tails and beady eyes, hoping the girls do not notice, and focuses on fins.

The fish, tiny and brightly colored, swim around spaces no bigger than coffee mugs. Red, blue, yellow, green, striped and feathery finned and sleek bodied, the little fish are beautiful. Flep's natural sense of aesthetics surfaces in a rush of affection for the morsels of symmetrical life turning in their water cups.

Displays of pamphlets and books stand next to a shelf of small fishbowls, food, and accessories like plastic treasure chests, kelp, and ground cover stones. The fishbowls are intriguing. They range from round bowls with no frills to window displays, wall-mounted tanks, and rectangles that light up.

The girls—seldom in agreement—latch onto one maroon specimen with feathery fins and a bright blue stripe running down each side. A stunning fish.

Carine coos and gasps. She talks to it while it flicks back and forth in the few inches of water.

"Look how graceful it is," Isabelle says to Flep. "Like a little dancer."

Flep watches them watch the fish.

He is not sure how he feels about the commercial trafficking of live animals. Even fish. But he smiles, hoping he will still see the girls as much with their new schedule.

"Look." Carine snatches Flep's hand and pulls him down to her level for a good angle of the specimen. "Sebastian, this is Flep. Flep looks after us. Even when we're up too late and making too much noise."

Squatting down to face the fish, he watches Ree as she leans in, touching the plastic container with her forefinger, drawing the attention of the maroon and blue fish.

"He knows his name," she says happily.

Isabelle has moved on to look at the bowls and trinkets while Flep straightens up, pulling his phone from his jacket pocket.

Torin will be in the thick of dinner service, unable to answer, but Flep tries a text.

OK to get the girls a fish?

He replaces the phone in his pocket. It buzzes before he has done more than pick up one of the slim books on Betta fish.

Startled, Flep checks it.

Fine. Can fix it tomorrow.

Flep almost laughs.

Not to eat. Pet.

Another response in seconds.

Oh. If you want to take care of it.

"Look." Bell has picked up a ceramic ballerina fish bowl adornment.

Flep smiles, pocketing his phone. "A perfect likeness. Ree, do you want to bring Sebastian home?"

"I think he belongs to the store," Carine says, casting her fish a tragic look.

"They'll part with him for the right price. If you'll feed him and make sure he has clean water on your weeks at our place, I'll look after him while you're at your mom's. Do you want to read about fish care for your next bedtime story?"

Ree shrieks and starts leaping around.

"Can we get the bowl with the light?" Bell asks eagerly.

"Sebastian, Sebastian, Sebastian!"

CHAPTER NINETEEN

Library, history research, tell Torin, and confirm his appointment with Dr. Kulmala—the psychiatrist who is blessedly willing to see Flep. Not in that order.

After saying goodbye to the girls on Saturday, Torin is morose, relieving his feelings by making sourdough bread generously laced with chunks and streaks of ninety percent dark chocolate.

Flep has no idea why he is still home when he should be at work. It is not uncommon for Torin to leave at 8:00 a.m. for a dinner service starting at 5:00 p.m.

A test day for others to prep instead? Lately, Torin has buckled down on training new or promoted sous chefs while also working at home on plans for the next place. He found the location, just doesn't have the budget yet. Torin attributes this delay to his ex, though Flep cannot imagine how he can blame Amélie for wanting out of the business—and also wanting to be paid for an exit from something that she does partly own.

Flep does not ask why he's staying.

The combination of tart bread and bitter chocolate melting in his mouth prompts Flep's forgiveness of any real or imagined indiscretion in Torin's past, present, or future. Flep could climb into the chewy loaf, eat nothing else for the rest of his life, die for it.

"Are you okay?"

Flep looks across the island from his place on the barstool.

Torin, pan frying crab cakes for lunch, frowns at him. "You're not hallucinating again? You looked funny."

"I'm fine." Flep chews another bite, resisting shoving the whole warm loaf into his face. Has he already eaten a quarter of it? No, Torin must have had a slice. "Just a foodgasm. This stuff is like crack."

155

"Hmm." Torin regards the chocolate-laden sourdough skeptically. He is proud of his crab cakes, his perfect duck, his unique vegetable creations, and famed savory sauces. Not his bread.

"I'm sorry they won't be over on Monday, Torin."

"It's fine. If they don't want to be here—"

"Quit it." Flep sighs. "You know it's not that. You get where Bell's coming from, don't you? They need stability."

"I didn't realize they were so lacking in it. We work our asses off so they have two places to call home, go to the best schools, can pursue their interests. They're not living on Skid Row without—"

"It's not all black and white like that. You don't think it gives them more security to have one week on, one off? Know what's coming and have expectations met?"

"I think we *had* a schedule. We weren't random with them."

"Sometimes. They needed more. You already know you're seeing them after school on Monday—"

"Right. To take them to their mother's place."

"And next week they'll be here."

"This is never going to work."

Flep opens his mouth, then shuts it. He turns his head, catching sight of Sebastian, ensconced upon the hall table beside the front door.

Flep spent much of yesterday evening setting up the fish's lodging and learning about Betta fish with the girls.

Torin takes the sauce off the burner, glaring into the pan, shoulders stiff.

Flep hates arguing with him, hates that Torin is upset about the change. He feels even worse because he knows Torin is fuming at him for dropping the argument. And for starting the whole schedule trouble in the first place.

Flep slices off another piece of chocolate bread. Just a small one. He slides from the stool to walk around the island, starting more coffee.

He turns back to Torin and hugs him from behind, leaning his head on Torin's shoulder.

"I'm sorry," Flep says. "Give it a month or two. We can try something else if it doesn't work out." He kisses Torin's ear. "Thank you for the bread."

"I didn't think to make two." Torin glances across the island to Flep's vacated spot by the knife, breadboard, and greatly diminished loaf.

"It isn't very big."

Torin twists to look at him. "Only a full-sized sandwich loaf."

"I...don't know what you mean." He takes a ready plate from Torin and returns to his seat.

Torin joins him at the barstools, bringing extra lemon and spicy dipping sauce. Flep thinks of Bell sharing the lemon croquembouche with him three months previously. So long ago, it seems. So glad he accepted.

As they eat, Flep tells Torin he wants that bread for Christmas. Nothing else. Just lots of sourdough chocolate bread.

Torin asks if the fish can't live somewhere less hectic.

"We didn't want to forget to feed it. Thought it should be in the thick of things. By the way: Sebastian? Any idea where that came from?"

"*Little Mermaid* probably. That and *Oliver and Company* were her favorites a while back. You probably missed it."

"Now it's all ponies, *Frozen*, and food shows." Flep watches the fish from afar.

He has to say something. Has to. Can't just...pretend. But he goes on eating, complimenting the food.

Torin talks about his chefs and how he is improving issues in the kitchen that have made things such a mess all year, having started with getting rid of Brent. Then explains to Flep who is going to be doing what, telling him about the new guys, Tai and...someone, and how Dominique is back to looking after her own job.

Flep hasn't the faintest idea who most of these people are. Nor can he recall the difference between a sous chef and other kinds just now. He is not called upon to contribute anything besides an occasional nod, so it hardly matters.

By the time their plates are empty, Flep has still said nothing relevant. He absently reaches for the bread, though he isn't hungry.

"Torin?"

Torin stacks their plates and looks at him.

"You know the dreams and…visions and stuff…?" Flep chews and swallows a small bite of sourdough.

"Yeah?" He once more sounds frustrated. An "Oh, that again" tone which makes Flep want to hit audio rewind and suck his own words back in.

Another bite.

Torin gives up on him answering and clears their plates.

"I met a student at Amélie's party a few weeks ago who is studying dream analysis," Flep rushes on. "We didn't have much of a conversation, but I just saw her for lunch yesterday to talk about it."

"Any insights for you?" Torin starts rinsing their plates for the dishwasher. The cooktop is on the island, the sink at the counter, so he has to stand with his back to Flep.

"She may know what's happening."

Dishwasher still open, Torin moves back to take care of the leftovers. "Can you eat another crab cake? Hardly worth refrigerating."

"No, thank you."

Torin grabs a fork. Facing Flep across the island, he eats the last cake from the skillet with a dollop of warm sauce.

Flep nibbles more bread. *Enough.* Going to make himself sick. And obese.

Torin's whole family is slender, balancing indulgences with diets overall heavy in vegetables and light proteins—and void of processed foods. There's an excellent gym in the building that Flep has hardly ever used. No more excuses with a solid week of evenings to himself.

"And?" Torin seems to be waiting for him. Impatiently. Not irritated now so much as wanting to get this over with. Move on to more interesting matters.

"I just wanted you to know I'm trying to get to the bottom of whatever's going on. To stop it. I hope."

"And your friend has a theory?"

"She thinks I'm dreaming about a past life."

Torin chuckles. "Why not?" He dips and swallows the last bite of crab.

Flep's back stiffens. "I don't know what this is, but it's completely screwed up my life. As long as anyone is trying to help, I'm trying to keep an open mind. It's worth researching."

"You sound like Amélie."

"Who has been more helpful and sympathetic in this whole thing than you have."

"What's that supposed to mean?" Amusement gone.

"It's not supposed to mean anything. It's just a fact."

"She's so damn helpful because she introduces you to a new age friend who's telling you that you lived before, died, were reincarnated, and now are dreaming about having been alive before? That's helpful and sympathetic? You're shitting me. I didn't know you wanted that kind of help. I don't know why you haven't seen a psychiatrist or sleep specialist or anyone to begin with—"

"When I went to a doctor, he gave me sleeping pills."

"You wanted them! You couldn't sleep!"

"Now I finally contacted someone who may know what's going on and be able to help—who *is* a psychiatrist, by the way. So I wish you wouldn't laugh when I tell you something like that."

"Excuse me for finding it a little hard to take seriously."

"I can't just dismiss everything Natalie said. I've got to know."

"Okay." Torin steps back to the sink with the skillet and utensils. "Don't let me stop you. If you need help with any ceremonies—swinging dead cats or sacrificing goats—just give me a shout."

Flep jumps off the stool. "Fuck you, Torin. I've hardly had a real night's sleep since January." He crosses to the entry to pull on shoes. "I'm tired and scared and starting to wonder about job security since I can hardly *do my job*."

"Flep—"

"This has me so messed up I'm hallucinating." He grabs keys and pulls on his jacket. "I terrified the girls. I walk to work now because I started getting freaked out on the subway—even though I've never been claustrophobic. I can't do a thing without something coming back to these dreams. It can't go on for another seven months, or it's going to kill me."

159

Torin stands at the corner of the island, one hand on the counter, the other on his hip. "Look, Flep—"

"No, you look." Flep whirls back from reaching for the knob. "I have no support system for working this out. Your ex-wife has done more to help than you have. I get that you're busy and working hard and under a lot of stress, and you spend your free time with the girls. But that does not rule out having a single shred of compassion. If you don't have the time and space to support me and understand issues in my life, the least you can do is pretend you give a shit." Flep yanks open the door.

"Think about what you're saying. A stranger told you you're dreaming about a life that you lived *before this one*. And you honestly expect me to say...what? 'Gosh, that's amazing. Let me help you find books on the subject. How about Wikipedia?' Is that what you want?"

Flep goes on through the doorway, but Torin rushes forward to catch his elbow.

"Because that would be a lie." Torin drops his voice, holding Flep's arm. "There are nine million people in this city. There are sleep specialists and doctors who could help you. But you haven't seemed to care all that much about seeing one. Now you meet a student and say you've got answers? You're grasping at straws. How can I take that seriously? And how would it be supportive to you for me to act like you hit on something helpful? You say this thing is ruining your life. So get professional help."

Flep looks around at him. "That's what I just told you I'm doing. I have an appointment a week from Thursday." He jerks his elbow free and starts down the hall.

"Where are you going?"

"Until then, I'm going to help myself."

"Don't just walk away."

Flep keeps going.

"Flep!"

He walks to the elevator, wishing he hadn't eaten so much bread.

CHAPTER TWENTY

Library, history research, tell Torin, confirm appointment. Two down. Two to go. Should have changed his order, told Torin last. Or scratched that part.

His heart still beating too rapidly, Flep actively avoids thinking about Torin and heads for the military history section in the New York Public Library on 5th Avenue. Civil War, World War One. Others? Further back? No, he is always carrying a pistol or revolver of some kind. And that rifle: the short-barreled rifle sitting in the mud with the young man as he stepped around the corner... These...memories can only be so old.

He starts with the Civil War, skims three or four pictorial works. He takes several books back to the chairs where other silent patrons read, but is only frustrated by the strings of meaningless images and extremely odd facial hair. After, Flep stays among the shelves, pulling down one volume at a time.

What else? Crimean War, Indian wars, Boer War—God, there were a lot of wars.

There, before a vast section on the Second World War, is a small shelf dedicated to the First World War.

Flep pulls down the largest he can find—a coffee table book claiming to host hundreds of rare and never before published WWI photos from the Imperial War Museum archives.

As he thumbs through, confronted again by faces of commanders and generals and political figures, all manner of strange attires and mutton chops, he thinks of Torin.

Flep has been afraid of this ever since Amélie's tone when she asked if he had told Torin. Now what?

He should have explained to Torin about the scientific evidence behind past lives. About the research of Edgar Cayce and Ian Stevenson. He should have stayed calm about the whole thing, maybe invited Torin to the appointment almost two weeks away. So many things he could have said.

He flips to the middle of the book, seeing black and white images of battleships and German U-boats.

This is ridiculous. What is he looking for? What is he supposed to do?

He skims deeper into the book, ready to close it.

Overleaf: No Man's Land, near the Somme, 1916.

He turns one more page.

"Sure we can get stretchers out today, sir?"

"We'll have a bloody good try, Daniels. Are the stretcher bearers ready?"

"Right here, sir. I'll go out with Attwater, sir. Give them a hand."

"Good lad. Let's give Fritz a wave first." He turned from the parapet and telescope to face Private Daniels. Behind Daniels stood Private Attwater and two stretcher bearers from B Company.

Having to press against Daniels and the cold, slimy earth wall—laden in spiders and slugs, stinking of mold and decaying flesh—he made his way back along the narrow strip of trench to a firebay. His boots squelched through mud that hid duckboards.

He shivered as he motioned the four men to the ladder.

"Stretcher up first, sir," one of the strangers said. A corporal by the insignia on his sleeve. He produced a grubby, white rag from his pocket. "Let old Jerry see this and they're often sports about it."

"'Often' is a handicap, Corporal."

The other B Company man placed a cigarette between his lips.

"*Private,*" he snapped.

"Not to light, sir. Just cuts those 'often' jitters, sir."

"Give me your flag, Corporal." He grabbed a ladder rung in one hand, taking the rag in the other.

"Best let me go up first, Lieutenant. Jerry gets ticklish some mornings." But the corporal passed up the stretcher as well.

With the young men pushing from below, he tied on the rag, then lifted the filthy canvas, rusted steel, and wood conveyance up along the ladder as he moved. He took care that the stretcher would precede him by a great deal, wiggling it to display the dirty cloth across No Man's Land.

He waited, listened, holding his breath. Sounds of booming shells came distantly down the line. Here, he could have heard a bird calling—if songbirds still lived in this sector.

He popped his head up. His steel helmet felt as substantial as would wearing a shilling in his hair.

"Right," he whispered. "No one ticklish today, lads. Come along, Corporal."

The two B Company men with Red Cross armbands followed him up with the second stretcher, tailed by Daniels and Attwater.

He lifted a hand to shade his face against the morning sun, looking across the lunar world of broken sticks that once were tall trees, and craters that once were horse pastures. Nothing growing, nothing alive besides the rats and crows feeding on the human corpses strewn in all directions.

They lay spread-eagle on the ground with limbs or heads blown away. They draped across belts of barbed wire entanglements like bloody laundry. They piled together at the bottoms of black shell holes, two feet deep in water and mud. Individual limbs and body parts dotted the landscape, bits of khaki and gray uniforms in semi-circles where shells had landed.

Not two feet from his muddy boots, several gleaming teeth lay. They looked so clean and white, unattached to face or skull. Perhaps a rat or fox spit them out. New, fresh teeth. Teeth of a nineteen-year-old boy. Maybe younger. So many snuck in underage.

"Right," he said again as the five men stood for a moment, taking in the nearest bodies to be collected. "After we tidy up a bit, we'll get in some midday rest. Double rum ration for you four. I shall inform Sergeant Burrell. Carry on."

The men moved out in pairs, one to each end of a stretcher. They soon stopped and bent to collect an intact soldier while crows flapped away. Bloated rats scuttled to the next body, their naked tails dragging behind like fat worms through the mud.

He turned, looking the other way, back to the second line support trenches.

Where the hell were their replacement stretcher bearers and runners? They couldn't keep relying on B Company's men. Captain Whitehead had his own casualties. Bleeding brilliant management. All apropos, of course.

He let out a breath as nausea was about to get the better of him. If he was going to be sick from the smell, he had to get away from his men first. It just didn't look good to—

Crack.

The nearby explosion of a rifle made him jump, grab for his Webley revolver, trip, and almost fall into the trench he had just climbed from. In the same moment as he whirled and the shot rang out, he heard Daniels scream, the corporal swear, and the sound of another rifle report.

Crack.

"Down! Get back in the trench!"

Daniels was on his knees, grabbing his own throat, Attwater trying to help him.

"Get out! Get out of there, Attwater!"

Still trying to help his friend, Attwater was nearly struck himself.

He ran forward, grabbed Attwater's arm, and jerked him back.

"Quick, Private! Go!"

More shots. The next second they were back in the trench, jumping, falling, men running to them. Several sprang to action, standing on firesteps to shoot back, covering for them, trying to spot the German snipers.

"Those fucking Jerries!" the B Company corporal screamed while he fell into the trench, holding his own knee. "Fucking blind Jerries can't see a fucking red cross!"

His fellow plunged in after him—stretcher gone. Blood soaked his face, dripping down into his tunic and gray shirt below, flowing from his neck and ear where a bullet had torn out a chunk of flesh as it passed.

"Bollocks, bollocks!" Again and again the wounded man shouted as the sergeant rushed forward to see what happened.

"Sergeant Burrell, get these men to the dressing station. Are you hurt, Attwater?"

"Don't think so, sir." The pimply youth was shaking, bone white under red spots and dirt streaks, eyes wide and flooded. "Daniels didn't make it back in, sir."

"It's all right, lad." Patting Attwater's shoulder, he turned away. "Nothing you could do."

He staggered off as the men shouted and cursed and shot and yelled in pain. Back past the narrow observation trench, past another turn and firebay. Past his own dugout, into a communication trench, past a latrine, and around a corner...before he was finally sick in the mud.

CHAPTER TWENTY-ONE

Torin makes phone calls, tries to get through résumés for one more hire, tries to finish cleaning the kitchen, tries to think, not to think, to find something to punch. Tries.

He eats a slice of the sourdough chocolate bread—not bad—and paces.

Might as well go to work. He told them he wouldn't be in until service. But he—unlike everyone else in the family, apparently—is flexible. He doesn't need each day and week and month planned out in stone. If he wants to go into work now, he can.

Torin turns from the kitchen to change clothes. His phone rings. Maybe one of the suppliers calling him back.

He grabs the phone from the counter and glances at the display before answering. *Flep.*

Torin stares at it.

It had crossed his mind—though he batted the idea away—that he wasn't going to be hearing from Flep anymore. Ever. Of course, all his stuff is here... But he just left a couple of hours ago. He's not calling to get his stuff.

Pulse fast, angry and guilty and scared at the same time, Torin answers.

"Flep?"

"Is this, um, Torin Cleary?" A woman's voice, speaking softly.

"That's me. Did you find this phone?" Torin is about to thank her for calling, tell her he will come pick it up. Not like Flep to lose things. But she goes on.

"Oh, no, he's right here. He asked me to call you for him. Can you come to the library? There's been...kind of an...accident."

Torin is already at the door, shoes on, key shoved into his pocket.

"What happened? Is he okay?"

Out the door, running to the elevator.

"I think so?" It sounds like a question, voice still very soft. Torin is unsure if she is trying to keep the subject himself from hearing, or is only self-conscious speaking aloud in the library. "He didn't want an ambulance. He says he's fine. I just told him I'd call someone for him to make sure he gets home okay."

"Thank you. I'll be right there."

"We'll be downstairs by security."

By the time Torin reaches the library, the woman from the phone has gone. Flep must have been able to convince her he is all right. He is sitting on the wide marble stairs with his back against the wall when Torin hurries through one of the large front doors.

Flep's eyes are shut, head tilted back. His face looks ashen aside from the dark circles under his eyes, only exaggerated by his black hair and lashes.

"Hey," Torin says softly as he sits down beside Flep.

Flep looks at him, then closes his eyes again.

"What happened? Are you sick?"

"I'm okay." He hardly parts his lips as he speaks. "Just...too dizzy to walk anywhere. Couldn't focus my eyes on the phone."

"Why did someone want to call you an ambulance?" Torin cuts himself off from saying "again."

"I kind of...passed out upstairs. I was coming back to my senses when a patron found me and wanted to call 911. I got her to call you instead. I'm fine."

Torin nods, watching him as Flep persists in sitting with his eyes shut.

"I'm sorry, Torin. It's not like any of this is your fault. I shouldn't have been—"

"It's okay," Torin says. "I didn't mean to lash out at you. I'm really sorry you're having such a tough time. I just...don't get it. And I don't know what you want me to do to help."

"I don't want you to do anything. It's not your problem. But I wouldn't mind a little courtesy when I try to talk to you."

About stupid, ridiculous things that he expects Torin to take seriously?

"Okay," Torin says. He kisses the side of Flep's head. "Want to come home?"

Flep nods, though he sits still and silent for another full minute before he opens his eyes, then stands shakily with Torin. Torin holds onto his arm to guide him out and down the steps.

"So what happened?" Torin asks.

Flep again has his eyes shut, letting Torin pull him along.

"I don't want to talk about it."

Torin has to keep his face by Flep's to hear him. Wasn't that what he was upset over? Torin not talking about this stuff? So is Torin not supposed to ask? How can he win if everything he does is wrong?

"Okay," Torin repeats, putting his arm around Flep. "Just let me know if you do."

He starts past the library's marble lions and down the crowded sidewalk in silence. As they go, he wishes for the first time that he had not laughed when Flep said he was remembering a past life.

STAGE THREE

Thursday, October 6

Today was my appointment with the psychiatrist turned past life researcher. The one who had a book published on the subject last year.

I got the book on my tablet, but found little time for it in the latter week. The girls were at our place. Every time I did sit down to read, I fell asleep. Grabbing snatches of time while I lay awake at night, I could never focus. My hands stayed numb with cold. A metallic rattle from machine guns filled my ears.

Dr. Gregory Kulmala was only squeezing me in out of interest in my story. Rapidly shooting questions, he took notes on a printed form and another blank sheet as I told him about my dreams.

He wore slacks and a button-down. I felt like this was just a quick business meeting for him. A terse job interview.

After his interest in my case and taking me on as an extra appointment, I fear I ended up being a letdown.

I watched his receding hairline, or looked around at the leather sofa and sparsely decorated room, while he made notes. Wood desk. Tall bamboo in pots to each side of the window. Little Zen rock garden on the granite-topped coffee table. I wished I could doodle in the sand.

I've done little in the way of art since becoming head of the art department. Despite the income, I sometimes wish I were still entry-level. I wish, at least, I had Craig's job again. I spent more hours sketching with Carine in the past six months than as part of my job. Maybe I should get my own sand garden.

Designing Torin's new place could be fun, really. If I had time for it.

I soon tired of explaining and asked the psychiatrist about what I was there for rather than the other way around.

Dr. Kulmala told me yes, cases like mine were unusual but not unknown. Though he had never heard of an adult spontaneously experiencing memories like mine. This was more typical—his word—in very young children.

He gave me book titles that he seemed to think I would already know. "*Across Time and Death? Many Lives, Many Masters?*"

I shook my head. "Do you think you can help?" I asked since there had been no indication.

"Of course. Your nightmares and flashbacks will only grow worse if you do not explore them and work through these memories. Although the reason you are not sleeping, and so on, is likely that you are remembering a past life, your symptoms—the panic attack on the 4th of July, triggered flashbacks—also match post-traumatic stress disorder. You first need a series of regressions to understand what is happening."

"A series? Would that help?"

"I have seen many complaints, from phobias to obsessive behavior, vanish after one regression. Your case is more complex. Until you reach that point—experiencing these traumas and exploring what happened to you—your nightmares will not go away."

Not go away. I inhaled a long breath.

"You're certain that's what is happening to me? That these are memories?"

"Have you ever fought in trenches in *this* lifetime, Mr. Andries?"

I remembered Natalie's brain tumor analogy. But, no matter how much I thought of this from different angles, I could not turn it into the flu either.

So the man had not exactly put me at ease by the time he told me to lie down. I felt like a living stereotype, lying on the stiff sofa, shoes off. My heart hammered as if I'd just woken from one of my dreams.

He guided me through breathing exercises while I looked at the white ceiling. He never asked if I wanted to remember. He never mentioned meditation with a rock garden to block the memories.

Still couldn't relax. Thought of opening that WWI book—the hundred-year-old photograph of No Man's Land, climbing from a muddy trench. Then the kitchen knife incident and fireworks.

For all his admitting that spontaneously remembering a past life was very rare, he did not seem surprised by what I told him. Not even by what I remembered in the library: that I knew *everything*—slang and terms and actions that I did not have to think about. Just knew.

There was no hypnosis or trickery involved, Dr. Kulmala told me.

He would only help me remember. I knew enough to understand these memories had come from intense emotions, or situations that were somehow related to the past events. Not from lying with my eyes closed on a sofa next to a stranger while I felt only hot, anxious, futile, and exhausted.

When he asked where I was, what I saw, I was bewildered by my own answers.

"I'm in the back garden, soaked in sunlight. There are honey bees everywhere. Men and women and children around. All in old-fashioned dresses and tailored suits. There's a sponge cake with strawberries and whipped cream. The air smells of honeysuckle and roses.

"The little girl with the blue eyes is there. And the woman. Mary has her arm around me. We watch the girl clapping at the sight of the cake. *Jesus Christ*." I sat up, eyes wide.

Dr. Kulmala leaned back in his chair, finally looking startled.

"It was her sixth birthday. That's when it started—God—see? See how it—I met them." I clutched my own hair with both hands. "Soon after I met the girls, Carine had her sixth birthday, then I moved in with Torin and it all started. It wasn't the move or the life changes. It was the damn birthday party." My voice broke.

"I promised her—*Christ*. I said I'd come home. I told her I'd come back. I wished her happy birthday and said I would come back." Tears ran down my face and I hardly felt them. "I was in uniform. At the party. Just now. Mary leaning on me. Insignia on my cuffs. First days of spring. A warm day and I promised her... Christ!"

Shaking and trying to stand, sitting back down.

"I told her I'd be home. I told her what we could do for her seventh. I said she would be ready to walk the fells with me then. How we could go to the seaside and the White Cliffs. She said she loved me. I said I'd be back."

Clenching my teeth, head bowed, hardly able to get the words out, choking.

"I didn't go back to her. I tried and tried to get back. It was almost her birthday again. I made it to late winter and didn't get back in time." Sick and trembling like a child. "I'm sorry, Lil. I'm so sorry."

He was saying something to me. I don't know what—remember only that he seemed calm. He has probably seen a lot of basket cases in that office.

I had to get out of there. Shoes on, out and away as soon as I pulled myself together.

He tried to stop me, told me to sit back down, insisting I could not move forward until I understood all that had happened. Didn't he realize I had just figured it out?

I never even offered a check. Could barely see all the way home. Was home before I realized I was supposed to go back to work. Shouldn't be home at all.

Have to call Craig. Have to email Dr. Kulmala and ask what I owe him. Have to pay online or mail the payment since I cannot go back and face anything worse than what I already saw. Have to die. So sick and in so much pain, I wish I had that frozen revolver in my hand.

I abandoned her. I made a promise, then left and never came back, and she had to grow up without me. She would never know how I tried to reach her. And we never really got to say goodbye.

Our goodbye in that sunny garden was "until we meet again." The goodbye I cried to her in the cold with blood streaming from my mouth was impossible for anyone but ghosts to hear. In the place I am now, desperate to say, "Goodbye, I'm sorry, I love you," I fear even ghosts cannot hear me.

Sorry, Dr. Kulmala, since you made an extra effort to see me, for turning out a disappointment after all.

CHAPTER TWENTY-TWO

"Happy birthday!"

Isabelle almost shrieks like a little girl when she sees her cake. She gasps, hugs her dad, and runs for her camera, but she does not shriek: she is twelve years old today.

"How did you make the ribbons? The shine—"

"Pulled sugar." Dad grins.

She knows he didn't do them himself. He is no sugar artist, only has amazing pastry chefs at Chaleur who must have added adornments for him. And he does make nice cakes that he learned from her great-grandmother.

"Do you want your picture with it?" he asks her.

"Yes." She pushes the little camera at him.

"Me too!" Ree runs forward and Isabelle puts her arm around her sister.

"I never saw it," Isabelle says. "When did you make it? You didn't do all that this morning." She cannot get over the perfect ballet slippers, the shining pink ribbons of sugar curling around the elegant white cake.

"I made it at Chaleur yesterday and brought it in last night."

"It's so beautiful."

"Eat it, eat it, eat it!" Ree shouts.

"No. I want to keep it."

Flep and her dad are both laughing as he hands back the camera. It feels weird to see Flep laugh. He hasn't been, well...normal for the last few weeks. Even by his usual sleepless standards.

He had old paperback books from the library at home for a while, though he never seemed able to read for long. Isabelle read the back of one that was lying on the kitchen table a week ago: a story about a woman who dreamed of past events for years. She finally went to

Ireland, where her dreams were set, and found out she had real family and real people from her dreams there. All from when she lived before.

And the book was nonfiction. A true story.

Isabelle never said anything to him or her dad about it, but she wishes she could have read that book. Lately, she wonders if Flep is thinking of going somewhere.

"We can leave the cake until your mom gets here after lunch," Dad tells her. "Most of the day to admire it."

"Okay." Isabelle smiles at her perfect cake, assuming first, second, then third position in turn. No time to worry about weird books. "I want her to see it whole."

Isabelle doubts her parents will bicker on her birthday. Probably safe for them all to have cake together before she and Ree go home with her mom for the evening.

"What does the birthday girl want for breakfast?"

"Eggs Benedict on those portobello mushrooms."

"I don't like them!" Ree shouts.

"It's not your birthday," Isabelle tells her smugly.

"We'll have tarragon potatoes also, with arugula on the side. Ree, we can put your egg on potatoes."

"Yes." Ree nods her approval. "When will you open presents?"

There are a few colorful packages behind the cake in the middle of the kitchen table, but Isabelle hasn't even had a chance to look at them. She wants to hug her little cake, frame it, and she definitely wants the girls at Nordisk Dance Studio to see it.

Her parents told her she could have a party with friends, something at the studio or restaurant. But Isabelle had friend parties and Chaleur parties for the past eleven years. She just wants to see her own family.

It has been easier lately, since Flep got them to change to solid week schedules. Way easier. She just wishes he didn't look like death in the meantime.

"Not until cake time," Isabelle tells her sister in regards to the presents. Though she is not sure she can resist. "Maybe just one or two with breakfast?"

"Go for it," her dad says. "Do you want orange juice?"

"With sparkling water in it." She hurries to take pictures of her gifts as well, Ree buzzing around. "My cake could get hurt if we sit at the table to eat."

Dad is already at work on their breakfasts, but Flep watches the ballet cake with a worried and thoughtful expression—a norm for him.

"We could have a picnic," he says.

"Picnic!" Ree yells.

"Ree, stop it," Isabelle says. "What do you mean?"

"Spread out a blanket and sit around the living room to eat," Flep says. "Then no one will touch the cake, and we don't have to move it."

"Sure." She snaps another picture, getting Flep at the corner of the table and Ree, in front of him, making a face at Isabelle's camera.

They share breakfast in the living room: Flep sitting with his legs out in front of him, leaning on the couch, Ree resting her plate on his shins, Isabelle sitting up cross-legged with hers, and Dad serving everyone, then sitting beside Flep.

She opens the biggest present only because she can't stand not knowing—a new messenger style school bag, not a kid's backpack—but leaves the few others for her mom's visit later.

"You can open your cards." Dad brings them over after the thrill of the grown-up bag.

He clears plates while Ree plays with the ribbon from the large box. She tries to get it to stay in Flep's hair while he continues sitting on the floor so she can reach his head.

A funny card from her dad. A crayon picture of Sebastian swimming around a birthday cake from Ree. A gift card from her grandparents.

Flep's card is not funny or in French. It is an elegant black and white picture of ballet slippers with a quote: *Life isn't about waiting for the storm to pass. It's learning to dance in the rain.*

Inside, only two lines of his handwriting: *Happy 12th, Isabelle. Love, Flep.* And tickets. Two paper tickets for the New York City Ballet.

She gasps and almost drops them, looking up sharply.

Flep has his eyes shut and his face screwed up as Ree struggles to tie the shimmery ribbon to his head. Dad is going on in the kitchen about...something.

She looks back down. Two tickets. For...*tonight*. In the first ring. The *first ring*.

She has been to performances at the New York City Ballet a couple of times before. She has never been in the first ring. Never. Because, as she well knows, those tickets can be over $200. Apiece.

"Happy birthday."

She looks up once more to see Flep squinting at her with one eye.

"Thank you..." Shocked, embarrassed, Isabelle doesn't know what more to say.

He smiles as Ree pulls his head sideways. "Sorry about the late notice. I know you like to have a plan, but there happened to be a performance tonight. I asked your dad if there was a show on you wanted to see and he said ballet. Your mom's going with you."

"She knows?"

"She knows," he repeats. "She's looking forward to it. Your dad has to be at work. I'll stay with Ree. Your mom's taking you out to dinner and the show." Though he still smiles, he looks really, really tired.

"That's...crazy. Thanks, Flep. That was...nice. Wow..."

"I hope you enjoy it."

"Didn't you want to go?"

"That's okay. Maybe we'll all see a Broadway show together sometime."

"I want to go," Ree pipes up.

"No, you don't," Isabelle says. "It's ballet."

"I do." Already lifting her voice. Why is she such a screamer?

"Ree?" Flep catches her little hands in his, turning his head so he can see her with both eyes as blue ribbon strands fall over his face. "It's something for your sister to do for her birthday. And I don't think you'd care about it anyway. But do you know what just opened for the season?"

Ree frowns.

Flep gives a gliding gesture with his hand.

"Ice skates!" Ree yells.

"That's right." Flep flinches.

"I'm going to learn to skate!"

Isabelle looks again at her tickets while her dad brings in more coffee and juice, telling Flep that color looks good on him.

CHAPTER TWENTY-THREE

Amélie stands with Isabelle and twenty-five hundred others in the roaring, packed theater as the final rounds of applause lift, then fade.

They move easily with the crowd from theater to street, talking about the show, Isabelle bubbling over, as animated as Amélie has seen her in years. She was never an ebullient child like her little sister. Since the separation, she has grown quieter and quieter.

Now she expounds over details of the performance that Amélie—a fan of ballet, though not a dancer herself—did not even notice.

The theater is close to home. Despite it being dark out and cold for October, they walk it, finding the sidewalks still busy. It's not far enough for a cab, and Amélie always avoids the repulsive and reeking subway if she can, especially with the girls along.

On the way, they talk about the day, the cake, her other gifts. At home, Isabelle subsides to yawning as she drops onto the sofa. Amélie puts on water for them both to have herbal tea before bed.

"I'm glad you had a good day." Amélie, sitting down across from her daughter, unzips her tall boots.

"I did." Isabelle is looking around. "It's weird without Ree here. I hope she had fun skating."

"Do you miss her?"

Isabelle grins. "No. Sorry."

"That's okay. Not wanting your sister in your hair every second of the day doesn't make you a bad person, Bell."

"Good thing, or I'd be terrible. Can I have more cake?"

"In the morning. Do you need a snack before bed?"

Isabelle shakes her head. "I'll get the tea."

She goes to fill their mugs with boiling water and peppermint teabags. When she brings them to the coffee table, her expression has changed. She looks thoughtful, her brows drawn.

She is growing up, Amélie realizes as she watches her. Finally getting taller—puberty about to hit. Amélie sees her now knowing that, in a year, even a season, her baby Isabelle, the tiny dancer, will be gone.

"What's the matter?" Amélie asks, leaning forward to lift her mug.

"Mom, why did Flep get us those tickets? He's never given me anything before."

"It's hard for us to interpret, sweetheart, but I think it could just be because he's a nice person. You've never known him for a birthday or Christmas before."

Even Carine seems to have accepted his good qualities. It has been a month since she stalled to keep her parents together in one place. No longer clinging to her past. Perhaps happy with what she has.

"I know, but..." Isabelle frowns at her steaming mug. "He's been weird lately. Weirder than usual. Is there something wrong with him? He doesn't sleep and he stopped taking the sleeping pills because of being dependent and side effects and stuff, but is he sick?" She looks up.

"I don't think so." Amélie watches her, sitting placidly with her own mug, though her mind races.

She had not known that Flep quit the medication. This possibly explains why he looked like the walking dead these past weeks—worse than he ever did in the summer. What else is Isabelle picking up on?

Since Amélie was finally able to settle the business paperwork with Torin, she has seen little of either of the men all autumn.

She is not, and will not become, that questioning, prying separated parent. *What's your father saying? Who's he seeing?*

But Isabelle is clearly upset about this.

"What's he doing, Bell? Do you think Flep is sick?"

"He's falling asleep all the time. He always looks like he's dozing off. He doesn't say much of anything. Lately, like, since the beginning of the month, he's just been...sad. The way he talks sometimes...I don't know." Isabelle bites her lip and looks away.

Amélie feels a rising concern, almost alarm as she watches her daughter. "The way he talks sometimes, what?" Voice smooth, not betraying tension.

"It's silly. I guess he just has insomnia, but sometimes I feel like he's...like...dying. I mean, not literally. But that's how he acts. I don't know," she repeats and shrugs, picking up her mug.

"That may just be a grown-up who is tired and also depressed. I doubt Flep is physically ill."

Isabelle nods, still not looking up, though she appears less tense. She takes a drink.

"Have you talked to him or your father about it?"

She shakes her head.

"I'll ask what's going on. Is that okay with you? I don't have to say you said anything. He seems to be sleepwalking every time I see him also."

"Yeah, a sleepwalker is what he's like. He didn't have to get those tickets. I feel like he thinks...he's not going to be around...later, you know? But I don't know why."

"I'll speak to him next time I see him, okay? I'm happy to. We just don't cross paths much these days."

Another nod. "It's really Dad's week. Am I going back to 2nd Avenue tomorrow after school?"

Tomorrow is Monday, but Torin is going to the restaurant because Dominique is away for her sister's wedding until Tuesday. Torin is irritated by this, of course—"only a wedding and not even her own." Even in that case, Torin would still probably expect the poor woman at work that night. He worked an easy hundred hours a week for the first five years of the restaurant's life. Even now, eighty hours seem perfectly reasonable to him—and not just for himself.

"Why don't you come to the office?" Amélie asks Isabelle. "I'll get you from school and bring you back. Then we'll go across town as soon as I can, get Ree from Mémé and Pépé, and drop you off with Flep. I'll get another slice of cake since I can tell someone here is going to eat my leftovers for breakfast."

Isabelle smiles. "Thanks."

Amélie feels glad to see she has reassured her.

Later, she lies awake, replaying her words. *He's not going to be around. Like he's dying.*

Images of his haggard appearance. Eerily familiar symptoms, though she has known few patients. Sleepless, fatigued, depressed, uncomfortable. Bouncing back, getting worse. Crimson blood drying on the counter, floor, and kitchen towel...

Amélie gets up early after a few hours of sleep and adds extra shots to her morning coffee.

CHAPTER TWENTY-FOUR

Amélie fights her own bigotry and paranoia, yet she has a hard time focusing on her cases all day. A hard time staying relaxed for Isabelle, who reads while waiting for Amélie at the office. A hard time smiling at Carine as she tells them about the skating rink.

"You must have had fun, Ree," Amélie says.

"I fell and fell because my feet went like—" She waves both hands straight out from her chest. She sounds proud of herself.

"Is that all you did—fall down?" her sister asks as they climb from the cab to 2nd Avenue.

"I held Flep's hands some. He kept saying I needed to hold on, but then I couldn't get anywhere."

Isabelle rolls her eyes. "You must be such a frustrating student, Ree."

"Other people went really fast. I wanted to go fast."

"Maybe you should listen to your teacher for the first few times out, fearless leader," Amélie says. "Those people had to work up to going fast also."

They greet Martin and take the elevator up.

Carine goes on about yellow leaves and how the Park looked fiery and she had to stay on the ice to be safe while treetops blazed. Amélie cannot keep following the story. Her heart pounds, though not because of her child falling on the ice. Carine seems perfectly perky and Amélie is sure it was her own fault.

Isabelle unlocks the door.

"We're home," she calls for Flep's benefit. "Ree, did you feed Sebastian this morning? He looks hungry."

Her sister gives her a funny face. "How does he look hungry?"

"I don't know. He looks skinny to me."

Isabelle pulls off her shoes. Carine feeds the fish.

Flep does not appear.

Isabelle goes straight to the kitchen to see what is for dinner. "Flep, did Dad leave anything to eat?"

Nothing.

She looks around at her mother. Amélie checks the couch and master bedroom.

"He's not here." She returns to the kitchen.

"It's after 6:00." Isabelle looks at the clock. "He's always here before that when we're coming over."

"Don't worry about it. I'm sure he'll be along. What should we do for dinner?"

Isabelle starts through the refrigerator. Amélie looks out the living room windows toward the river. Now she is the one who is worried—who cannot shake the feeling of dread and pressure on her throat. A tension headache at the back of her head travels down her neck. Her muscles feel tight.

"Ravioli!" Isabelle steps from the refrigerator with a glass container in her hands. "He made us ravioli. Can you put the pot on, Mom, and I'll fix our salad and sauce?"

She has just set the large pot on to boil and Carine has dashed back from her room to turn on the TV, when the door opens.

Amélie lets out her breath but gives her eldest daughter a quick smile. "See?"

"I'm really sorry," Flep says, leaning on the doorway to kick off his shoes, panting and red-faced. He clearly ran here. "I didn't mean to keep you."

"That's fine," Amélie tells him. "We just got in a few minutes ago."

"Your dad made us fresh—I see you found them," he says breathlessly to Isabelle.

"Flep!" Carine scrambles over the arm of the couch to run to the foyer. "When can we skate again?"

"I'm surprised you want to." He shrugs out of his jacket. "Did you feed the fish?"

"Yes. Can we take Sebastian to see the ice?"

"Do you have a minute?" Amélie crosses to them. "Go on, Ree."

"Sorry—" Flep repeats to Amélie.

"It's nothing. But I was hoping to talk to you."

"Oh." He looks around as if longing for a sinkhole. Cheeks sunken, haggard, eyes exhausted. Has he lost weight? A noticeable amount in a few weeks? He looks like he should be in a hospital bed.

"Come on." She reaches to rest her hand on his shoulder, her own pulse still fast. "Why don't you sit down for a minute? Bell is getting dinner."

He nods wearily, though he looks as nervous of her as ever.

She wants to take him downstairs for privacy, but the lobby is a long trip from up here. She cannot leave the girls alone with pots of water and sauce on the stove. At least Carine has the TV loud, and her sister is working away. She confirms with Isabelle that she can handle dinner, tells her to be careful with the water and call if she needs anything—that she's just going to have a word with Flep.

Isabelle nods, looking guilty, as if feeling bad for setting her mother on Flep's case. There cannot be any pretense about a private conversation around here though.

Amélie leads him to the bedroom, closes the door, and tells him to sit down on his own bed. Nowhere else to sit so she steps to the window, looking toward the river. She stands, not directly in the light to appear in silhouette to him, but beside it.

"How was the show?" he asks, sitting back on the edge of the neatly made bed.

Flep must be a bedmaker. Torin certainly never was.

"Exquisite, thank you. Bell loved it."

He nods, leans an arm against the wood footboard, rubs his eyes with thumb and forefinger. His left hand looks fine now. Maybe a small scar left over, but she cannot see it.

"Flep? Are you sick?"

"Sick?" He looks up vaguely. "Not that I'm aware of."

Isn't that comforting? But her own sense of political correctness and hating feeling prejudiced keeps her from asking him if he has been tested.

She tries to be more delicate. "Not aware of?"

He shakes his head, looking up at her. "It's just the same stuff. So a trick question, isn't it? I guess some people would say that's a sickness, but I'm not sure about a mainstream diagnosis..."

"Nothing else?" They both keep their voices soft.

He frowns. "What else would there be?" He looks confused, not put out with her.

"I just wondered if there was something new happening. You look horrible. Have you lost weight?"

"Maybe." He looks down at his own midriff.

"Did you stop taking the sleeping pills?"

"I was getting too dependent. Anyway, they weren't working. I tried some natural stuff, but that hasn't helped either."

"Are you having nightmares every night?"

"And all day." A whisper.

"Excuse me?"

He says nothing, eyes unfocused as he looks blankly toward the corner of the window beside her.

"Flep?"

He blinks. "Natalie referred me to a psychiatrist to do a past life regression. He said remembering what happened could eliminate the problem. But he meant people like...having a fear of water in this life and doing a regression in which they drowned and not being afraid anymore because they dealt with it. My stuff... I started a regression with him and I...remembered things that made it worse. A lot worse."

"Did you go back? You need to keep seeing this guy."

"I don't *want* to remember. I want it to stop. I remember more and more and it never helps."

"What are you remembering?"

Silence.

"Have you talked to Torin about it?"

"I gave it a couple tries. He has come as far as telling me he hopes I can work it out and to let him know if he can help with anything. But it's not much use turning to someone who doesn't believe the diagnosis is possible."

"I don't know if past lives are real or not," she says slowly, "but I'm certain you need to do something. Do you have any reason to believe that's *not* what this is?"

"Oh, no." Flep shuts his eyes. "I'm positive that's what it is."

"Then go back for another regression."

"That's what made everything so much worse." He rubs his temples. "It's not the answer. I know it's not. I just...don't know... I can't think. I'm afraid I'll lose my job. If I do, I may have to leave the City. I can't afford to stay here very long on savings. I thought about quitting to relieve them of my incompetence. Craig, and even my interns, are doing more work than I have been for the past month."

"This is insane. You've got to go back to this guy. Even if you don't want another regression. What could be worse than this? You're talking about your entire life. I don't think you realize how you sound, Flep—"

"Sorry, I—"

"Stop it! What happened when you went before?"

He only sits there, looking helpless and miserable, shaking his head.

She wants to shake him, make him see however he imagines he is coping is not working or helping him. Mostly, she just wants to hug him. But that she can do least of all.

"If you won't go back, why don't you see another psychiatrist? If your only goal is to make it stop and you don't want to remember and don't want to have another regression, you would be better off seeing someone who can give you ideas for how to do that and move forward."

"I don't want to keep—" he stops, eyes once more closed.

"What *do* you want to do?"

"I want to go there."

"Where's 'there'?"

"I've been thinking, since I saw Dr. Kulmala..." He clenches his teeth for a second, and she is horrified to realize he is trying not to cry. "There was a place I had to say goodbye to...someone I loved...in the past. And a place...I died, where I was saying goodbye with no one to hear. Since I saw him, I can't...

"I want to go back. To find those places, and people. Find out what happened to them after I said goodbye."

Her pulse is fast again, though she keeps her voice calm. "Real places? In your regression? You know where you could go right now to these real places from your past?"

"Yes."

"Then, for God's sake, why don't you go?"

"They're in Europe. France and England."

Amélie almost laughs, catching in her throat. "That's it? I go to France every other year. It's not that hard. We have airports here."

"I just told you, I could lose my job. Holidays are coming up... I've never been to Europe—"

"Fuck your job," she hisses. "Do you have a passport?"

"Yes. The studio wanted me to have one, but I've never been out of the country besides Canada."

More baffled than upset with him now. She cannot grasp knowing so clearly what needs to be done and sitting on your hands instead.

Amélie had been in her mid-twenties, married and a few months pregnant with Isabelle, when she was due at a conference in New Jersey. Rail first, then a bus to get there—a simple journey. But she never left home.

She was overcome with a sickening sense of dread that turned her stomach and sent her to open the windows in their studio apartment and clutch the ledges as if having a panic attack. Torin had told her it was just morning sickness, to go on anyway, that she would soon feel better. She said that was bullshit and went back to bed.

By evening, she had learned the exact bus she was supposed to have been on had crashed in one of the worst local traffic accidents in years, killing nearly everyone on it, leaving the rest in critical care.

How can anyone know what they must do, feel it so intensely, yet do nothing? On the other hand, she knows what it is to live with Torin. It takes a strong personality to fight the tide.

She thinks of telling Flep this story, sharing her support of following his intuition, but it hardly seems the time to talk about her.

"Do you need the money?" Amélie asks. "I'll get you the ticket."

"I have the money. But I can't go on a trip like that right now. I can't just go there for a couple of nights and come home. It could take weeks just to find the places and figure out what happened to them—if they were even real people."

"If you don't go, who's going to find that out?"

He finally looks up at her. The expression in his eyes makes even her want to cry.

Damn this. She crosses the few steps to sit beside him, wrapping her arm around his shoulders.

"I'm sorry," she whispers as he bows his head. "But it sounds like you already know what to do to fix things. There are a couple of airlines you can check for the cheapest tickets to Paris."

"I don't speak a word of French."

"Heathrow then. Or I'll give you a few lessons. You don't need French to go."

Nothing.

"Promise me you're going to do something."

Flep nods.

CHAPTER TWENTY-FIVE

Sitting on her hip on white ice below a backdrop of golden trees, Ree holds both her hands up for Flep to lift her onto her skates. And he sees two other small hands, two other blue eyes upturned toward him as he reaches down.

Gliding and twirling gracefully around the kitchen as she adds ingredients to a bowl of ground turkey, Bell tells him about her afternoon at the dance studio. And he moves with a grown woman in a slow dance around another kitchen.

Stepping up behind him to rest an arm around his chest and kiss the back of his neck, Torin sets a plate of crumpets and scrambled eggs with spinach, mushrooms, and Beaufort cheese before him. And he tastes a wet and frozen crumpet while his breath steams, snow builds up on his helmet, and the earth quivers below his boots with shell concussions.

He sketches a concept for a living room set on his Wacom tablet and instead draws a trench with firestep and sandbags and duckboards.

He works with the rest of his team on schedules and plans and cannot hear their answers.

Simon brings him coffee and asks if he is okay—everyone is worried about him. Flep can still hardly hear him over the ringing in his ears, the endless high rattle of machine guns.

He cannot ride the subway at all anymore. Too many panic attacks from the close, suffocating pressure flattening him into a grave with the mass of humanity, all about to be blown apart. Can't even take a bus. He is up and awake so early anyway that he walks to work, though it takes him nearly an hour on his slower mornings. So dazed, and half the time needing to pick up the girls after work, he starts taking a cab home.

He still shares breakfast with Torin, but only from force of will, eating little else since everything he eats tastes of aluminum or cordite or blood, while everything he drinks tastes of mud and gasoline.

With Torin working, Amélie takes charge of the girls on Halloween.

Leading up to the event, Bell stalks around the apartment pointing at things like the TV and Sebastian's bowl and ordering, "Off with your head!" She is going as the Queen of Hearts.

Flep suspects Ree's costume will make its way into her daywear until she outgrows it. She is going as a lobster.

He waits up for Torin on Halloween night, watching silly monster movies to fill the ringing in his ears. He is not sure how much more Cooking Channel and Food Network he can take. Although *My Little Pony: Friendship is Magic*, which seems to be the only non-food TV program the girls watch, is not half bad. Better written than whatever movie is running now.

On his laptop, he goes back and forth between the websites he has already checked, and new ones—new searches, slightly different dates. Narrows it down. Why is Paris cheaper? By hundreds. Why not English-speaking London?

Checking again, turning his credit card in his fingertips as his eyes lose focus on the screen.

By the time Torin gets in, long past midnight, Flep has abandoned the card and laptop at the coffee table. He dozes through visions of cold, molasses-like mud dragging him back as he tries to walk through a frozen earth corridor, all to a soundtrack of the incessant chattering of TV vampires.

He does not hear the door open. Torin is simply beside him all at once.

"Hey." Smiling to see him up, Torin bends to kiss him. "What are you doing?"

Flep reaches vaguely for the remote to kill the TV. "Just waiting for you. Not much point in my going to bed these days."

Torin pulls off his coat and sits down beside him.

Flep cannot read his face, confused for a moment by a look in Torin's eyes he cannot place. When Torin strokes Flep's hair back from his temple, brows creasing, it clicks. He is not used to seeing Torin look worried.

"Are you sure you shouldn't try that shit again? What's it called? You were at least sleeping some on it."

"It's not the sleep." Flep pulls Torin's hand down to kiss his knuckles. "Torin..."

"Do you want leftovers? I have vegetables and lamb *ragoût*."

Flep hates eating lamb, only ever tried it to humor Torin. And veal. And killing spiders when they could be shooed out.

Among many things that just...don't add up about the two of them.

So why does he still love Torin so much? Why does he always see the easy smiles, the gentle kisses, the nurturing side that brings his reinvented family together with meals, when he looks at Torin? Amélie thinks he should see the self-interest, the brashness, the truth that Flep is third on his list of priorities.

But he knew that going in. Torin has never lied to him about who he is. At the end of the day, Flep cannot agree with Amélie because he does not want Torin to change. It is he, Flep, who walked into this with his eyes open and he who, perhaps, must walk out the same way.

Seeing Torin now, worried, gentle, presenting him a meal because that is how Torin fixes what is broken and heals what is sick—if food and love are not enough, Torin hasn't any idea what to do—Flep is not sure if either offerings can do anything anymore.

His throat hurts. His head hurts. His back feels like he was hit with an aluminum bat. He feels unsure if he can say what he must, risk what he must.

When he does not answer about the food, Torin asks, "What were you going to say?"

"Nothing. And I'm fine, thank you. I ate." A lie. He has eaten nothing since breakfast, too sick to his stomach to try.

He still says nothing as they go to bed.

Torin takes a quick shower. Leaving the bathroom, toothbrush in his mouth, he brings Flep the long-unused pill bottle.

He lifts his eyebrows, speaking indistinctly. "Shleep?"

Hopeful, like offering food. A small attempt to help, though he feels helpless—which is why he mostly never tries, of course.

195

"I love you." Flep, sitting up in bed, does not reach to take the bottle.

Torin cocks his head. "Luf oo too." He rattles the pills.

"It's okay, Torin. It really doesn't help much now, and I was too dependent."

Torin turns back to the bathroom.

Climbing into bed a moment later, he checks his phone for texts, then switches the sound off.

"I hope the Lobster Quadrille went well," Torin says.

"I'm sure they had fun. Bell will be too old in another year or two."

"Don't say that." Torin shudders.

"Sorry." He presses his face against Torin's neck, yawning.

Torin leans away from him to turn off his lamp, then back, kissing Flep's hair. "Did you give out candy to the building's hooligans?"

"I did. Not a lobster in sight."

Torin laughs softly, sliding down in bed with him.

"Have fun on the dinner service?"

"Blood everywhere. Dominique went to town on pastries. She's outstanding."

"It's not everyday I hear you say that about one of your people."

"She could be the only one. But we have 'good' to 'superior' in the kitchen also. We've got things running well again with her and the new sous chef and Tai on board. Best we've been in years. What do you want for breakfast? Didn't you say you have an early meeting?"

"That was today. Not that early. I got a cab."

"Seriously? You're not even trying buses?"

Start of an argument. Flep kisses him.

"Torin? What's your favorite place?"

"Why?"

"Just...wondered." Foreheads together, resting on the pillow, looking into one another's eyes in the dark. "Thinking about...where we, people, call home and visit and marry and raise kids and live and die. If you could be anywhere, what place would you be?"

"Manhattan," Torin says, fingers stroking down Flep's head, jaw, shoulder. "Where would you be?"

"I don't know," Flep whispers—the ringing in his ears fading, smelling Torin's coconut shampoo and feeling his warmth rather than decay and snow.

"Do you miss Connecticut?"

"No."

"Don't you like the City?"

"I do a lot more since being here with you and the girls."

"Good." Torin runs his hand down Flep's arm, twining their fingers together. "Outstanding, even," he adds, smiling against Flep's lips.

Flep returns his kiss, pressing Torin's hand until Torin twists his fingers free to pull up Flep's T-shirt.

Sitting up in bed to tug off one another's shirts, Flep feels dizzy. From hunger, he assumes, but it could be from so many things. He feels so accustomed to living with the sensation, he hardly notices.

As Torin kisses him, he closes his eyes, unlacing the white dress. As Torin caresses him, he lets his jacket fall to the rug while Mary unknots his necktie.

Fascinated, terrified, elated, he kissed her on their wedding night, while, exhausted, grieving, in love, he holds Torin's face in his hands.

"I love you."

Who says the words? Where? When? An echo? A vow? From his own lips? From his lovers'?

Words that come before "Us." Before "I promise." Before "Goodbye."

He wakes without waking, for he lives in a world of gray: almost awake, almost asleep, almost alive, almost dead. He never really wakes up anymore.

All so interconnected. Torin against him in the dark while he faced Mary. Gentle Mary with her blue eyes and hair like wheat, upturned nose and dimpled cheeks when she smiled. Intense Torin holding him, kissing him, inside him, saying he loved Flep. His voice after all. Or many voices. How many were there?

Now, looking from the blinds to Torin asleep beside him, Flep wonders if Torin will ever have the last laugh in his bisexual debate with society.

Are they not all, if they remembered long enough, bisexual in the end? Is this what happens to transsexual people? Old souls, previously born as another gender and carrying that subconscious memory to this life? And asexual people? Maybe they are the oldest souls of all. Maybe they are just...tired.

Flep kisses Torin's brow, slides from bed to shower, and takes his time in the hot water. Still slow and careful when shaving and dressing, focused on each task to avoid injury or embarrassing attire.

Torin has just put on coffee when Flep emerges in slacks and button-down, shaky and lightheaded. Torin, in his shorts and T-shirt from bed, frowns as he watches Flep lean on the counter. The unexpected look again—worried.

"You should sit down." Torin pulls out a chair for him at the table. "What do you want?"

You. Not to say what I'm going to say. Not to do what I'm going to do because of what it will do to us. For this to end. At all costs.

"I don't know," Flep says softly. "Maybe those left over vegetables and an egg? That's cooked all the way through, please." The last time he saw a runny egg yolk oozing over skillet potatoes on his plate, Flep saw intestines oozing out of a man's torn abdomen and almost vomited.

"Okay." Torin still watches him. He does not even roll his eyes or argue about overcooking eggs.

Worried enough, at last, for them to get through this morning and still have a tonight?

Flep pushes through most of breakfast—which helps slightly to clear his head—before he calmly tells Torin he is going to Europe.

Torin looks at him across the table, his own plate empty. "What?"

"I'm flying into Paris in less than a week. The last-minute tickets were crazy expensive, and Paris was cheaper than London."

"You what?" Torin still appears too bewildered to get beyond his first question. "Is this for work?"

"I'm quitting. Well, I'm asking for...leave, kind of. So I assume I'm quitting, or being fired. It's not going to work out when I tell John I'm leaving next week without notice—"

"What the hell are you talking about?" He doesn't sound angry yet. Still stupefied.

"I have to resolve what's happening to me. I would say I can't keep living like this, but I'm not living." Flep looks helplessly at the men in soaked khaki uniforms all around him, sitting on muddy crates or upside down buckets or heaps of sandbags, eating out of mess tins while rain clatters over their helmets. Clouds of cigarette smoke fill his nose and sting his eyes.

He looks back at Torin across the table. "Not figuratively. Literally. I cannot keep living like this. You don't know how bad it's been, especially for the past month. There's nothing to talk about when there's nothing to be done. Now, I'm doing something."

Torin pushes his own plate away and rubs a hand through his disheveled hair, leaning forward in his chair.

"If you need help, why haven't you gotten it in the City? I don't—I didn't—Christ. I still don't get what you're talking about."

"I'm going to France, and England, to find out what happened to my family."

Torin looks blank.

"From my past life."

Mouth slightly open, staring.

"It's the only thing I think could...heal..."

"Bullshit." Torin's voice is now just as soft as his.

"That's what I thought you might say. I'm sorry, Torin."

"When are you going?"

"I told you. Next week."

"For how long?" Anger flowing in.

"I bought a one-way ticket."

"Jesus Christ. Are you serious?"

Flep says nothing, inhaling slowly, trying not to cough on smoke.

"What about the girls?"

"Hopefully their grandparents can watch them some. I'm sorry to leave you in the lurch with them. I know they're supposed to be here next—"

"Not you babysitting. I mean, you telling them you're taking off, saying goodbye. You don't suppose they're going to notice?"

"Torin, I don't think..." He has to stop, eyes shut. Elbow on the table,

Flep presses the bridge of his nose with thumb and forefinger. The lump in his throat chokes him and he sits still, silent for several seconds until he can trust himself to issue normal speech. Finally, he sits up straighter, opening his eyes and dropping his hand.

"I don't think that would be a good idea. For me or for them. Not like this. I can't say goodbye to them. And there's nothing else I can... I'm sorry. I love them and I love you and I hope to be back before long and maybe still...have something... But I don't know if that will be the case. I don't know what's going to happen over there. And I know you're not...impressed by this decision."

Torin opens and closes his mouth. He gets up, takes his plate to the sink, walks around the kitchen, presses his palms to his skull, and walks around again. He stops, gripping the edge of the counter with both hands. Muscles stand out in his arms and shoulders with the force of his hold.

"You're telling me, seriously, that you are quitting your job, buying a thousands of dollars plane ticket to fly to a country you have never been, stay who knows where, not knowing the language or ever having navigated Europe, to 'find' nightmares and hunt for a place that matches a place in your *dreams*, all on your own?"

Flep stands slowly, as has become his habit to minimize the dizziness. He holds the back of his chair until he can get his bearings.

"That sounds about right," he says, letting out his breath. "I've got to get to work. Thank you for breakfast." He makes his way to the bedroom, taking more steps than usual.

Ready for work—his teeth brushed and his small messenger bag stuffed with his phone and external hard drive, keys, water bottle, and protein bar—he again passes Torin in the kitchen. Still in the same place, still holding on.

When Flep comes back after work to pack, Torin will be at Chaleur.

Flep walks to the door, stopping there to look back. "Goodbye, Torin."

Then down the long hall to the elevator. Down the elevator to the lobby, to the street, to the morning sun.

Sunday, November 6

Waiting to board my plane. Typing on the tablet screen. Like those first dream journal entries. I feel as if lifetimes have passed between.

Stayed in a hotel across from Time Marks for the last five nights. Packed at Torin's place. Some stuff still there. Craig kept my work desktop and other things from the office for me.

Surreal being homeless and jobless, sleepless and sick and alone. I've never taken well to unemployment. The least of my concerns right now. No car, school paid off, no dependents, no extravagances. Rent has been my only marked expense in the past years. Living well below my means. I can manage for a while. For however long I have.

If I come back—maybe it's the insomnia talking—but I wouldn't mind entertaining the idea of working with the restaurant. Design the new place, perfect my WordPress skills, develop graphics and branding.

Just the insomnia. Even if I did want to walk away from pursuing new options in set design and artistic director areas, my thoughts are stuck in the past. Torin badgered me about working with him in the restaurant—*for* him—for months. Not recently. Even Torin gives up an infinite argument eventually. Only because he has moved to the next one.

It doesn't matter. We broke up. I guess. Not entirely sure. The basis I'm working under for now.

Maybe they'll take me back at Time Marks if I want it. If I get things sorted out. Right now, I don't care. I just want to sleep. Then to find Mary and Lil and the places we said goodbye and know what happened to my family after I was gone.

CHAPTER TWENTY-SIX

"Bourride, chef?"

Torin grabs the tasting spoon from Chef Ava. "Fine."

Her eyebrows jump. "Thank you, chef." She steps back to her station to finish plating.

Torin calls for service, then heads back to check orders.

Two minutes pass before Mason races in. "Sorry, chef!"

Torin hardly hears him.

As the evening slows, Torin finds others doing more around him than he is. New sous chef Christopher manages the place as if he has been doing it all his life.

When Vic flies into a panic that custard has almost run out and Roman, Dominique's second, shouts at him that he cannot drop everything to make custard, Torin starts a pot and tempers the eggs himself. He blast chills the mix before adding it to the ice cream machine. It's still warmer than room temperature, but it will turn out.

"Your custard's in the machine," Torin says as he passes Roman working frantically to plate soufflés.

Roman, like Ava, seems startled. His chocolate soufflés look exquisite. Torin wishes he had one for Flep.

He is already past Roman when he thinks to tell him they look perfect.

Roman glances at him, hands still working. "Thank you, chef."

He returns to the tickets as Roman shouts for Vic to get the soufflés out.

At the end of the night, Torin remembers in a vague way to tell Chris he likes his work and ask Zade how her dog is managing.

"Jasper's walking on his own." She glows as she talks about her pet.

"Glad to hear it," he replies, forcing his own smile.

While sure he does not actually feel glad, he could not say, if asked, what he does feel.

Back home late, Torin turns on the TV, though it has never been a pastime of his.

He stands for a moment in the doorway of one bedroom, then the other. The little apartment seems to echo with voices and laughter he cannot quite hear, just out of range.

He opens a German beer that he would normally use to cook with and sits on the couch. Has to start somewhere, but he sighs and returns the bottle to the refrigerator still half-full.

He switches off the TV, showers, and goes to bed.

Cannot sleep. Just like he hasn't been able to sleep for the past week.

After two hours, he gets up and takes one of Flep's sleeping pills from the bathroom. After another hour, he is wide awake and jittery—he clenches and unclenches handfuls of the sheet, turns around and around, sits up, checks his phone, lies back down, sits up again.

By 4:00 a.m., Torin feels like he could leap tall buildings and sprint several marathons and still be looking for something to do.

What are the side effects? They knocked Flep out. At least, at first, when he started taking them...

Hands shaking—aching to run, climb, swim—he turns on all the lights in the apartment, opens all the blinds, turns on NPR and the TV at the same time since he cannot decide, finishes the beer, and starts to cook.

It's noon when Torin looks at the clock again. Christ, he's late for work. Or is it Monday? Yes. Monday and he has to pick up the girls from their schools, and take them back the next morning.

At 2:00 p.m. he must meet Ree. But...he feels like he has been hit by a truck.

He sets his phone alarm for 1:30 p.m., lies down, and passes out so completely that the alarm sounding in his ear seconds later terrifies him.

Cursing, head feeling as if bowling balls keep bouncing against each side, he races to dress before dashing out.

Running through rain, only a minute late.

Ree leaps in puddles as they walk along the sidewalk, Torin holding her hand. Noise, light, hubbub, rain...too much. How can she feel so normal?

When she asks what they are going to eat today, Torin cannot remember what he cooked last night. Strange. It will come to him. Just the headache.

They wait a short time for Bell and catch a bus home.

Bell is neither hungry nor jumping in puddles. She is silent, sullen—not speaking to him unless he asks her a question. She has been just the same for a while now.

At home, she goes to her room. Ree stands on a chair to help him cook and tell him about her day. Very loudly. She also does not hesitate to correct him when he does something she disapproves of—like not taking proper safety precautions by using a kitchen towel rather than an oven mitt.

The two share dill chicken salad on toasted crumpets—both of which he must have made at 4:00 a.m.—and Torin takes aspirin while Ree shouts to her sister that she missed lunch and runs for the TV. She watches too much TV. Especially lately.

She used to draw pictures, or work on her easy readers, or play games with her stuffed animals or cards—go fish, memory games. The TV was off and on. Now it's constantly on.

"Hey, Ree? Want to work on your reading?" Torin offers, starting the dishes. Though they just got home, the kitchen looks like a train wreck.

"When Flep gets back," she says absently, already riveted by *Cupcake Wars*.

Because those were things she did with him. Because she is waiting patiently for his return.

Torin and her mother explained to her that Flep had to travel to France. Ree understands France. She has been on the long flight, visited family. Then, she came back. So Flep will be back.

Bell drags herself out of the bedroom to collect her sandwich and sit down with her sister before the TV. She does not say a word to either.

"You're not supposed to eat on the couch," Ree chirps at her.

Bell ignores her.

Torin goes on cleaning.

No one explained anything to Bell. Or, what did her mother tell her? That Torin drove Flep away? That he's not coming back?

It would explain how she has been treating him lately. If someone told her the truth—that Flep is an adult who does whatever he wants and travels if he wants and takes off all at once if he wants—maybe she wouldn't be so tetchy.

Torin hasn't the energy to do or say anything about it.

By the time he is halfway through the dishes, his head feels like several hatchets are wedged into his skull. Much worse since the painkillers.

None of them make much conversation that evening, not even Ree. The TV stays on.

CHAPTER TWENTY-SEVEN

In the morning, Bell remains cool to him. Ree feeds the fish and collects her school bag without protest. Also without enthusiasm.

At the entrance to her school, with other parents and six- to eight-year-olds flowing past, she lets go of his hand after a goodbye, but turns back while Torin is still watching her.

"Daddy?" She tilts her head to look up at him. "When will Flep be back?"

"I don't know, sweetheart."

"Is he still sick?"

"I hope not."

"Will you tell him all the lights are up at the Park? I'll show him on our next skating lesson."

Torin opens his mouth, having no idea what he is about to say.

"Ree! Race you!"

A little girl with long braids bursts past Torin.

Ree runs with her, feet flying, shouting gleefully, "No running in the halls!"

Torin returns to Bell waiting on the steps out front.

She sits on the handrail, texting with one hand, holding onto the rail with the other, swinging her feet in tall boots that her mother got her.

"Don't sit on that, Bell."

She hops to the sidewalk, tossing her head to swing hair out of her face, still texting.

After he drops her off, Torin walks to the station to wait for the first southbound train. But he gets on a northbound line instead.

At her office, the secretary informs him that Amélie is with a client.

He waits forty-five minutes, looking at an email on his phone from Flep saying he is in a town in northern France called Arras and he misses them—"All of you." Does that include Amélie or just the girls? They seem strangely friendly. Torin hadn't cared, knew Amélie's liking Flep was critical to his own relationship. Flep could go to all the soirées at her place he wished, and Torin had previously thought nothing of it. Previously.

He never can think how to answer these small emails. He can't just say, "I'm happy for you," or, "Sounds great." He would come across sarcastic. But he can't say more because he does not know what to say.

Perhaps tell Flep that Ree is waiting to show him the Christmas lights in Central Park when he takes her for her next lesson? Waiting because no one has told her Flep bought a one-way ticket, and he and her father are not exactly together anymore?

Which is so...crazy. So impossible. *Not exactly together anymore.*

Flep was just here. Perfect. And he would be. Forever.

Torin would marry him in a heartbeat. The thought makes him wonder, for the first time, why he never broached the subject with Flep. Why it never occurred to him to ask. They hadn't known each other long—a year and a half? Yet Torin cannot convince even himself that this has anything to do with his lack of planning.

He didn't need to plan for Flep. He had to plan for his restaurant, for the second location, for his daughters and their futures. Not for Flep.

He lets his phone go to sleep, looking at the screen long after seeing only his own reflection in black.

The sound of Amélie's voice makes him look up. Perfectly New York, that voice. He has seen her dumbfound people when she starts speaking French.

It makes him think of Flep alone in France—unable to speak the language—in rural areas that have few English-speakers. He wishes that he had come up with something in response to his note.

Amélie bids goodbye to a couple at the front desk. She talks to the secretary about changes to the schedule next week, then turns to see Torin standing behind her, waiting.

She does not look surprised to see him. Amélie never looks surprised. Her lawyer face doesn't even flicker as she turns.

"Are the girls okay?" she asks, tone cool.

"Fine. At school. Can we talk?"

"I don't have time for legal advice today, Torin. I told you, you have to make an appointment."

The secretary types at her computer, only feet from them. A young man sits just as agonizingly close in a chair near where Torin was just seated.

"It's not about the restaurant," Torin says.

"If it's not about the girls and not about restaurants, it must be about you. I'll call during lunch." Her eyes remain cold, disinterested. Perfect dark auburn hair frames her face—thick and full, with a slight wave to it—falling past her shoulders. It makes him think of Bell tossing her hair as she jumped off the handrail, ignoring him. Ignoring him for long enough.

"I just want a minute, Amélie."

"And I'm 'just' at work. Have I *ever* walked in on you during dinner service and said, 'Can we talk?'"

Torin looks at her. Her beautiful hair, sharp features, cold eyes. Her solid stance, planting herself against him—shark to shark—and he can think of no argument to that.

The feeling bewilders him. He does not feel angry or indignant about what she might have said to Bell anymore. Or to Flep in all their coziness. But he doesn't want to go away without answers either.

"I'm sorry," he says after a blank moment of having no words to shoot back, leaving him with an unaccustomed feeling of openness. Nothing to catch onto. Nothing with which to attack.

Amélie's eyes open a touch wider. She leans back maybe half an inch. No more. But, for one of the first times in his life, he has seen her surprised.

"You're right," he goes on. "I know you're busy. Just five minutes, please."

She looks at him, turns. "Come on."

Torin follows her to her office. Leather chairs, black-and-white abstract photographs of the City on the walls, a spectacular view of Central Park out the wide windows.

"What's wrong?" She walks around her desk to sit.

Torin closes the door and takes one of the leather chairs.

"What have you been telling Bell about Flep and me?"

"I don't know what you mean."

"She's been pissed off with me for a week. I didn't want to make a big deal about it, but she's giving me the silent treatment now, getting worse and worse. I thought I should ask you about her. You haven't talked to her about Flep and me at all?"

"We've talked." Amélie speaks carefully, tone measured. "She's upset about him being gone. I haven't been 'telling her' anything. She's twelve years old. She's not stupid. Or unobservant."

Anger flaring again, Torin tenses in his seat. "Meaning what?"

"Meaning no one has to tell her—"

"For her to get the wrong impression and take it out on me?"

"What do you think her impression is?"

"That I drove Flep away and don't care where he is, or if he's coming back."

"And what did you actually do?"

"Nothing." He catches himself as he raises his voice, pulling back. "I didn't do a damn thing."

"That's right. That's what I thought you did also. Never ask anything you don't already know the answer to in court. *Now*." She leans forward, forearms on the desk, hands together. "Tell me this: what's the difference?"

"What?"

"What's the difference between you 'driving him away' and 'not caring' and you doing 'nothing'?"

Torin sits still.

"Do you know what nothing implies? Indifference. Indifference is noticeable to impressionable young people observing it around them, as well as to those upon whom it is directed. That should answer your questions. You've got two more minutes."

"I am not indifferent. You don't think I care about what's happening? You don't think this—"

"I think you care when it affects *you*, Torin. You don't care when your daughters are looked after and happy. Or when you come home each night to someone you get to sleep with and cook for. Or when the restaurant is thriving. You don't care when everything falls into place. You don't care when a great person walks into your life who is there for you and makes your life easier.

"Because you expect it. Just like you expect perfection in your kitchen. When everything is perfect, you roll along on the waves. You don't nurture it. You don't thank it or praise it or pay it forward. But, when things fall apart, you start shouting. Because you have to lose it to be bothered about it. Look at what happened with Keon—"

"What the hell does Keon have to do with any—?"

"You had the perfect sous chef, Torin. Your staff loved him, he was a mellow counterpoint to your own temperament, be brought in a flair to Chaleur's profile with his own Pacific Island background. And you let him walk away."

"He was starting his own place! I didn't 'let him' do anything. He just did. These people are not puppets under my control—"

"Do you wish Keon were back?"

Torin closes his mouth, jaw tight.

"Have you regretted him being gone every day for the past two years as you struggled to find a new chef to live up to your standards and fill his shoes? But did you try to stop him? Did you try to get him back? Did you sit down with him when he gave you notice and say, 'How can I make it worth your while? What do you need to earn? How many days off do you need?'

"Did you ask him that and did he say, 'There's nothing you can do. I've got my heart set on this. It wouldn't matter if I brought home twice what I do now, I've got to go'?"

Torin still keeps silent, only looking back at her.

"I don't talk behind your back to the girls," Amélie says. "Bell is upset because she is worried about Flep. She came to me saying she was worried, while you were busy taking everything good in your life for granted. The last time I had a real conversation with Flep, he seemed suicidal. I'm glad he went to France. I hope he's finding answers about the people he's looking for. If he had to leave his job—and you—to do it, and you don't know if he's coming back, that's just too bad for you.

"I'm sorry for the girls. And I'm sorry for him. Because it looks to me like you behaved just how he was afraid you would. But I am sure as hell not sorry that you had to open your eyes and face what you failed to appreciate—if you're not so selfish and proud that you can't see that even now."

She sits back, glancing at the clock on her desk.

"You're past your minutes. I have an appointment."

Torin gets up stiffly—breath shallow, muscles tight—wanting to kick over the chair. "Thanks for your time."

"I'll send you my bill."

He has his hand on the knob when Amélie adds, "We've talked about setting examples for our children since before they were born. I hope, one day, they can see their father admit he can be wrong, like any other mortal. If he could do that, I could admit I was wrong about him."

Torin walks out, his fingers bunched painfully against his palms, headache returned.

STAGE FOUR

Wednesday, November 9

Everything has stopped.

I sit at a sunbaked table among a few French and British visitors in the breakfast room. The quantity of fresh bread, croissants, and cheese is extraordinary. The coffee tastes fantastic. But my attempt to ask about omelets or sausage in English fell flat. Cheese, it seems, is your "protein" here. And butter.

I eat wedges of creamy cheese, and slices of dry, on croissants with fruit. Still starving. And tired. Though I must have slept for fourteen hours last night. How soon before I can find lunch?

Ordering is a problem. The people seem mostly pleasant in this small town, accustomed to stupid Americans. Once you leave the urban areas, not many people speak English. But Arras is large enough to have places to stay and eat and a bus and train line. I won't perish. Only feel like I might.

I got out of Paris as quick as I could, hardly functioning, hardly knowing how or where to go. Yes, there were signs in English—some of the time. No, they were not much help. It was, in the end, American college students who helped me onto the correct train and told me where to change from the airport.

Amélie, communicating with me by email, offered contact information for a couple of relations of hers. They will likely be no help, being in the south of France, but it means a lot to me to know they are there in case of a major emergency.

I have her Parisian sister's phone and email as well. Amélie told her I would be here. Though Marcelle is in Zurich on business and won't even be home until after Armistice Day, which is about to be celebrated—as British tourists explained to me. I am some distance from Paris anyway.

Still, the fact that she offered, the fact that she told her sister about my being here on my own and I could call her if I had to, means more to me than I can tell Amélie. I have no idea why she ended up being so kind to me.

I sent Torin an email as well, just to tell him where I am—that I'm already starting to feel better, that I hope he and the girls are well. But I'm trying not to think about them. And I don't expect a reply.

Now, I should have already started looking for...things. Landmarks, battlefields, museums, memorials, and graves from WWI. I am finally here. The right places.

Yet I have done nothing but sleep and forage since I arrived.

Because everything has stopped. Everything.

Since I stepped off the plane at Charles de Gaulle, I have seen nothing erroneous. I have not smelled cordite or felt the earth tremble with shells. I have not craved black tea or tasted mold. I have seen no human faces which were not around me here and now.

I have not even had a dream which I can recall.

Not once.

But I must get something done. I cannot go on sleeping for half the day in my quaint room on the third floor—there's no elevator, only creaking, narrow stairs which rise as sharply as a ladder. From here, I look over the gray streets of Arras and green pastures beyond.

There are places here I must see, things I must find. Although I remain unsure how. I was too terrified by repercussions to do more than quick, fragmentary research back home. I know only that I am in a B&B alongside what was, one hundred years ago, the Western Front. I know there are battlefield tours and military cemeteries here. I know I have to get out there.

But, first, I hope I can find a filling lunch.

Saturday, November 12

I went to an Armistice Day—Veterans Day—memorial event at a military cemetery. I walked through towns along the Western Front. Miles on narrow country roads and footpaths through farmland. Buses and trains to neighboring areas.

A sense of urgency, of foreboding, oppresses me. Like storm clouds. A ticking clock.

But I don't feel sick. I don't have nightmares. I have not had a single night in which I slept less than eight hours since arriving in France. I hadn't had an eight-hour night in the past year before this.

Seeing rows of white crosses, flat farmland and slightly rolling hills, old roads and historic churches and inns—it all feels familiar. Like I might feel visiting Connecticut. Not exactly where I grew up, but the same type of geography. Comfortable—despite my own bewilderment at nearly everything going on around me. I haven't even been able to find anyone speaking English in a grocery store.

Familiarity and urgency. No great realization. No breakthrough.

Should I go on to England? Looking for what? A name in old marriage or death records? I don't know the names. A first name, a nickname, and a sunny garden in Kent.

Kent. I don't know how I know that. I don't know the names of more than a few English counties—Cornwall, Yorkshire... But, somehow, for a long time, I've known to look in Kent.

Kent is easy. Cross the Channel into Dover by ferry, start looking. I can always come back to France. These B&Bs are cheap off-season.

After a shower in a hallway bathroom the size of a New York City closet, I searched online with my shaky internet connection and found some local tour guides. I emailed a couple of private individuals that are offering WWI battlefield tours in English around the Arras, Amiens, Albert, and Somme regions.

Dinner in the only place in town that greeted me in English when I walked in: an Irish pub. French onion soup and wild rabbit on fresh greens. I have not tasted a single bite in France that was not spectacular.

Yet every meal makes me think of Torin and the girls, often making it difficult to eat at all.

Tomorrow, I should hear from a guide. A tour. Some insight into what I might be looking for. Go into museums and libraries—I may have to make a real effort about all this.

Everything used to be so intense. I thought I could show up and immerse myself, like taking a dive. Instead, I've been standing in a puddle, wiggling my toes in warm mud. Nothing unpleasant—besides that sensation of a ticking time bomb. Nothing creating forward momentum either.

I may email Dr. Kulmala, or even Natalie, for thoughts. But that would only be because I don't want to do what I know I should: be more proactive.

I don't want to find exact battlefield lines with guides. I don't want to see hundred-year-old photographs or model displays in museums. I have never even had the courage to read about the War online. Not after what happened at the library from looking at a single picture.

I listen to British English and rapid French around me in the pub, warm beside a massive fire. This hearth is open to the room at large and would never be tolerated in a public building at home due to American safety fanaticism. I watch whirling flames, thinking of crème brûlée and Bell's dances.

Time to be proactive. Time to take the plunge and face deliberate triggers.

But so many of the triggers I know are the people. Without Torin, Bell, or Ree, what if I have come halfway around the world in search of answers that can only be found back home?

Tuesday, November 15

Clear thinking is both a gift and burden. Far too much time to think. To wonder what I am doing, contemplate the past, worry about the future.

I met up with Charles, an older Englishman, who took me on a personal tour of the Amiens and Somme battlefields today. I knew the hills. I knew the river. I knew names of the towns before he said them. I knew, but I did not *remember*.

As if reading a book I had not seen since childhood. Familiar story, knowing what comes next. No more.

I thanked Charles for his time, paid him in euros, and took the opportunity to grill him about nuances of local public transportation and more resources for research.

"Trying to learn about a great-grandfather?" he asked jovially before we parted. "We've seen a lot more Americans out here lately with the War's centennial."

"Something like that."

"You'll find names in regimental histories and memorials. Not just out here, but in the hometowns. Hundreds of towns in Britain have Great War memorials with names of the dead from each town."

I couldn't very well tell him I didn't know the name. Much less the regiment. Or the hometown. Kent alone was like saying I was looking for Bob in New Jersey.

Tomorrow: museums. Deep breath.

CHAPTER TWENTY-EIGHT

Flep remembers, as he walks through dim rooms—among French and British and a few German tourists—what it was like to hold a pen in a dark dugout while the ink froze. He had to resort to sharpening a pencil with his knife with numb fingers. He recalls feeling sorry for mules and horses, muddy to their ears, as they carried ammunition to the artillery that could never get through on lorries. He shudders to think of the clang from a gas alarm and sheer terror of the scramble to get his gas mask on.

In the same way he remembers breakfasts with Torin, skating with Ree, and picking up Bell from the dance studio, the memories do not overwhelm him. They do not own him.

He looks at photographs, knowing men like the ones in the stills. He sees helmets and feels the weight on his head. He sees mess tins and thinks how they burned his fingers if he tried to hold his Maconochie straight from the brazier. He wishes, as he walks and reads plaques, that he had someone along. An old comrade with whom he can talk.

"Remember that? How cards fell into the mud and were marked forever? Remember how that one trench mortar hit the firebay we'd been sitting in two seconds before? Just in the dogleg when it hit? Sparing the lives of five men by chance? Remember how Daniels used to start pools with the men watching dogfights overhead, though betting was against regulations? After Daniels was shot down, his best mate blew a hole in his own head one night. Remember how Attwater had a box of pasties or fruitcake every bleeding week from his dear old mum? No wonder all the lads liked him."

Instead, Flep walks in silence through the museum.

It was hard. God, it was horrible. But there were good times too. Good men there with him. Good friends he would never forget. Never.

But how? He looks through a window at modern cars and parking lots and people on smartphones. How is he remembering those friends?

The officers' mess on a rainy evening. Captain Whitehead had a problem with overindulgence—though he wasn't the only one. The other junior officers looked the other way when Whitehead had one too many, only trying to keep him out of sight of the major. Then half his head was sliced cleanly away by shrapnel, and no one had to cover for Whitehead any longer.

Second Lieutenant Southern wrote the most horrific poetry ever penned, yet felt no shyness about sharing his work. He insistently solicited feedback for each line, implying an interest in improving his skills. Admirable, but where to start in a critique?

Lieutenant Costen, there was a good fellow. Maybe they got on so well because both had a young wife and child at home. For Costen, two: a five-year-old and a three-year-old. They showed one another photographs and spoke of how bright and superior their children were to the common man's in every way.

Flep's heart does not pound. His head does not spin. He feels only regretful, confused, and in need of a drink as he leaves his second museum.

Mostly, he feels incredibly alone.

All these memories and emotions are here, part of him. Why can he not remember his own name? His own address? For the urgency remains. The grief at his own failure. He was going to be there for her birthday. For her life. He was coming home. And he failed.

He must find her. Lil, his daughter. Her grave, her grandchildren, her home—because he cannot live his own life until he does. But he cannot find her without more memories resurfacing first.

Later, in the Irish pub for dinner—feeling guilty for not expanding his mind with local French establishments—Flep sits quietly over his fish and chips and tries to remember.

Images and sounds float by as he closes his eyes before the fire's warmth. He remembers her bright eyes and reaching hands. Along with Ree's. He remembers Mary in a sunny kitchen, laughing while pretending not to after he added salt instead of sugar to his tea by mistake. Along with Torin chuckling over his attempt to hold a knife in another kitchen. Torin gently taking his hands, showing him what to do.

Each detail he remembers of that other time feels muddy, hampered by the present. He just cannot catch a break...

CHAPTER TWENTY-NINE

The day before Thanksgiving. Raining in a steady drizzle as Flep again wanders battlefields.

Much, of course, is private land these days. After a second walk with Charles and time on his own looking at local maps and information from the museums and pub owner, Flep knows his way around.

He walks until his socks are soaked inside his "waterproof" hiking boots. Until rain has seeped through the zipper of his raincoat to saturate layered cotton shirts. Until his hands are numb and his face stiff with cold.

He has few memories out here because this is not the place he knew. He understands that now. Seeing a helmet in a museum is closer to home than seeing a green pasture when all he knew were muddy walls. But this—drenched socks, numb fingers, steam before his face as rain settles over him—he knows.

So much cold. He was out in summer as well. He remembers the heat and stench, flies, bodies, and the dry, chalky ground. But not like the cold. The frozen ink, blank mind, and deathly cold that stole his breath and will to push on and drove him nearer to despair than ever the enemy managed.

Strange, too. He has seen little mention in museums of the intolerable cold. They tell of rats and lice, noise and rations, mud and wire. They don't seem to know there was nothing worse than the stench and the cold.

He can feel it now, moving in toward his lungs, his bones. His joints are cold. His teeth are cold. And this is only autumn rain. Not death cold.

Did he die of cold? Is that what this is about? No. Blood in his mouth. He died of injuries. He only...cannot quite remember.

It gets dark so early now, the sun setting behind clouds of rain over

225

lush fields. As light fails, the world falls silent and monochrome. Such sameness in his waking world. So many gray skyscrapers. Now sodden, dull fields. Only memories reveal colors of life: burnt orange of Torin's crème brûlée, scarlet blood on snow, pink of Isabelle's ballet slippers, bluebird on a battered French postcard, yellow of Carine's favorite shirt.

He longs to merge these worlds, aches to reclaim one, put the other to rest.

Flep walks along a public footpath which seems to have turned into a farmer's backyard. There is a hedge, a hill to a road. He can follow the road back into town.

He climbs the slope toward the hedge, hoping for a stile, not to have to turn back, hoping the farmer will not see him.

He trips, falls to his knees, throwing out his hands to catch himself on muddy ground, and he remembers.

The wire was there, running up to the top of the slope. Entanglements fifty yards deep, partly destroyed and tossed by shells.

Beyond the wire, the German line: Fritz waiting for him and his men. Over the top, leading the offensive with dozens of other officers, dozens of platoons and companies. A small attack to get their hill back. Their captured hill of strategic value for this tiny strip of the front.

They waited until past the morning hate and stand-to, past the earliest gray of snowfall. Then up and run—take those hills, retake what was theirs.

The sequence of events blurred into impossibility. First his knees hit snow, then he was thrown back, then the bullets caught him: a line of machine gun spray across his abdomen. He felt the impact, the force like a kick in the stomach, but no pain.

Someone stopped, bending to grab his shoulder as he failed to stand and follow his men.

"Back into the trench, sir! We'll get you to the dressing sta—"

Attwater's head sprayed blood into his face, a spatter of hot liquid released by the wave of bullets catching his brow as he bent over to help. Attwater toppled against him, then into snow.

Again, he felt only surprise. Attwater was there. Then he was not. Or, he was still there, but he was not Private Attwater.

He should call his batman. He should pick himself up and go on.

He looked down, still on his knees, to see blood oozing from holes in his own tunic. Attwater's blood trickled down his nose and chin.

Then fear. The fear came in a rush, terror at what could happen, at the poor prognosis for stomach wounds. Fear for her, for his promise, fear for what would happen to both of them, for never seeing her seventh birthday.

She was right there. Across the Channel, waiting for him in the garden in Kent. Running to him. "Papa! Papa's home!"

Lifting her, swinging her in the air, kissing her cheek while she laughed.

He had to reach her, protect her. He had to be there for her birthday, only weeks away after the snowmelt and the first warm bloom of spring. And for Mary, depending on him, waiting.

But he looked and saw blood on his tunic and knew the letter might be all he had.

Dizziness mastered him, pain stirred in his gut, and he pitched forward, hitting snow on hands and elbows. Shaking, with blood welling up in his throat like bile, he fought to open his breast pocket while his breath came in panicked gasps. Bullets sped over him, fanning a trail through the falling snow.

After biting his gloves to pull them off, he got that paper into his hands. A letter. Not a letter from home.

His letter.

A letter he had just finished before it was time to launch the attack. A letter to his baby girl. No envelope, no address. If found by the stretcher bearers or MOs or nurses with no destination, it would never be mailed. It would go into the fire with piles of bandages caked in viscera and bits of unrecognizable uniforms.

She would never even see his last letter.

Attwater's blood was already freezing on his face. He could not feel his lower body. Lying on his side, he fought for support from his elbow, working to open the paper, to find his pencil.

The folded letter fell into snow—picked up again, dropped again. Still no pencil. He reached for Attwater's pockets.

All the while, the snow around him changed colors. White, crimson, black.

Attwater had a purple pencil. So blunt, he could not get it to show on the paper.

He rubbed it on a frozen rock, bit it, and scraped it across his belt buckle, dropping it many times. Nothing helped.

Blood ran over his lips, bubbling up from his insides, leaking away as he scrambled with the dull pencil. He tried writing again, only making the paper damper.

Leaving his letter on Attwater's puttees, the pencil in his own bloody lips, he crawled several feet to the nearest barbed wire.

Pain then. Like ravenous beasts savaging his insides. Like he was going to die.

He could not die. He had to get back to her. And get this letter sent off so she did not worry. Then he would wait. The stretcher bearers would come and he would have a Blighty for sure. So he could go home to her.

Grasping the wire, he used one of its razor blade spikes to shave off the pencil tip. He cut his own fingers half a dozen times groping with the rusted metal, staining it with his own blood, but he sharpened the pencil.

His own legs lost to him, he returned the pencil to his lips and pulled himself to Attwater's puttees on his hands. He pressed fingers and pencil into clean snow, then Attwater's trousers. He could not get blood all over her letter. At least his hands were so frozen that the bleeding had slowed.

He read what was already there as pain and shock and blood loss crowded out the world.

My Dearest Lil,

Papa is enjoying hot soup tonight while it snows outside. I hope you have soup to warm you up on nights like these. Do you know what you want for your birthday, little bluebird?

My thoughts and prayers are with you and Mum every moment. Know that I am more proud of you than I can say, and love you more than I can say. I miss you, but I will be seeing you soon—and you'll never know we were parted.

Goodbye for now.
Hugs and kisses,
Papa

Letter by letter, grasping the stubby pencil in his fist like a javelin, he added four short lines to the bottom:

Lillian Taft
44 Hillier Close
Ashford
Kent

The pencil slid from his fingers on the jagged T, and he could not bend his knuckles for another attempt to pick it up.

Hands nearly rigid, he clasped the letter to force it back into his tunic pocket. Try after try, falling onto his back, he still could not manage. He dropped it onto his own chest, his arm across the page, holding on.

Being on his back seemed somehow to keep him from breathing. Pain boiled through the only part of his body—his middle—that he could still feel. Pressure bulged against his chest, blocking his throat, stopping his air.

They would find him, send him out with a Blighty—home to his bluebird.

If he could just turn over. If he turned, he could spit out the fluids and breathe and wait for them. He could make it.

Snow fell into his eyes, his mouth, coating his skin and wool uniform.

"I'm sorry, Mary. I'll be right there." He mouthed the words, though he could not be sure his lips even moved. "I'll be home soon. See you soon..."

Only wait.

Without breath, he could not wait. He had to roll over. He felt nothing anymore besides pressure and fear that he was not going to get home for this birthday, or the next, because he was about to drown.

Body frozen, letter pressed into his chest, he fought with an effort of will to turn as blood filled his mouth and throat, panic claiming him. But he had used the last of his strength for a pencil that lay in a pool of blood below him.

And his will was not enough.

CHAPTER THIRTY

Flep walks back to the bed and breakfast in the rain and twilight—still scared, still numb and sick from the taste of blood in his mouth and the despair of failure, holding back tears. Soaked and cold to the pit of his stomach, all the way back he thinks of packing tonight and getting a train to the airport, so desperately in need of another human being who speaks English and pays in dollars.

Anyone.

Torin, mainly, but Torin never even answered the couple of short emails he sent. It really is over with Torin. But anyone, really. Any casual friend, any former colleague—Amélie, Craig, Dr. Kulmala, any stranger on a bus. Just to not be so powerfully alone.

He cannot leave yet, of course.

He can do this. Hold himself together. Can go inside, up the vertical stairway to his tiny room, make notes about what he remembered, shower, and go to bed alone.

In the morning, he will make plans to reach Calais to take the ferry across to Dover. Maybe, if he is really desperate for human contact, he will call his guide, Charles, or Aunt Marcelle.

He knows, at least, where he is going. Ashford. He will find out what happened to her. Maybe things won't be so isolating in England, so depressing. They speak English there. Kent is easy to reach. And he can see London. He always wanted to visit Paris and London.

Yes, he can get through this.

Then he looks up as he dashes across the street to the bed and breakfast, lit by streetlights and sparse traffic and windows, and sees Torin standing in the doorway, watching him approach.

Not Torin, obviously. Memories and visions and dreams. But a lump fills Flep's throat as he sees the handsome man in the raincoat and...jeans. They don't seem to wear a lot of jeans out here. Just a tourist.

The man moves down the stairs into the rain, apparently coming to meet him.

"Flep?"

Flep stops. Something metallic hums in his ears.

Torin is at the restaurant on a Wednesday night. He is in New York on a Wednesday night. Not in France. Not in Arras. Not right here in the rain at this bed and breakfast. Flep never even emailed the exact place—though...he told Amélie.

Flep cannot speak or move, riveted to the sidewalk by his frozen feet.

Torin's shoulders are hunched, hesitant. He remains by the foot of the steps.

"Happy Thanksgiving." He looks down. "I'm sorry, Flep. I..."

He really is standing there.

Flep rushes the last steps to him. Torin's arms go around him, as tightly as Flep holds on. Finally, he cannot stop the tears.

CHAPTER THIRTY-ONE

Flep wakes and sits up in bed in the same moment, hands and feet icy. Same guest room on the top floor. Tiny bed and space. Gray of early morning through the square window, rain gone.

Dreams mix like oil and water—together, yet distinct.

Lil standing at the garden gate, watching for the postman down the lane, waiting. Waiting for him.

And Torin. Torin here last night.

Flep dreamed he walked back to the bed and breakfast and found Torin waiting for him on the steps. Torin hugged him and Flep cried on his shoulder in the rain. Torin took him indoors, up to Flep's room where Flep shivered violently, trying to towel off and change into something dry. Torin left.

He returned with a heavy mug of scorching bone broth and an electric space heater which he plugged in, quickly raising the temperature in the little room.

Torin sat with Flep, put him to bed like a child, kissed him.

He made a second trip downstairs, to whatever nearby establishment he was visiting—the kitchen below served only breakfast—and returned with another mug of broth and a hot sandwich.

Flep marveled at him, hardly able to speak or think. He ate in bed while Torin told him he looked like he needed an early night and that they could talk in the morning.

So very Torin: nourishment equals everything all better. Only...more. Torin better. Torin enhanced. Dream Torin was not only here in France, but he was soft-spoken, gentle, and concerned in each word and motion.

Flep had held onto him, clutching his warm hand after finishing the sandwich, yet Torin slipped away. He kissed Flep—his brow, his hands—

and told him good night. Not goodbye. Then Flep blinked and he was gone.

Only dreams of the waiting girl remained. Looking down the lane, waiting for him. His own sense of urgency seemed to be a tangible force in his chest. *Find her.*

The Torin dreams were stranger, more impossible than anything he has dreamed in the past year. And so much better.

Real Torin would not have been here. If he had, he would not have been so worried by Flep's tearful and frozen condition. He would have been rational, expecting Flep to pull himself together with a meal. And he certainly would not have left in the end. He would have stayed in the bed with Flep—tiny or not—and still been here now.

Shivering, Flep takes stock of the room from bed, meaning to grab his bath towel and hurry to the shower down the hall if it's not occupied.

There is a space heater. He could reach out from here and turn it on. The space heater Torin brought up.

Flep jumps, almost falling in his scramble to get up and dress, forgetting about his hot shower. He runs down the hall—grateful to find the bathroom unoccupied—to splash frigid water on his face and rinse his mouth before dashing to the stairs.

He must find the owner, ask about the American man who visited here last night—whether he's staying. Can't ask the woman who brings out the breakfast pastries and refills juice. She only speaks French. Find the owner to figure out what has happened.

Is Torin really here? He must be, yet...

Again almost falling, this time on those impossible stairs, then down the wider flight to the lobby. Sharp left to the breakfast room, find the proprietor—

"Flep!" Carine springs away from a table to run at him.

Isabelle follows while their father stands up beside the window table, smiling to see him.

As Flep hugs both girls, kneeling in the newly sunny room, he nearly weeps again—finding reality more impossible, more wonderful, than any hope or dream for the first time in his life.

CHAPTER THIRTY-TWO

Flep still feels caught in a dream—in limbo between what he wants and what is possible—throughout breakfast with the three of them. He asks why and how repeatedly, hardly tasting coffee or toast, though feeling better with the hot drink.

Isabelle watches him and Torin from the corner of her eye, not eating much, pulling out the insides from a fresh croissant, then nibbling the shell. Carine heaps a croissant with cheese and honey to eat as a sandwich, then another with berries and honey. Her father will not normally allow her to eat so much sugar at breakfast. Now he has eyes only for Flep. Bell is the one telling her to lay off the honey.

"We all missed you." Torin has only black coffee before him. "I should have come with you in the first place, Flep—"

"You couldn't. I don't understand how you're here now. You haven't had an unbroken twenty-four hours off work since I've known you." It had stopped occurring to Flep that Torin knew of such things. Besides that, the girls have school. Only a couple days off now for Thanksgiving.

"Dominique, Renard, and Chris are there. Amélie is helping us out also. She has a bit of experience in managing things from the good old days."

"A bit?"

Torin smiles. "I thought I'd just come out for a week myself and see you." He arches one eyebrow. "You can imagine how that went."

"He didn't want us coming to France," Carine tells Flep happily. "Because it's a long, long, long trip and no fun at all. But it is. We already saw Aunt Marcelle and rode the train, and we have the big room with the pink wallpaper. Have you seen it?"

Flep shakes his head.

"Amélie's sister met us at the airport and put us up the first night,"

Torin says. "We got in late. Then got here yesterday afternoon while you were out."

"They said you were very polite," Isabelle says.

Flep looks at her.

"The owner," Torin explains. "We said we were with the other American staying here, and they told us you were a lovely guest."

Flep feels another rush of giddiness. Torin speaks broken French; the girls: perfect French. He wants to hug them all again.

"I feel like an oaf not being able to do more than thank them in their own language. How long are you here?"

"*Here* just a couple nights. I didn't know if you were staying. Our return flight from Paris is nine nights out. This was two. What are your plans? What's happening with you?"

Flep feels speechless, looking helplessly at Torin. Not Torin—this man asks questions and still looks concerned.

"You're right. I've got to get to Calais to cross over to Dover. I was thinking today, but maybe one more night here, since you've booked it. I do know where I'm going in England now. A town called Ashford?" He adds the last hopefully.

Torin shakes his head. "Never been in England. With luck we can reach it on the train from Dover. I'll help you make plans today, find a place to stay, figure out the ferry, and we'll all come with you in the morning?"

Flep nods, still rattled by all their help, questions, and proximity.

"Be right back. See if I can cajole an egg from our hostess," Torin says in a low voice and slips from his chair.

"All the lights are on in the Park, and all the fire leaves fell off the trees," Ree says to Flep. "I'll show you when we skate."

"We're going on a ferry from France to England?" Bell asks.

"Ferry!"

"Shush, Ree." Isabelle blushes, glancing around at other breakfasters.

"Bell, what happened? Why are you all here? I didn't think your dad had any...interest in coming to France right now." Even as he asks, he realizes he longs most to know what is happening with Torin and himself.

Torin failing to answer his emails confirmed they had broken up, hadn't it? Yet Torin is here now to do...what? Show his sudden support and commitment?

"Oh, you know," Bell says. "Everyone argued about it for a long time, then he got tickets."

Flep just looks at her, more confused than ever.

She starts on the tender insides of her shredded croissant. "I think Mom and Dad argued about it. Then he told me I had the wrong impression about...pretty much everything in the world. He said you were trying to deal with a bunch of stuff, and I said half of it was him being a jerk."

Flep recoils. "You said that to your dad?"

She shrugs. "He just pouted. He doesn't shout at us. Only at other adults."

"Gives you something to look forward to, I guess." Flep smiles weakly.

"We can handle him." Bell looks up from the crumbs on her plate. "But we'd like it a lot better if you were there with us."

He takes a breath. "That might be the nicest thing anyone has ever said to me. Maybe I can handle him also...with you two there."

She smiles.

But should he be saying any such thing when he does not know what's next with Torin?

Torin soon returns to them, empty-handed. He grimaces when they look at him.

"I'm apparently not as charming as you. She told me there are plenty of cafés in town if I want something else to eat."

"We should get lunch soon anyway," Flep says. "I've been lazy about visiting local establishments with hardly anyone speaking English."

"Bell will get us around," Torin says. "She was phenomenal in Paris."

Isabelle flushes again, looking at her plate.

After splitting up—Flep getting his hot shower and a shave while pulling himself together—they reconvene in the lobby and set out to explore the town. Flep still feels bewildered facing Torin, self-conscious and full of questions he is unsure he would ask even if they were alone. Intimate strangers—not exactly one thing, yet not another.

He feels further embarrassed to discover how few of the urban sights he can explain. Flep has only been in the little corner grocery and a couple of the restaurants, namely the Irish pub. They take side streets, walk over a bridge and out of town to country roads, then to a memorial cemetery that he knows.

He picks Ree up so she can see over a hedge to farmland beyond, telling the girls about the War.

"One hundred years ago, millions and millions of people were drawn into a war that was partly fought right here." Flep points out landmarks, invisible paths of trenches, and the location of a former field hospital. He tells them it was a terrible time in history that deserves to be remembered and understood. "Learning from the past honors those who died here."

The girls run ahead on the footpath after seeing a red fox, Isabelle trying to take a picture.

Flep and Torin follow along the muddy track, the sun high while the day remains sharply cold. Their breath steams in the air. Flep remembered to wear the gloves he bought in town since arriving, but still has his hands jammed into his coat pockets.

"You've done a lot of research," Torin says. "I didn't know you knew anything about World War One."

"I went to a couple museums and an Armistice Day event. A British guide met me for tours on the Somme. He knows his stuff."

"And explained where everything was?" Torin gestures to where Flep had been pointing out landmarks.

"We...didn't come up here..." Flep trails off. He had not even thought about it. As changed as the landscape may be, he can still find sites of such memorable locations as hospitals and reserve lines.

His heartbeat quickens, thinking of Torin's last reaction to Flep knowing things he should not.

Torin says nothing. He pulls a hand from his own pocket to wrap his arm around Flep's shoulders, walking beside him as they return to town. Flep consciously tries not to question or worry over the exact nature of this gesture, feeling grateful, more than anything, that Torin is here.

Back in a populated area, the girls stop strangers on the street.

"*Excusez moi, s'il vous plaît,*" Isabelle says to a young couple. "*Est-ce que vous pourriez me dire quel est le meilleur restaurant en ville pour déjeûner?*"

They smile and jabber away in return.

Torin informs Flep that they are telling her the best places in town for lunch.

Following the couple's directions, they find the place easily. Not what Flep would have picked, but he feels comfortable in the shabby brick and mortar establishment. Isabelle orders everything for all four of them, the waitress speaking to her in dizzying French.

They eat *cuisses de grenouille, boeuf bourguignon,* exquisite autumn ratatouille of squash, onion, and peppers, and a cheese plate for dessert. Torin is already saying they must find a suitable substitution for Thanksgiving dinner this evening, yet Flep feels he has never had such a wonderful Thanksgiving meal as it is.

In the afternoon, Torin takes them back to their family guest room. One double bed and a single in a normal sized room—as opposed to Flep's closet. Even en suite.

The girls pile onto the large bed they must be sharing and switch on the TV. Flep is surprised by their fascination with a nature program—having to remind himself that the girls understand its narration.

He and Torin, with their tablets, sit on the small bed and desk chair, respectively, planning their morning train and ferry trips.

"We'll have to leave early. Look at these crossing times." Torin shows Flep his screen.

"Make sure that one takes walk-on passengers. I saw one the other day that you could only drive onto."

Torin raises his eyebrows. "That would be convenient."

"The train does go into Ashford," Flep says. "I'll check for places to stay."

"How come we can't see the parade?" Ree asks from the bed.

"I told you, if you came, you wouldn't have Thanksgiving with Mom or see the parade," Torin says to his screen.

She scowls.

"Wouldn't you rather eat frog legs than turkey for Thanksgiving anyway?" Bell asks.

"Yes!"

"We'll see the parade next year." Bell changes the channel, starting an argument. They land on a French cooking show. Ree is all smiles again.

Flep has never had such a strange Thanksgiving and Black Friday. But why eat pumpkin pie when you can have chocolate soufflé?

On Friday afternoon, he stands on the deck of the industrial and decidedly unromantic ferry beside all three of them. That crushing urgency leaps to excitement, even joy.

Flep sees the White Cliffs of Dover across the English Channel, watches gulls wheel through sunlight and icy wind, smells the ocean, listens to the engine, and welcomes the heady euphoria of going home.

CHAPTER THIRTY-THREE

After an hour by train from Dover, they finally step out from Ashford International railway station long past sunset. Carine is falling asleep. Torin carries her while Flep gives a cab driver the address of their new bed and breakfast and Isabelle points out a pizza place across the street. Should they get one before going to the room?

Flep asks the driver, "Is there much around here? Will we be able to get dinner?"

"Not half. Two minutes from here. Best tandoori place in Ashford's across the street from The Gatehouse. You'll find shops and all sorts at your door on North Street."

Flep wants to kiss the old man just for speaking English.

"Thank you." He waves the others to the car.

Flep is disconcerted to see, not British pubs and old-fashioned street lamps by church towers, but a bustling city of headlights, fast food chains like Domino's and McDonald's, and seemingly dozens of Indian restaurants.

He knows the street names. He knows he is in the right place. But nothing looks the same.

At the cab driver's recommendation, they eat a late dinner at the Indian place across the street from the bed and breakfast after leaving their bags. Two rooms again, both en suite—Flep alone while Torin stays in a family room with the girls.

All are exhausted, taken aback by the surprising tastes of England—cumin, cardamom, and turmeric—but get through a cheap and delicious meal before going to bed.

Flep longs for mince pie and Eccles cakes with clotted cream, though he has never tasted the first two in this life. The feelings no longer surprise him.

Torin lets Ree switch on the TV while Bell changes for bed. He talks to Flep in the doorway about their plans for tomorrow. Flep wishes they could discuss plans in bed. Still, he would not trade that with the girls being here.

In the morning, they are served eggs, sausage, bacon—slices of hot ham, really—coffee, juice, fried bread, tomatoes, fruits, and all kinds of spreads. They are also offered what looks like white beans in ketchup and served hot on dry bread. All four refuse this offer.

Flep, relieved to find not a croissant in sight, gorges and finds he enjoys tomatoes on scrambled eggs.

Even the textureless sausages, which Torin and the girls will not eat, are lovely. Carine gags, saying they're like meat mayonnaise. More like hot pâté, with skins that pop against his teeth. When they see he is the only one indulging, the other three roll their sausages onto Flep's plate in silence.

They all look at him strangely, Torin trying to keep a straight face and Bell incredulous, as they finish breakfast. Only Ree appears glad of this opportunity to share.

"What?" He might as well try a few slices of fried bread for dessert. The local strawberry jam looks delightful. They even have both lemon and lime preserves.

"Nothing." Torin is clearly repressing a smile.

Bell, it seems, cannot resist. "This is the worst food we've had since we got to Europe, and you're eating like—what?" She looks at her dad, who shakes his head.

"It's the best breakfast I've had since landing." Flep is surprised, but not offended. He cannot help it if she was raised to be a French food snob. "Do you think we can find a real English pub for lunch?"

"We can't go in a pub." Bell is indignant.

"What's a pub?" Ree asks, offering him sweet lemon preserves.

"I think you can here," Flep tells Bell, taking the jar from Ree. Why not? *Just lemon.* It won't hurt him, and she seems to like it. "Different culture and rules."

"I've noticed." Speaking under her breath, Bell glances toward a plate at the next table heaped with ketchup beans over toast.

"Are you all ready to go?" Flep asks. "You don't have to stay with me. I'm trying to find this address that wouldn't come up on the map searches. Then I may end up in libraries or anywhere I can find to hunt through old archives for names."

"We'll come," Torin says. "If you start poking through dusty file boxes in basements, we might split up to see the sights."

Flep nods, eager to get going. Still in a rush, but knowing now he is close.

Sunday, November 27

I dreamed about her last night. Not the War. Not the snow. I haven't felt that bitter cold since the day I remembered the end, in the French field at dusk. Just about the girl. Sunny garden, blooming honeysuckle. And Lil waiting for me.

I almost forgot my haste during breakfast with Torin and the girls. Everything rushed back as we stepped out. He brought them along as we started to walk, then stopped a cab for 44 Hillier Close.

There was no 44 any longer, but a Hillier Close remained, and the driver let us out, asking what we were looking for.

While Torin paid, I stood on the sidewalk. I looked to the corner of my familiar Hillier Close and to Redman Road, which led out of town through green fields, running along the river for miles. Used to.

What faced me now was a block of red brick row houses dropped onto the sidewalk. You could step out your front door and be hit by a car—if they were not parked up and down the street.

Torin noticed me staring. I hardly heard him ask the driver to wait a minute while I walked to the corner.

I looked down the road for green fields. More brick and concrete. I turned back and almost ran into Bell.

"Did you live here?" She looked worried under the wool hat protecting her from the drizzle.

How could she know? I never talked to her about any of this. Would her parents have spelled out what I believed was happening? Certainly not her father.

"Yes," I said after a pause. "A long time ago, before this life." I looked back to the row where there once were cottages with neat gardens. Where bees droned and honeysuckle bloomed. "But it didn't look like this."

"You'll find your old family. Like finding ancestors." She had clearly thought this over.

"Come on." I put my hand on her shoulder as we returned to the waiting car. "I'm glad you're all here, Bell."

"Me too."

I bent to address the driver. "How about the city library?"

I thought he might take the girls to sightsee, but Torin let them look through British children's books while he asked about accessing newspaper archives, and I asked about public records. I was told that if newspapers did not help, I should contact the GRO, and was given their website.

Torin told Bell and Ree where we were and not to go anywhere besides the kids' section or to us. We took side by side desktops, searching archives, first by year, then for "Mary Taft" and "Lillian Taft." Starting in 1916, going month by month. Torin jumped ahead to start at 1926.

I went through a full year, already discouraged, when I started into 1917, reached February, and blinked as a tiny piece was displayed on the screen. I read, swallowed, read again.

"Torin." I could scarcely speak.

He leaned over to see.

February 12, 1917
OBITUARIES
Ashford resident Lieutenant Gabriel Taft was killed in action in France on Thursday. He leaves behind wife, Mary Taft, and daughter, Lillian Taft, age 6.

Torin regarded the screen calmly for longer than I did. He leaned past me for the mouse to print the page, then squeezed my shoulder and returned to his own search.

Nine more years, month by month. Nothing. Not a hint.

The girls returned. Torin told them we would be done soon. Bell read to Ree in an undertone for us.

Torin was on 1932 when he said my name. I almost jumped in my chair. He printed the page and stood to fetch it while I read from his screen.

Lillian Taft of Ashford, daughter of Gabriel and Mary Taft, to wed Thomas Winship of Canterbury, son of Albert and Margaret Winship, on Sunday next. The couple will be married in the parish church and plan to set up house in Canterbury near Mr. Winship's family and work at the local paper.

"Checking out in the morning?" Torin sat back down. "I have heard of Canterbury." He smiled.

I could only nod dumbly as he handed me the second page, my hands shaking.

"How about that real pub lunch? You look like you need it."

Again, I nodded.

We searched more, but both girls were growing put out with us and we soon paid for the prints and left for the pub.

The food was as excellent as breakfast, but, this time, I could hardly taste it.

Now it's early Sunday morning. Sun just up. All heading for the train to Canterbury.

CHAPTER THIRTY-FOUR

Canterbury is so sickeningly charming and historic that Ree seems to think the city is an amusement park.

She first asks if they have to pay to go in, then if they are in Hogsmeade, because Muggles aren't allowed. Bell tells her to shush. Torin takes one of her hands, Flep the other, and she flies above the cobblestones so no one will know she is not magical.

Torin watches Flep pause as they pass a churchyard. This cemetery is much too ancient. Still, if Lillian Winship moved here as a newlywed in 1932, it seems possible she may have stayed, and died, in Canterbury.

With bags dropped off at another bed and breakfast, Torin lets Flep set out for the library on his own. He emailed a couple of places based in London last night, trying to find the death record of either Mary Taft or Lillian Winship.

Torin knows Flep hopes to find something to lead him, not only to a grave, but to survivors. Did she have children? Grandchildren?

But what does Flep plan to do if he finds relations? Introduce himself? Tell them...what?

Torin was shaken to find the obituary of a man Flep believes he used to be. Could he find more? Could he find people he thinks are his own grandchildren, though Flep was born after them?

Torin cannot think about it. That part doesn't matter. This is Flep's journey, like a religious awakening. Torin figured out, before buying those outrageous tickets to Paris—half-funded by Amélie—that it isn't about whether he himself believes, agrees, or understands.

He gets takeout pizza with the girls. The three of them have a quiet afternoon following too much travel and commotion. Introvert Bell, though she says nothing, is hitting a wall. Ree, who thrives on chaos in the short-term, is becoming anxious and clingy by this fourth stopover among planes, trains, taxis, and ferries, hauling baggage all the way.

Torin worries about their time frame. Flep will still be looking by the time he and the girls have to return home. Which Torin had wondered about when making the booking, though hoped they could avoid it. He does not want to abandon Flep here.

He also worries about the restaurant as he checks email. No news. Presumably everything is okay. Christopher, a fourth generation chef, has been performing well. And Dominique is there. He gave her a raise in the same private conversation in which he explained he was going to be gone for a while, needing her again to perform beyond her job description.

Hoping Amélie will never find out, and never mention Keon's name to him again, he increased Dominique's pay by twenty-five percent—retroactively effective from November 1st. He hasn't any idea how the restaurant can afford this, but he'll figure it out later. The idea that she, too, could leave one day made him want to close the doors now.

If Chris holds things together with Dominique, he is already due a bonus as well.

Now...keeping Flep. He can't exactly offer Flep a check. Or hide his pursual of Flep from Amélie. No pretense here. No pride.

He still feels like he's on pins and needles with Flep, walking a wire. A frightening game of "He loves me, he loves me not" with an endless flower.

Not that Torin has any doubts about Flep being glad to see them and have them here. It is the after going home part—the next month, next year—that has continued to keep Torin awake at night since reaching Europe.

He must get them all home, to show Flep he is not taken for granted. Which Torin always showed, of course. Amélie was not in on their early dates and walking breakfasts and sourdough chocolate bread. Obviously Flep knows he was—is—appreciated. Torin only has to make sure there can be no doubt. Not just now and then—like when he has time to make bread or go to work late. Every day.

If Flep will give him a chance—coming home with them rather than remaining here alone.

Torin opens the calendar on his tablet while the girls watch game shows and finish the pizza. He lies back on the family room's double bed.

After tonight, they have only three nights left. One of those must be spent in France at Amélie's sister's place on the way out. So, two more nights in England, a day devoted to traveling, then a night in Paris, and an early flight.

Torin wishes he got the tickets for later—the girls have school, but it's not as if a week at home would have been as educational as traveling in Europe. He answers emails, updates Amélie on their new location, and tosses his tablet aside.

Bell and Ree can Skype with their mother tonight. Maybe she will babysit from the screen as well. Torin hasn't had a moment alone with Flep since the first night they met on the front steps in Arras.

"Daddy!" Ree shrieks and Torin jumps.

"What?" He sits up. Had he really been falling asleep? Maybe they are not the only ones who need a break.

Strange—at home, Flep was sleepwalking through the past months. Now he is by far the most energetic of the lot. He even ate those baby food sausages.

"*Chopped* is on," Ree tells him excitedly.

"That's great, sweetheart. I didn't know they showed it here." Torin yawns and drops back onto the bed. "Do you want to talk to your mom tonight before bed? I sent her a note. It's morning there."

"Uh-huh." Ree watches the screen.

"Can't we call now?" Bell asks, glancing into the empty pizza box. She seems to always be hungry lately—finally growing. "Then we could go to bed."

"She might already be at work. I bet you'll have to wait."

"We'll only talk for a minute."

Sighing, he blindly grabs his tablet again.

The girls are able to get in a quick chat with their mother before she has to go, leaving Torin short even a digital babysitter. Late afternoon when they hang up and all three are falling asleep. Jet lag still clinging on?

Torin thought they coped well, the girls bouncing back in a couple of days. Maybe that was the problem. Now crashing after too much, too fast. And going back in only a few days. Why didn't he get the tickets for longer?

Because he can't afford this. And he thought they all needed to get home. Especially Flep. But that is not what this is about.

It's dinnertime and dark out—both girls having drifted off together on one twin bed—when Flep taps at the door. It could only be Flep. No one else would knock so apologetically.

Torin opens the door quietly and steps into the poorly lit hall. This passage between the few guest rooms, lined in carpet that should have been ripped out twenty years ago, smells of antiques and cooking grease from endless breakfasts.

"Well?" Torin speaks in a whisper.

"Are they okay?" Flep sounds anxious.

"They fell asleep. Find anything?"

"Only about the husband. He became an editor of a local paper. But he died in the seventies."

"Still living here when he died?"

"Yes. Leaving behind a wife, Lillian Winship, children, and grandchildren. Over forty years ago. Then, no more mention from the local archives. I heard back from both places I wrote to. One said they couldn't help and to contact the second. The second said that a Mary Taft died decades ago in Ashford, but no other relevant record of a death in this country." Flep shakes his head. For the first time since Torin found him, he looks defeated. "I went to the courthouse for public records. I even went to tourist information before they closed. Those people know how to find things." Still shaking his head.

"Did you stop for lunch?" Torin longs to be closer to him, to kiss him. He keeps still, hands at his sides.

"Too busy." Flep regards the abused carpet, the old fatigue back in his face.

"I would take you to dinner, but stepping out of the room is about all I can manage right now. Takeout? Lots of pubs and inns in town."

"That would be wonderful." He looks up. "Thank you, Torin. I'm really, really glad you're here."

"Bangers and mash?" Torin lightens his tone. "Toad in the hole? What do you fancy?"

"You know, I passed a Thai place just now that smelled amazing." Flep smiles.

"Green beans and cashew chicken, medium spice, or comparable alternatives?"

"Sounds right. I'll stay with the girls."

They eat in Flep's room with the door cracked, a note lying beside Bell to inform her they are in the corner room, in case she should wake.

No green beans on the menu so Torin brought them broccoli beef, cashew chicken, veggie spring rolls, and rice. Not bad, either. Not as good as some of the New York places, but less sweet than American Thai, which he appreciates.

They sit cross-legged on the double bed, facing one another, trading cartons. Flep talks about his fruitless searches, about the husband having his own name all over the place from working in the press, and Torin tells him to stop worrying about the girls.

"If they called for us, or dropped a hairbrush, we could hear it."

"I've just never traveled with kids before. It's nerve-racking. We should have rented a car—"

Torin is laughing and Flep stops himself, grinning now.

"I know," he repeats. "Sorry."

Neither of them drives. Torin, who has lived in New York City his entire adult life, never even learned to drive a car.

Flep knows how, but has not had his license renewed in six or seven years. And that's in their own country, where everyone sober drives on the appropriate side of the road.

"Anyway, don't say 'with kids.' You've never even traveled."

"I went to Canada for work a few times," Flep says. "And Virginia once."

Torin snorts. "Let's see more of our own nation sometime."

"I'd love to. If you ever have the time." Smile sad now, almost shy.

Torin remembers too late that they don't know where their relationship stands.

"I'll make time. You know, it's a lot more affordable to go to, say,

Vermont or San Francisco, than Paris and Canterbury." He stops himself short of adding, *You could have just said you wanted to travel.*

He has been trying to think before he speaks since finding Flep. It might sound amusing to him, but too easy to read into it.

"That's a good point." Flep closes an empty container. Portions seem to be smaller here. "All through school I thought I'd be working in Hollywood. Now I've still never been."

"First trip." Torin passes him the last spring roll. "I had pizza. Go on."

He soon leaves Flep with only a good night kiss and assurance that they will figure something out in the morning, wishing he were staying in Flep's bed.

Bell is awake, TV on with the volume low. Ree remains passed out beside her.

"What are you watching?" Torin frowns at the screen.

"*Star Trek*. Did Flep find anything?"

"Do they only have American shows?"

"BBC Four is showing a British documentary about the Amish in Pennsylvania."

"Of course they are. Need anything else to eat?"

"I just want to go to bed. What about Flep?"

"Brush your teeth. I'll shift Ree. And not much. He found out she lived here until at least forty years ago, but no death record."

"We have to go back soon. What if he doesn't find out what happened to her?"

"Then he'll stay longer while we go. Nothing we can do about it, Bell."

He lies awake after getting Ree up to change into pajamas and brush her teeth. The room is dimly lit by streetlights. Noise from neighboring TVs, voices, and traffic.

Now, of course, he feels wide awake.

He should have told Flep about trying one of those sleeping pills and becoming a maniac. Though he is not sure his pride is ready to admit he didn't sleep after Flep walked out.

He should have thought of something to say to get Flep to come back with them, but he cannot push Flep. Again, not the point of being here.

Torin lets out a long, silent breath, muscles tight in his back and neck as he lies still.

He grabs his tablet, looks again at the calendar, and checks emails. One from Flep: *Thanks for dinner. I love you.*

That's all. Haven't been saying that to each other lately. Torin writes back.

Thanks for the company. Go to sleep. We'll figure out what's the next step in the morning. Love you too.

He opens the digital map, checking how long it takes to get from Canterbury back to Dover by train. The entire time, he thinks about Flep's words.

The husband. His own name. All over the place.

In the screen keypad, Torin taps in: *Lillian winship canterbury uk.*
He hits "Search."

Slow connection. He looks to the glowing window drapes, listens to cars.

He looks back at the screen, sharp in the dark room. His gaze drifts over the results.

Then his heart catches in his throat and he leaps from bed.

CHAPTER THIRTY-FIVE

"Flep, *Flep*. Open the door."

Flep scrambles from bed, slipping on his shoes to cross the rug.

"What's wrong?"

Torin bulls past him through the doorway, glowing tablet in his hand, breathless.

"Look at this, look—sit down." Pushing him back to the bed, Torin shoves the tablet at him. He switches on the bedside lamp.

Flep blinks and flinches at the light, then tries to take in the webpage. A British news site. A local Canterbury paper—Flep knows all their names by now, at least from many years back.

His eyes focus on the headline as Torin remains eager beside him.

CANTERBURY RESIDENT TURNS 106

Flep's breath comes short as his gaze races to the small print above the header. March. This past March. Eight months previously.

Hands trembling, he looks up at Torin.

"You couldn't find her in all those records," Torin says, "because Lillian Winship isn't dead."

CHAPTER THIRTY-SIX

Flep's mouth feels dry—the ringing back in his ears, visions back in his eyes. Damp spring garden alive with bees and blooming buds. Laugh of a little girl, kiss of a woman bringing a tray of sandwiches. A letter in his frozen hand. Holding on, crawling north, just across the Channel to the garden.

Torin leaves the girls in a waiting area with his tablet and earbuds to share, impressing the gravity of the situation and need for their best behavior. Flep cannot hear exactly what he says.

The middle-aged woman behind the desk asks him to sign in as a visitor, smiling when he says he is here to see Lillian Winship.

"Our most famed resident at the care home. How do you know Mrs. Winship?"

Flep's mind is blank, hardly able to keep his hand steady to write.

"Distant relations," Torin says, stepping up beside Flep and taking the clipboard to fill out his own name. "Finally got across the pond. It's a charming city."

"Isn't it? And you've come at a good time. Not so many tourists around and we're even getting sun." She takes the board back, all smiles.

They start down a hallway of maroon carpet and yellow paint and turn left, following her instructions.

"Friendliest Brit we've met," Torin says under his breath.

"That's not true. For one, what about the last cab driver?" Still hardly breathing.

"Immigrant. Are you okay?" Torin stops him. "You look like you're going to throw up."

"Just...dizzy. We shouldn't have lied to them..."

Torin cocks his head. "Right. Because you had a ready reply. I assume you have something you're planning to say to the old lady?"

"Uh..."

"Can I help you?" A nurse stops in the hall.

"Lillian Winship?" Torin says. "It's our first time visiting."

"Let me check that she's up." She leads them down another hall, to the far side of the building.

Here, morning sunlight streams into a room of puzzles and board games. Elderly men and women sit around these in chairs or wheelchairs.

Flep can hardly see them. If asked, he could not have said if the woman leading them is tall or short, blonde or brunette. One more corner and she knocks on an open door.

"Mrs. Winship? How are you feeling this morning? Would you like visitors?" She steps in while Flep and Torin wait at the door. "I see you have your cards out."

Blood pounds in Flep's ears—*swish-swoosh, swish-swoosh*—as it did when he fought to sharpen the pencil. Tunnel vision shows him an open door, a patch of sun hardly large enough for a cat to curl up in, and the foot of a small bed.

"Now—" The nurse stands beside him, speaking softly. "Her eyesight is very poor, as you probably know, and she gets tired easily."

"We won't stay long. Just wanted to say hello," Torin says.

She nods and returns to the game room.

Torin looks at Flep, apparently waiting for Flep to faint or...probably to go into the room first, really.

Flep walks in.

The ancient lady—tiny, chalky-skinned, wrinkled and bird-like with her boney hands—is sitting up in a neatly made bed with a tray on her lap. Scattered on the tray are dozens of postcards, all faded and worn with age.

She looks up, smiling faintly as she manages to track Flep's approach with cloudy blue eyes.

"Good morning," she says, her voice breathless but pleasant. "Do I know you?" She turns her head, trying to see him better.

"I'm...not sure..." Flep sinks to his shaking knees beside the bed, reaching to lift her hand while she watches him. "Did you get a letter from your father before your seventh birthday in 1917?"

She blinks, her uncertain gaze lifts from his hand on hers to his face. "How do you know that? Are you a friend of Rosemary's?"

"Who is she?"

"My granddaughter. She's here every week. You just missed her yesterday. I didn't think anyone else knew that much about my letters."

"But I know more," Flep says, almost whispering. "I only...need you to tell me if I'm right. Please."

"I'm sorry." She looks confused, but not troubled by him, leaving her cool hand in his. "I'm not sure what you mean."

"'My Dearest Lil.'" Flep closes his eyes. "'Papa is enjoying hot soup tonight while it snows outside. I hope you have soup to warm you up on nights like these. Do you know what you want for your birthday, little bluebird? My thoughts and prayers are with you and Mum every moment. Know that I am more proud of you than I can say, and love you more than I can say. I miss you, but...'" He swallows and opens his eyes to look up at her.

Tears roll silently down her cheeks as she watches him, her hand now tightly clamped on his.

"'I will be seeing you soon,'" she picks up, "'and you'll never know we were parted.'"

"'Goodbye for now,'" Flep finishes. "'Hugs and kisses...Papa.'"

"I never showed that letter to anyone since my mother and I received it. Never."

"I never saw it after that either. I only saw it before. When I wrote it. Lil, my bluebird, do you believe souls live on after an individual body dies?"

"Yes, I do," she whispers, still holding on tight, still staring at him. "Bluebird, bluebird, sing me a song..."

He remembers, flowing with her words to the garden, the party, sunlight, birdsong, lifting her, swinging her around, singing with her.

He continues where she leaves off. "I'll build you a house if you'll sing up the dawn."

"Don't cry for twilight," she says, "for sun comes so soon."

"No matter the distance, I'll see you by noon..."

She shuts her eyes, tears flowing over colorless cheeks and dropping to her nightgown, clutching his hand in a surprisingly strong grip.

"Papa," she whispers, face bowed. "I waited, Papa."

Flep moves to sit on the edge of the bed, the tray shifted down to her knees, and wraps his arms around her.

"I'm sorry I didn't return to you, Lil. I'm so, so sorry. I promised I'd be there for your birthday."

"Mum got the telegram from the War Office and she tried to tell me." She leans into his shoulder. "I wouldn't listen. Then your last letter came, saying you'd be home. So I went on waiting—"

"Lil—"

"And you did. I knew you'd come back."

Monday, November 28

I spent the morning with my daughter, Lillian Winship. She is seventy years older than me, but I have learned to love nontraditional families lately.

She knew who I was.

She vividly recalled her sixth birthday with her mother and me, down to the sponge cake with strawberries and my promise to take her to the beach next year.

I thought her memory shocking—nearly as shocking as my own. But she has my letters. Dropped into a tattered manila envelope: a stack of postcards and single-sheet letters sent out of France one hundred years ago.

Fragments of this former life now fall together like a puzzle assembling itself after months of chaos.

Carine's sixth birthday arrived just at the time that Lillian's health started declining—right before her own hundred and sixth. Then I began to remember through dreams of war which grew worse and worse, forcing me to never forget, not let her go.

Gabriel Taft was born in 1889 in London to a prosperous businessman and a farmer's daughter who married up and raised six children in Brighton. Gabriel went into business after his father and married Mary Chummny in 1909. They had only one daughter the next year—Mary's health preventing more children. Having hoped to raise a large family, Gabriel focused all his paternal spirit into Lillian, their miracle.

As an educated man, he enlisted at the outbreak of war and was commissioned into the infantry. He left for France in the summer of 1915. Receiving one long leave pass in March, 1916, he spent a fortnight with his wife and daughter. In April, he returned to the Western Front.

Though he should have been granted more leave as an officer, various situations prevented this: deaths of peers, last-minute orders, minor wounds which sent him to field hospitals, but not to Blighty—not home.

In February, 1917, he was killed by machine gun fire during a small offensive to reclaim a captured strategic position from the Germans. His leave home had been due to start the next day.

Lillian received his last letter, along with another written by the company captain to Mary. Her mother told her Papa was never coming home.

But Lil said he promised. So she went on waiting. For one hundred years.

She grew up, married, had children, stayed home with them while her husband worked. While he traveled—writing for his paper on matters of travel or foreign correspondence—he sent back cards to her. Sometimes every day; each time he saw a new sight or reached a new place, he wrote a postcard.

Lillian had these cards on a tray when I arrived at the care home.

She explained to me, pointing out many invitations and faded pictures of the Wonders of the World, that Thomas had always wanted her there.

She never left the children. She never traveled so she never had to say goodbye. She stayed in Kent, still impossibly waiting.

In the whole of her hundred and six years, Lil told me, she has been outside of England twice. Once for a family vacation to France by ferry, once to her daughter's graduation in Edinburgh.

"I wouldn't do it again," she told me. "I don't know why more people don't love what they already have. You always did. I used to sit on your knee on the garden wall and you'd say, 'See those fells, Lil?'"

"'See the rabbits and the birds? See the emerald grass and the sapphire sky?'" I said, looking up from her long-dead husband's postcards.

"'Can you tell me a place better? Can you find a place you'd rather be?'"

"And you would say, 'Here. I'd rather be right here with you, Papa.'"

We talked and I told her parts she did not know or remember, and she told me parts I did not know or remember.

264

Four grandchildren, seven great-grandchildren, nineteen great-great-grandchildren, and so on. Some here in town, some in London, some in Scotland.

"I wish you could have seen them when they were small," she said, smiling sadly at me where I sat at the foot of her bed. "I know how much you loved children. I know you wanted more. Even then I knew. I wanted to be your angel, to be enough."

"Of course you were enough," I said. "More than enough. I was so blessed with you and your mother. I was happier in those years between your birth and the start of the War than I ever had been in my life. Of course you were enough."

She lifted a postcard from France. "Remember this one?"

A picture of bluebirds.

"'Each time I see a bluebird, a blue scarf, a blue-eyed lady, I think of you, Lil, my little bluebird. I don't see much blue here at the front...'"

"'So I bought two of these cards,'" she went on for me, running her fingers along the soft, faded image. "'One for you. One for me. So we can see the same blue and be a bit nearer. Goodbye for now. Be seeing you soon.'"

"I'm sorry for all the goodbyes, Lil," I said, looking down to the many yellowed pages.

"No... Don't be sorry for that. The places we say goodbye are the places that bring us closer together. If we don't have the goodbyes, we don't value the hellos, the 'I love you's' and 'I missed you's.' It's okay to say goodbye."

I watched her, listened, never wanted to leave. I could hardly see the old woman on the bed. I kept seeing my little girl smiling back.

"You don't seem troubled by me," I said. "You're accepting this much faster than I did myself. Do you really believe in past lives?"

"I believe that love goes on. I believe that no goodbye spoken in love is ever permanent. I believe that you have brought my father back to me. And I have learned, in these years, that life is more than granite facts and proofs."

"I wish I were as smart as you when this whole thing started. I could have been here sooner."

She leaned forward to press my hand between hers. "Give it another few dozen years. In this case, never too late, right?"

I would have gladly stayed all day, all week, but her breathing was shallow, her cheeks showed a hint of blue, and I knew she was exhausted.

One of the care home nurses stopped in twice to shoo me away, Lillian insisting to her each time that she was fine and to leave us be. Torin was long gone.

He witnessed the first part of our meeting and conversation, waiting near the door, silent. When I finally remembered him and glanced around, Torin looked like he'd seen a ghost. And then some.

He soon excused himself, leaving the two of us alone to return to the girls. I told him I would meet him back at the rooms.

Now, he brought me dinner once more, hardly saying a word while I showed him the letters she gave me, her whole manila envelope of my own letters to read.

I have never spent so many minutes with Torin and heard so few words in return to mine.

I'm reading the letters, finalizing all those moments of my past that showed me fragments and scenes of a broader stage. I'm remembering the morning I spent with Lil and am looking forward to going back, meeting her family, my many times great-granddaughter, who she assures me looks just like she did. And I want her to meet the girls, my twenty-first century girls. If they don't mind. She has told me all about what happened to her after I died. I want to tell her what I've done since I was reborn.

Bed. Or I will be as tired as her tomorrow. Goodbye for now, Lil. Be seeing you soon.

CHAPTER THIRTY-SEVEN

The receptionist looks up from behind the counter. No smile this morning.

"You were in yesterday to see Mrs. Winship, weren't you?"

"Is she okay?" Flep feels the warm force disintegrating in his chest.

"I'm sorry..."

Feet sinking to earth, weight returning in a sickening rush.

"Her family's here now. Mrs. Winship passed away in the night. She had a smile on her face when they found her."

Her words reach Flep through miles and heartbeats, the sight of her lost to him. Torin's arm at his back.

"Come on," Torin murmurs. He guides Flep back to a chair in the waiting area where the girls sat the day before.

Isabelle tugs Carine after them. She looks grave. Carine appears only confused, opening her mouth before her big sister hushes her. Flep wonders if Ree understands what the receptionist meant. Her parents don't say things like "passed away." If someone died, Torin and Amélie would say they are dead.

Strange thing to be thinking, Flep thinks while he sits and looks around as if waiting for someone in a restaurant. Like Torin's. Flep remembers he was thinking of telling Torin that he could give it a try—working for the restaurant. He has said nothing about it yet.

He looks at Torin, watching Flep from close range, sitting beside him, brows drawn. His eyes are as worried and sad as Flep has ever seen them.

Flep feels like he missed a beat, a question, a ghost of words. He knows Torin said something to him.

Her family is here. He can still meet them. And say...?

Flep shuts his eyes, rests his head on Torin's shoulder.

Torin showed up in France. He remains here now.

Flep waits until the dizziness fades, and the world is back in color.

He stands, taking a deep breath.

"Let's go," he says softly.

"Are you sure?" Torin stands after him, uneasy.

"That—yesterday—was all she was waiting for." Flep looks at him. "I think...it has to be enough for me also."

With another breath, he walks back to the desk.

"Do you have any idea when the funeral will be?"

"She has family coming in from up north. They'll wait at least a few days. It should be in the paper. I'm sure they'll do another story on Mrs. Winship. Everyone in town knew of her."

"Thank you." Flep nods and turns.

He holds out his hand as he reaches the girls. Ree lifts her free hand to take his, Bell still holding her left. Torin opens the door for them. They walk out together into December sunlight of a twenty-first century day.

CHAPTER THIRTY-EIGHT

On the train toward Paris, back to Marcelle with the girls before the morning flight, Torin feels much as he did in November back at home. Like he does not know what to do. Or knows, but cannot do what he must. Both feelings leave his world inverted.

He can't go back alone. But he is not alone. He has a six- and twelve-year-old to take home. And Flep would not leave before the funeral. Torin never even asked.

Ree shows him her coloring book—a work in progress—and he admires her skill. Bell sits in silence, earbuds in place, gazing out the window from her backward-facing seat across from Torin and her sister. They have four seats and a small table to themselves on the decrepit train. A good place to think, to figure this out.

Like Bell, Torin looks out the window, seeing farmland through rain. But seeing so much more.

Everything has been impossible this week. No home, no kitchen, no table to sit around. Yet all four of them have been together—a family—and...happy. Despite everything, Flep has been as happy, and awake, as Torin has ever known him. Not just finding answers he needed, but away from a demanding job that drained him and receiving constant attention from three people he loves.

No, not despite everything. Because of everything, the three of them have been happy here.

"Bell?"

She looks at him. Just a look. No "What?" or "Yes?"

God, she looks like her mother. Especially when she does that. Not a belligerent expression. Just a bit condescending. Can't bother wasting breath with a verbal reply.

Destined to be an unbearable teenager? Or is destiny, and other people's choices, not as black and white as all that? Can he shift the tide himself?

He raises one eyebrow before saying anything else. Bell pulls out the earbuds.

"Do you wish I wouldn't cook so much at home?" Torin asks.

"What?" Her eyes widen, shocked. Not one of Amélie's expressions. Beside him, Ree also looks up.

"I wondered if you'd rather we do other stuff," Torin says. "Grocery shopping and cooking, then cleaning up, takes up the time we spend together. I thought you all liked that. But we don't have to be that way. We could grab something out and go to the Park more, or a movie, or..." He shrugs. What do other people do with their kids?

"Why?" Bell asks. "Why would you want to stop cooking?"

"I can cook, Daddy," Ree says. She seems worried, grasping a red crayon as she looks up at him.

"It's not that I don't want to. I only wondered if you didn't want... If it takes up too much time?"

"Food is better at home than going out," Bell says.

"We never get lobster out—"

"I wouldn't mind going to a movie now and then," Bell goes on. "Getting pizza or pho or something."

"Movie—!"

"Don't, Ree." Not even looking at her sister. "We don't always have to cook at home. It was kind of fun seeing all these places and going in libraries and getting food out. But it's not like we want you to stop cooking."

Torin nods. "Just checking. It was weird to not cook for so long."

"Dad—" Speaking with a drawn-out tone, almost rolling her eyes, Isabelle puts the earbuds back in. "We've been gone barely over a week. It hasn't been 'so long.'"

"Seems like it." Torin smiles.

"When can we see a movie?" Ree asks, going back to her book.

Isabelle ignores her, looking out the window. "Dad, ever heard the song 'Let Her Go' by Passenger?"

"Never even heard of them. Why?"

She shrugs, watching rain and green fields. "No reason."

Not that cooking isn't vital to being a family. Of course it is. Only, this past week, Torin has witnessed, for the first time in his life, that a kitchen is not required to make his family. That you can feed a relationship and still not be nourishing it. Food only helps. All that is *required* to bring this family together is love.

"Bell?"

Another silent look.

Torin shakes his head. "Never mind."

He can tell them when they reach Paris. By then, he better have a plan. Because he is not going back to 2nd Avenue without his family complete.

CHAPTER THIRTY-NINE

Icy rain falls upon the wood casket while dozens of mourners look on from behind hats, hoods, and umbrellas, all in a sea of black.

Flep keeps to the back of the gathering, watching the children and the grandchildren—right down to a toddler carried by her mother. He speaks to none of them, maintains a respectful distance, but he clutches a bundle of old letters protected by a layer of plastic and an envelope.

Torin stands beside him, silent. He was not supposed to be here, having taken the girls back to Paris four days ago to catch their flight back home.

Saying goodbye to them was horrible. Ree had asked why Flep wasn't coming with them, wondering when they were going to ice skate again.

Bell said, "You won't take one hundred years to see us again, will you?"

Flep hugged them both. "Not even close." But he could hardly say more.

They had spent a night at their aunt's while Flep remained in England, then left for the airport.

There, Torin and the girls and Marcelle explained, begged, and wheedled—Carine in tears—until the airline transferred the ticket into Marcelle's name so the girls did not have to fly alone, and Marcelle did not have to buy a standby ticket and scrap Torin's. It was against policy, but Flep, shocked to see Torin show up for a second time, was hardly surprised the family could get ticket agents—even French ones—to bend to their wills.

So their aunt took the girls home. Torin came back to Flep for the funeral. And Flep was nearly as bewildered as the first time he ran into Torin in Europe.

"Why are you back? What happened?" Flep had asked, standing in the doorway of his room in Canterbury.

"Marcelle's taking them home. I guess I had a one-way ticket also..."

"But, the restaurant...you can't stay gone—"

"Screw the restaurant." Torin had kissed him. "I'll sort it out. But I'd rather be an accountant, and have you to come home to, than own a dozen restaurants."

The new nicest thing anyone has ever said to him.

Later last night, Flep booked them two tickets home with a last-minute deal—relatively cheap—out of Heathrow. They have only a few more nights. And Flep has a decision to make.

Everyone is clearing from the cemetery—the first earth having been dropped into the grave, the rain thicker than ever—when Flep finally approaches.

Clutching his parcel below his jacket, he sinks from Torin's arm, kneeling on drenched grass and mud at the edge of the grave.

With rain soaking through his hat to his skin, he remembers his last night on the front line, trying to reach her. But he does not feel the cold. He remembers longing to see her again, hear her sweet laugh. But he does not feel the fear.

"Know that I am more proud of you than I can say, and love you more than I can say," Flep whispers, hardly breathing the words. "I miss you, but I will be seeing you soon—and you'll never know we were parted. Goodbye for now. Hugs and kisses...Papa..."

When he stands, very slowly, Torin puts his arm around him. Leaning on him, Flep walks back toward the churchyard gate.

A young woman of thirty waits for them there, watching them.

"Hello." She offers a dripping, gloved hand. "Have we met? You must have known Lillian..."

Flep shifts his parcel to shake her hand, nodding.

"Flep. This is Torin. I'm sorry for your loss. You must be her...great-granddaughter?"

"Great-great. Won't you step in with us?"

How to explain? How to talk to any of them?

"I'm sorry. We need to go, but...she gave me something that really

274

belongs to you. Or a museum."

She looks only puzzled as he passes her the plastic bag.

"Those are letters your many times great-grandfather, Gabriel Taft, wrote to Lillian and her mother while he was serving in World War One."

She gasps, covering the bundle with her black coat. "Brilliant. Mum said no one could find them in her things. Only granddad's postcards from all over the world. Where did you get these?"

Flep looks toward the grave through screens of silver rain, then back to the young woman with her great-great-grandmother's eyes and nose and small chin.

"I came here...researching the Great War. Your grandmother was very helpful. And kind. I wouldn't have been able to finish what I came for without finding her. But those are yours."

She thanks him again before Flep and Torin walk back to the main street leading to the bed and breakfast.

Flep pretends to take a long, sweltering shower. Only pretends. There do not seem to be decent showers in Europe. Or not in bed and breakfasts. He takes a short, lukewarm shower—water descending in a brittle spray that soothes two square inches of skin at a time.

When he gives up, Torin trades with him. The bathroom itself is hardly large enough for both to occupy at the same time, and the shower is out of the question.

Flep wears a towel to bed. They can go out later for dinner. Now, he needs to stare at the wall for a few hours, a few days, a few weeks.

Shivering in the cool room, hair dripping, Torin crawls into bed beside him minutes later. Flep rolls to face him, sliding down to rest his head against Torin's chest while Torin kisses him.

Flep suspects he has been a disappointment to Torin since Torin's unexpected return yesterday, when Flep wished only to hold onto him, to not be alone. Whatever he may be thinking, Torin still does not push him. Arm around Flep's back, he lies motionless.

After some time listening to traffic, rain, and Torin's heartbeat, Flep hears Torin say, "I'm sorry you had to say goodbye again so soon."

Flep moves to look at him, thinking about those words. Mostly, the "again." Because Torin does not mean Flep saying goodbye to Lillian last

Monday.

"She...didn't need to wait anymore," Flep says softly, stroking the backs of two fingers down Torin's jaw, gazing into those eyes. He must be the world's leading sucker for blue eyes. And for the longest time. "This kind of goodbye...is never forever. I'll see her again sometime."

Torin does not turn his head or take Flep's fingers in his mouth. He only looks back into Flep's eyes, his serious expression unchanging as he says, "I'm sure you will."

Chapter Forty

They check out of the bed and breakfast the next day, moving to a final stop for a few nights in Greater London, south of the city center.

Flep composes a long email to update Dr. Kulmala and Natalie. He meant to keep in touch with her, owes her another lunch at the very least.

He thinks of Lil—of memories, gardens, his wife's kisses and his daughter's laugh—as he and Torin visit Oxford Street and Westminster Abbey. None of it takes him away. None of it haunts him. He only remembers and loves them and knows they are at peace and all connected.

He and Torin note how old, yet squat, London is—after Manhattan, it seems they could stand on their toes to look over the tops of most buildings—and also sample as wide a range of food as they can find to indulge Torin.

At night, they leave the TV off, watching people and city lights from their window, talking about London versus Paris and New York City. In the dark, they undress one another, remaining by the window since, at the slightest motion, the old bed sounds like a train stopping on rusty tracks.

Flep marvels at Torin's solicitude. Gentle and loving and slow. Torin after a long night, finding Flep still awake and greeting him in bed. Not Torin after a month without sex, or even time together. Since being here in Europe, he has been asking questions and making suggestions. Now he finally talks more.

Kissing the back of Flep's neck, Torin says how much he missed him, that he couldn't sleep with Flep gone, didn't care about going to work.

Uneasy, Flep wishes he would stop. Like an Olympic diver saying he does not want to look at a pool again.

"Okay," Flep cuts him off. "I love you too." He reaches to his own shoulder to touch Torin's face so Torin can bite his fingers. Torin doing so makes Flep smile.

He has felt vaguely unsettled by Torin since Thanksgiving in France. Unconsciously waiting for the catch. Tonight, he stops questioning this change.

Torin hasn't changed after all.

The evening they met when Torin first started cooking for him, late nights and slow mornings, dropping everything just to gaze at Flep across a table. Torin has always been affectionate, always devoted. He just used to mostly show it when it was convenient for him. Now, he is trying it when it is convenient for Flep.

On their last day, they pack and Flep takes Torin to Alain Ducasse at The Dorchester for lunch—having been unable to secure a dinner reservation and settling for the earlier time. Flep has no idea what Alain Ducasse at The Dorchester is, but he found it at the top of some London lists.

He surprises Torin with their lunch location, stepping off the red double-decker bus to lead Torin down the street alongside Hyde Park.

"That's the one." Flep points, biting his lip, hoping he has pleased Torin, yet never sure how Torin will feel about a given food or chef.

Torin looks, recoils as if bracing himself in a strong gust, and catches his breath.

"Jesus Christ," is all he says.

Flep relaxes. He made a good choice.

Stepping forward, Torin shakes his head. "Never without a reservation, even at lunch."

"I have one," Flep says.

"You do? What is this about?"

"A surprise for you. You don't know how much it's meant, having you here."

Torin seems hardly to hear him as he holds the door for Flep, looking around.

By the time lunch is nearly over, Flep feels both impossibly content and again uneasy. He did what he came for. Time to go home. To rediscover his modern life, pick up pieces, decide who he is now. Employment will help, though he feels more interested to know where he stands with Torin. Obviously going home with him, and things seem all right. Yet a fresh history of extra baggage makes Flep wonder.

Wasn't it little more than a month ago when Flep decided he and Torin were not such a great match? That leaving was for the best?

Flep reminds himself once more that Torin has always been honest with him. Flep could, and can, take Torin at face value. He may be one of the most open people Flep has ever met. No, this is about each of them. Flep has made plenty of his own mistakes in the past months. High on the list are the unfair expectations Flep made of Torin when he was not even doing a passable job of looking after himself.

He owes Torin an apology of his own. And owes both a real discussion about their relationship and expectations. If they mean to maintain that relationship.

Chatting with Torin about the London Tube and their food as they eat, Flep feels a new pressure in his chest, desperate to know answers to questions he does not ask.

They refuse the wine included in their meal, but take coffee along with luscious ice cream. Torin watches him eat. The chocolate is not lost on Flep either. He smiles across the window table at Torin.

"The first meal we ever shared."

Torin only looks back, unsmiling. "I wanted to do something for you—"

"Like being here?"

"But you're the one doing stuff for me," Torin goes on. "So I guess this is as good a time as any." He holds out a tiny box, removing a lid. "Will you marry me, Flep?"

Flep sits like marble, stunned as if the building had flipped on its roof.

"What—?"

Not a ring. A golden flower.

"I got it in Paris. An engagement ring would be traditional...but I wasn't sure you'd be any more into that than me. So it's a charm.

279

Another type of symbol."

A poppy. Symbol of the Great War—of loss and love and memory, of coming together, never forgetting. Beautifully made, half an inch long, in polished gold.

When he only stares for several seconds, Torin swallows. "Flep, I know I've—"

"Yes," Flep says, breathless, almost light-headed to know the entire conversation he dreaded has been concluded with a single word.

Wednesday, December 7

On the flight home with Torin, we laughingly plan ahead, neither of us being good planners. I'll try working with the restaurant on a probationary period. It will mean a massive pay cut, but I'm not worried about that as long as I can meet obligations. We both understand this is temporary—a year, even if all goes well. Help with the old place, redo the image, and free rein over the new place.

Already thinking of this as a year off. Looking forward to it far more than I will admit to Torin. Back to set design either after a month, or a year, however long the restaurants maintain their novel charm for me. And Torin remains bearable to work around.

Torin agrees—only if I will also agree to a honeymoon in Los Angeles.

Thursday, December 8

Getting there was even better than the flight. Amélie met us at the airport with the girls last night, though the plane arrived late.

Ree ran at me after customs, shouting, "Flep's home!" Ignoring her father as I caught her in the air. I'm sure she took it for granted that he would be back.

I remembered that other little girl. Loving arms across the English Channel. Again, it was not bad. Only a memory.

Bell hugged us both. Her mother also seemed glad to see me, also not paying much heed to Torin. She returned my embrace.

"Thank you," I whispered and she pressed my shoulders.

"What are families for?"

Perhaps strange, our reunion. Or, perhaps, that is how families are. If not a kindly dragon, a sober, bisexual chef, a man who remembers

281

past lives, and girls who love cooking over dress up, we would be something else—maybe just as odd. I'm grateful for how we are.

At the kitchen table soaring above Manhattan, golden poppy beside my coffee mug and laptop, I feel for the first time in a long time that I can look ahead, not back.

Ree jumps around like a cricket, shouting about holiday lights. Her father and sister fix lunch before he leaves for work. I look forward to grabbing my skates and walking the girls to the Park.

Most of all, I look forward to the end of this journal, and many upcoming years of peaceful dreams.

AUTHOR'S END NOTES

Although this is a work of fiction, there is factual precedent behind *The Places We Say Goodbye*.

In many parts of the world, and according to many religions—including Buddhism, Hinduism, Jainism, and others—reincarnation is considered a matter of fact. Researchers have documented accounts of young children remembering past lives, while people of all ages have been cured of phobias and medical complaints through past life regressions.

Edgar Cayce, Ian Stevenson, MD, and Brian L. Weiss, MD, mentioned in this novel, were, and are, real people involved in past life studies.

Soul Survivor by Bruce and Andrea Leininger (2009, Grand Central Publishing), *Across Time and Death* by Jenny Cockell (1994, Fireside), and *Many Lives, Many Masters* by Brian L. Weiss (1988, Touchstone) are also real books, all of them nonfiction. The first two detail stories of young people remembering past lives which were then traced to actual events and people who were still alive.

For more information on children and past life recall, see Carol Bowman's *Children's Past Lives* (1997, Bantam), or Ian Stevenson's *Children Who Remember Previous Lives* (1987, University Press of Virginia). *Through Time Into Healing,* by Brian L. Weiss (1992, Simon & Schuster), covers various forms of healing through past life regressions.

ABOUT THE AUTHOR

Jordan Taylor is the author of numerous novels and stories from the bestselling *Angel Paws* shorts to the historical fantasy series *Lightfall*. An avid reader and writer, Jordan also enjoys photography and graphic design, old bookstores, researching World War One, travel, and tweeting about her smooth fox terrier.

Website: www.jordantaylorbooks.com
Twitter: @JordanTaylorLit

ALSO BY JORDAN TAYLOR FROM NINESTAR PRESS

Guardian

NineStar Press, LLC

www.ninestarpress.com

www.ingramcontent.com/pod-product-compliance
Lightning Source LLC
Chambersburg PA
CBHW050711180626
46814CB00002B/382